Ida McKinney

The year book of English authors

Ida McKinney

The year book of English authors

ISBN/EAN: 9783337280024

Printed in Europe, USA, Canada, Australia, Japan

Cover: Foto ©Andreas Hilbeck / pixelio.de

More available books at **www.hansebooks.com**

THE YEAR BOOK OF
ENGLISH AUTHORS

WILLIAM SHAKESPEARE

1564–1616

THE YEAR BOOK OF ENGLISH AUTHORS

WRITTEN AND COMPILED BY IDA SCOTT TAYLOR AND ILLUSTRATED WITH TWELVE HALF TONE PORTRAITS OF PROMINENT AUTHORS

NEW YORK

RAPHAEL TUCK AND SONS

COMPANY, LIMITED

MCMI

PREFATORY NOTE

It has been my purpose not only to make this volume a helpful Year Book, but also a compilation of popular selections, which may render it useful for reference. So far as possible, I have affixed signatures to the quotations. In a few instances the writers quoted are not of English birth, but these cases are so few that it is practically what its title says it is — a Year Book of English Authors. It may be understood that all of the prose, as well as a few bits of verse without signature, included in this work, belong to the author and compiler of it.

I. S. T.

"OLD TIME'S GREAT CLOCK, THAT NEVER STOPS,
    NOR RUNS TOO FAST NOR SLOW,
HUNG UP AMID THE WORLDS OF SPACE,
    WHERE WHEELING PLANETS GLOW,
ITS DIAL-PLATE THE ORBIT VAST
    WHERE WHIRLS OUR MUNDANE SPHERE, —
HAS PUSHED ITS POINTER ROUND AGAIN,
    AND STRUCK ANOTHER YEAR!"

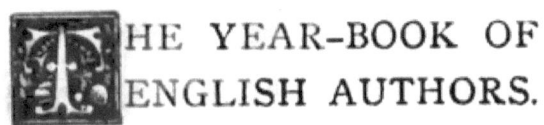

THE YEAR-BOOK OF ENGLISH AUTHORS.

JANUARY.

AND now across the hills of Time, falls the glory of a new Day, the royal birthday of a glad New Year. Make way for his coming — this messenger of promise! Open the gateways of the skies, let down the bars of sunlight in the meadows of the heavens, hoist your flags of triumph, and hail King January, the ruling sovereign of the year! Look up! see where the horizon is brightest, there is a motto for you and me, which reads, "Be thou faithful unto death, and I will give thee a crown of life!"

Oh, glorious promise, arching above us like a rainbow of Hope, — a promise like the pillar of fire to go before us all the year! let us indeed be "faithful unto death."

> January, bold and dauntless,
>   Scales old Winter's rugged height,
> With his spangled garments gleaming
>   In the iridescent light;
> And he walks with step majestic —
>   While we hear the joy-bells ring,
> As they greet the happy New Year
>   Whom they honor as a king.

So here hath been dawning another blue day;
Think, wilt thou let it slip useless away?
Out of eternity this new day is born;
Into eternity at night will return.

T. CARLYLE.

JANUARY SECOND.

OUT of the darkness into the light! Rejoice and
be glad, for you are allowed to see the radiance
of another morning, and its blessings, opportunities,
and duties are yours. From silence and sleep have
sprung thought and activity, and the busy world has
once more begun its round of daily cares. Put your
shoulder to the wheel, take up the dropped stitches of
yesterday, and don't be disheartened; thank God, and
take courage: come what may, He will help you to
bear it, and give you strength for to-morrow when it
comes.

Again the Lord of life and light
   Awakes the kindling ray,
Unseals the eyelids of the morn,
   And pours increasing day.

This day be grateful homage paid,
   And loud hosannas sung;
Let gladness dwell in every heart,
   And praise on every tongue.

To Thee, my Saviour and my King,
   Glad homage let me give;
And stand prepared, like Thee, to die,
   With Thee that I may live.

          ANNA LETITIA BARBAULD.

Come, Light serene and still!
Our darkened spirits fill
   With Thy clear day:
Guide of the feeble sight,
Reveal the path of right,
   Show us Thy way.

          ROBERT II. OF FRANCE.

[8]

JANUARY THIRD.

LET us be true to ourselves; true to our principles, our convictions, and our religion. A man who lives up to a true moral standard of right, provided his conscience is unimpaired, is a man of untold influence: other men look up to him, quote him, and endeavor to imitate his example. They are proud to claim his friendship, for his word is as good as his bond, and a man like that is a friend worth having. If we would be true ourselves, we must seek the truth. Unless we can discriminate between right and wrong, we are unable to know the truth. Let us therefore cultivate our consciences, and do only those things that are pleasing to God, who is Himself the Divine Truth.

> This above all — to thine own self be true,
> And it must follow, as the night the day,
> Thou canst not then be false to any man.
> > SHAKESPEARE.

Truth is as impossible to be soiled by any outward touch as the sunbeam. — MILTON.

Happy the man taught by the truth itself;
Not by the shapes and sounds that pass across his life,
But by the very truth.
Our thoughts and senses often lead us wrong;
They see one side alone.
> THOMAS À KEMPIS.

There is nothing so strong and safe, in any emergency of life, as the simple truth. — DICKENS.

[9]

WE are never happy so long as we are unforgiving. If we cherish an unkind thought or feeling, our hearts are never quite right in the sight of God. And what are we, that we should deny forgiveness to our neighbor? Have we done nothing to be forgiven ourselves? Think of the mistakes we are continually making, of the impatient words we say, and the number of times we have grieved and offended those around us. Oh yes, you say, we have much to be forgiven: if so, then, shall we refuse to forgive others? How many times does the Bible tell us to forgive? Have you exceeded the number? Ah, but you say, "I was not to blame." No one who refuses to forgive ever thinks himself blamable, and even if he is innocent of any wrong-doing in the act itself, he is sinning against God so long as he denies forgiveness to his neighbor. I believe it to be sacredly true that no one can keep the Golden Rule or catch the real spirit of the Lord's Prayer, if he is unforgiving towards any one, — no matter what the cause may be, nor who may be the offender.

"Forgive us all our debts," we say,
  "As we have all forgiven";
Ah, help us indeed to pray —
  "Father which art in Heaven!"

Help us to pray, for only Thou
  Can'st trace the secret sin,
And only Thou can'st wholly know
  The pride that lurks within.

HELEN MARION BURNSIDE.

DEATH and life are in the power of the tongue.
PROVERBS 18 : 21.

Whoso keepeth his mouth and his tongue keepeth his soul from troubles. PROVERBS 21 : 23.

A word spoken in due season, how good is it!
PROVERBS 15 : 23.

A word fitly spoken is like apples of gold in pictures of silver. PROVERBS 25 : 11.

How much the Word of God dwells on the " power of the tongue," and yet it is referred to as a "little member." With what care should we guard our tongues, that they speak no ill, that they carry no sting, and that they always find an opportunity to say a word in " due season." A wise tongue echoes the thoughts of a wise intellect, an eloquent tongue paints word-pictures in glowing language; a truthful tongue is persuasive, and carries conviction, — though its utterances may sometimes lack culture and polish; but a kindly tongue speaks the words that can never die; surely they are "like apples of gold in pictures of silver," sweet and precious to an aching heart and wounded spirit. O words, words! let us be careful how we speak them!

> Words are mighty, words are living;
>   Serpents with their venomous stings,
> Or bright angels crowding round us
>   With Heaven's light upon their wings;
> Every word has its own spirit,
>   True or false that never dies;
> Every word man's lips have uttered
>   Echoes in God's skies.
>   ADELAIDE PROCTER.

[11]

BE patient at all times. When the cares and duties of the day are weighing you down, when the night is long and dark, and when your cross is heavy and hard to bear. The day with all its burdens will end with the setting of the sun; the night will soon wear away, and there will be a glorious dawn; and God shall exchange your cross for a crown. Then be patient; there is a reward awaiting the faithful.

Sweet Patience, come;
Not from a low and earthly source, —
Waiting till things shall have their course, —
Not as accepting present pain
In hope of some hereafter gain, —
Not in a dull and sullen calm, —
But as a breath of heavenly balm,
Bidding my weary heart submit
To bear whatever God sees fit:
Sweet Patience, come!
HYMNS OF THE CHURCH MILITANT.

There is no crown in the world
So good as Patience: neither is any peace
That God put in our lips to drink as wine,
More honey-pure, more worthy love's own praise,
Than that sweet-souled endurance which makes clear
The iron hands of anger.   SWINBURNE.

Be still, my soul! — the Lord is on thy side;
Bear patiently the cross of grief and pain;
Leave to thy God to order and provide, —
In every change He faithful will remain.
HYMNS FROM THE LAND OF LUTHER.

WHAT though we stand in the shadow with our souls sadly yearning for the light; know ye not that in God's time it will come? We shall find the waiting hard at first, for we are by nature impatient; there will be doubts and complainings, and troublous murmurs from restless, wilful hearts, but by and by we shall find His way is best; and when we cease to rely on self, He will calm all our doubts and fears, and hush our tumults into rest. He will gently lead us in the paths of Peace, and reveal to us the light of His love that shines like a beacon in the Christian's sky. Let these words find an echo in our souls : —

I do not ask, O Lord, that life may be
    A pleasant road;
I do not ask that Thou would take from me
    Aught of its load;
I do not ask that flowers should always spring
    Beneath my feet;
I know too well the poison and the sting
    Of things too sweet.
For one thing only, Lord, dear Lord! I plead, —
    Lead me aright,
Though strength should falter, and though heart should
    bleed,
    Through Peace to Light.
ADELAIDE A. PROCTER.

Under Thy wings, my God, I rest,
  Under Thy shadow safely lie;
By Thy own strength in peace possessed,
  While dreaded evils pass me by.
ANNA L. WARING.

IF the heart is full of happiness and joy, the lips will sing. A volcano must have an outlet somewhere: it may lie smouldering for years, but by and by, when we least expect it, it will burst forth, and its fiery eloquence shall reach far into the clouds. The music of the glad heart cannot be silent forever; God will tune the key and measure the rhythm, and the happy songster shall respond to its great Master Musician. Sometimes, in the lowliest walks of life, surrounded by humblest walls, and in the midst of homeliest tasks, the singer shall catch the divine key, and the melody shall mount up, as with wings, and chord with the Heavenly Symphony; and if earth does not recognize the strain, the listening angels shall know and rejoice, and the heart of the singer shall be blessed and gladdened by the song. God interprets melody one way, and man another: music to Him is acceptable when the heart sings out its joy and gladness, — when there is love and praise and contentment in it, though the voice be poor and trembling and the tune sometimes uncertain. Man only accepts as music that which talent and culture bestows. "Man looketh on the outward things, but God looketh on the heart."

> There are in the loud stunning tide
>   Of human care and crime,
> With whom the melodies abide
>   Of th' everlasting chime;
> Who carry music in the heart
> Through dusky lane and wrangling mart,
> Plying their daily task with busier feet
> Because their secret souls a holy strain repeat.
>
>   J. KEBLE.

DO not depend too much on earthly friends. Circumstances often change them and alter their friendship for you. Do not, however, misjudge them: sometimes they are carrying burdens of which you may never know, and you may deem them untrue when they are only absorbed with other things. On the other hand, circumstances may influence them so that they grow indifferent to us. New and more prosperous friends may take our places in their thoughts and affections, and we may become unnecessary to them. Absence and distance sometimes estrange friends, and in the lapse of time we are almost forgotten: yet the true and steadfast friend will never fail us through all life's vicissitudes, and the separation of years will make no difference in his love and loyalty. Such a friend is Christ. He changes not, but is " the same yesterday, to-day, and forever."

> There's naught on earth to rest upon,
>   All things are changing here,
> The smiles of joy we gaze upon,
>   The friends we count most dear:
> One Friend alone is changeless,
>   The One too oft forgot,
> Whose love hath stood for ages past —
>   Our Jesus changeth not.
>
> .   .   .   .
>
> One sky alone is cloudless,
>   There darkness enters not,
> 'Tis found alone with Jesus —
>   And Jesus changeth not.
>   WHITEFIELD.

This God is our God forever and ever: He will be our guide even unto death. — PSALM 48 : 14.

IF we can only cling to the Cross of Christ, we shall be safe. In the midst of temptation, of doubt, and danger, it is a Rock of defence; in the waves of sorrow, and underneath the clouds of darkness, it is a comfort and a beacon of light to lead us onward. When weary and discouraged with the journey of life, let us rest in the shadow of the Cross and drop our burdens there. Its radiance shall illumine our souls, and give us renewed faith and hope. Blessed are they that hide their hearts in its refuge.

Never farther than Thy cross,
　　Never higher than Thy feet;
Here earth's precious things seem dross,
　　Here earth's bitter things grow sweet.

Gazing thus, our sins shall see,
　　Learn Thy love while gazing thus;
Sin which laid the cross on Thee,
　　Love which bore the cross for us.

Here we learn to serve and give,
　　And, rejoicing, self deny;
Here we gather love to live,
　　Here we gather faith to die.

Symbols of our liberty
　　And our service here unite;
Captives, by Thy cross set free,
　　Soldiers of Thy cross, we fight.

Till amid the hosts of light,
　　We in Thee redeemed complete,
Through Thy cross made pure and white,
　　Cast our crowns before Thy feet.

ELIZABETH R. CHARLES.

TRUE contentment is an ornament to the mind. It is a jewel that brightens with the using, and imparts a lustre to all around it. It combines peace and happiness, and its possessor has a treasure which kings might envy. To be contented, in the midst of gaining and losing, waiting and serving, loving and hating — what a rare thing it is! How few of us learn, even in the longest lifetime, the sweet lesson of content, and yet it should be our chief care to cultivate so desirable a trait of character. God tells us " to be content with such things as we have," but we are continually reaching out after something which is not worth having. It is right that we should be discontented with ourselves, — we should aspire to a higher growth and more noble living, — but to be discontented with what God gives us, is wrong. Let us make the best of our surroundings, and meet each day's duty with a cheerfulness that is the outgrowth of inward peace and calm content.

Happy the man, of mortals happiest he,
Whose quiet mind from vain desires is free ;
Whom neither hopes deceive nor fears torment,
But lives at peace, within himself content.

GEORGE GRANVILLE.

The noblest mind the best contentment has.

SPENSER.

My crown is in my heart, not on my head,
Not deck'd with diamonds and Indian stones,
Nor to be seen ; my crown is called Content :
A crown it is that seldom kings enjoy.

HENRY VI., PART III., ACT III.

[17]

THROUGH all the changes of life have a purpose, and stick to it. Let no outward circumstances cause you to become discouraged and lose heart, if your aspirations are noble and true, but go resolutely forward, and be contented to face dull monotony day by day. No man can ever obtain wealth, power, and honor without fixedness of purpose, and to accomplish these he is obliged to do a great deal of plodding. If you are willing to climb, you will sometime reach the summit. You cannot walk around a difficulty expecting to find an easy place to surmount it: you only waste time in the attempt. Take in the situation, and begin the ascent: God allows no obstacles too great and no mounts of difficulty too high for us. Purpose and perseverance, with faith in Him, shall break down every barrier and leave us no excuse for failures.

> Onward, onward may we press
> Through the path of duty;
> Virtue is true happiness,
> Excellence true beauty;
> Minds are of supernal birth,
> Let us make a heaven of earth.
>
> JAMES MONTGOMERY.

The man who seeks one thing in life, and but one,
May hope to achieve it before life be done;
But he who seeks all things, wherever he goes,
Only reaps from the hopes which around him he sows
A harvest of barren regrets.

OWEN MEREDITH.

> Our lives are measured by the deeds we do,
> The thoughts we think, the objects we pursue.
>
> ANONYMOUS.

NEVER allow yourself to be too busy to look after your conscience. It needs more attention than your toilet. Put it in order every morning for the day, else if neglected it will become diseased like any other part of you. Examine it carefully at night, and see how it has stood the test of the day. Keep it clean and pure, keep it tender and impressionable, and always remember that it is an open window to the eye of God. Listen to the gentle monitor within; a good conscience is a safe counsellor, and to follow it is to steer in a right direction. God has given us our consciences that we may educate them in the best schools and give them a good moral training. A neglected conscience is like a garden full of weeds; nothing good has room to grow in a man, for the weeds of his evil nature get the better of him, and his conscience becomes hardened and unresponsive for want of pruning.

Yet still there whispers the small voice within,
Heard through Gain's silence, and o'er Glory's din;
Whatever creed be taught or land be trod,
Man's conscience is the oracle of God.

BYRON.

Conscience is harder than our enemies,
Knows more, accuses with more nicety.

GEORGE ELIOT.

Let Joy or Ease, let Affluence or Content,
And the gay Conscience of a life well spent,
Calm ev'ry thought, inspirit ev'ry grace,
Glow in thy heart, and smile upon thy face.

POPE.

Every subject's duty is the king's, but every subject's soul is his own. — SHAKESPEARE.

[19]

JANUARY FOURTEENTH.

IN the beginning God created the heaven and the earth. — GENESIS I : I.

The heavens declare the glory of God; and the firmament showeth his handiwork. — PSALM 19 : I.

Eternal Wisdom! Thee we praise,
   To Thee our songs we bring;
While with Thy name rocks, hills, and seas,
   And Heaven's high arches ring.
Thy hand, how wide it spread the sky!
   How glorious to behold!
Tinged with a blue of heavenly dye,
   And starr'd with sparkling gold!

There Thou hast bid the globes of light
   Their endless circles run;
There the pale planet rules the night,
   And day obeys the sun;
The stormy winds stand ready there
   Thine orders to obey;
With sounding wings they sweep the air,
   To make Thy chariot way.

Infinite strength, and equal skill,
   Shine through the worlds abroad;
Our souls with vast amazement fill,
   And speak the builder — God.
But the sweet beauties of Thy grace
   Our softer passions move;
Pity divine in Jesus' face
   We see, adore, and love.

ISAAC WATTS.

[20]

OH, the blessedness of giving! How it enlarges our hearts and sweetens our toil to share our bounty with others! There is always some one poorer than ourselves to need our help, — poorer in more ways than one. Perhaps some one we know is starving for sympathy and kindness, or hungering for an encouraging word: we surely can give these things without impoverishing ourselves or our dear ones.

Or, if they lack temporal blessings, let us do with a little less, that we may divide with them. It is the sweetness of silent alms that gladdens the heart of the Master and enriches the heart of the giver. It is the every-day life of self-sacrifice and self-denial that makes benevolence beautiful.

Is thy cruse of comfort wasting? Rise and share it
    with another,
And through all the years of famine it shall serve thee
    and thy brother.

Love divine will fill thy storehouse, or thy handful
    still renew;
Scanty fare for one will often make a royal feast for
    two.

For the heart grows rich in giving; all its wealth is
    living grain;
Seeds, which mildew in the garner, scattered, fill with
    gold the plain.

Is thy burden hard and heavy? do thy steps drag
    wearily?
Help to bear thy brother's burden; God will bear both
    it and thee.

ELIZABETH R. CHARLES.

[21]

WHY should we boast of what we have and are? All that we have God has given us; all that we are has only been reached through our acceptance of His opportunities. He has endowed us with body, mind, and soul. If we possess physical beauty and symmetry, it is His gift: if our minds are active and receptive, He has made them so: if our souls are singing the music of Heaven, it is because He has given us the chord. Worldly possessions should only be regarded as a blessing and means of doing good. As God has prospered us, let us benefit others. Riches are short-lived, but good deeds that spring from right motives are as immortal as Heaven. Let us then divest ourselves of pride, and keep before us the thought of the Eternal Goodness. Life at best is short, and will soon vanish away; but, thank God, He has provided a home for the faithful, an inheritance that shall last forever.

O why should the spirit of mortal be proud?
Like a swift-fleeting meteor, a fast-flying cloud,
A flash of the lightning, a break of the wave,
Man passes from life to his rest in the grave.

   .   .   .   .

For we are the same that our fathers have been;
We see the same sights that our fathers have seen;
We drink the same stream, and we see the same sun,
And run the same race that our fathers have run.

   .   .   .   .

Yea, hope and despondency, pleasure and pain,
We mingle together in sunshine and rain;
And the smiles and the tears, the song and the dirge,
Still follow each other, like surge upon surge.

WILLIAM KNOX.

[22]

GOD has given us His peace to comfort us, His faith to uplift us, and His Word to enlighten us. We have daily proofs of His care for us, and of His provision for our well-being and happiness. All this is because He loves us! O, what divine condescension, that He should stoop to remember us in our low estate! He rules the celestial Kingdom, and His footstool is the world; His strength is in the clouds, and His dominion and power are beyond comprehension. The Almighty and Infinite God hath for all His creatures a deep and boundless love, which we in our humanity cannot fathom or measure.

On the great love of God I lean,
Love of the Infinite, Unseen,
With naught of Heaven or earth between.
This God is mine, and I am His;
His love is all I need of bliss.

H. BONAR.

Lord, Thou art Life, tho' I be dead,
Love's fire Thou art, however cold I be;
Nor heaven have I, nor place to lay my head,
Nor home, but Thee.

CHRISTINA ROSSETTI.

What myst'ry clouds my darkened path?
I'll check my dread, my doubts reprove;
In this my soul sweet comfort hath,
That God is Love.

Oh, may this truth my heart employ,
Bid every gloomy thought remove,
And turn all tears, all woes to joy,—
Thou, God, art Love.

ANONYMOUS.

[23]

A MAN should guard his honor more than his gold. If it is impossible to possess both at the same time, let him part with his wealth and cling to his honor. Better, a thousand times, be a penniless beggar with a blameless character than a prince with a stain on his name. Better fall low in the estimation of the world than lose caste with God and the angels. The man who would honor his Maker must also honor himself; he must make a name and keep it above reproach, so that in after years it shall be found unsullied in the Records of Heaven.

Honour is purchased by deeds we do ; honour is not won,
Until some honourable deed is done.

CHRISTOPHER MARLOWE.

'Tis the mind that makes the body rich ;
And as the sun breaks through the darkest clouds,
So honour peereth in the meanest habit.

SHAKESPEARE.

Honour and shame from no condition rise ;
Act well your part, there all the honour lies.

POPE.

The sense of honour is of so fine and delicate a nature that it is only to be met with in minds which are naturally noble, or in such as have been cultivated by great examples or a refined education. — ADDISON.

Glory is sweet when our heart says to us that the wreath of honour ought to grace our head.

KRUMMACHER.

I could not love thee, dear, so much,
Loved I not honour more.

RICHARD LOVELACE.

BOOKS exert a silent influence on our lives. They are like friends, — we choose them, and all unconsciously they mould our characters after their own similitude. A man's thoughts usually flow in the same channel with the books he reads. He who chooses only the purest and best books will certainly be the better for their influence. If, then, our minds are so susceptible, let us be careful how and what we read, selecting only books that will elevate and improve us and broaden and expand our intellect.

> Of all those arts in which the wise excel,
> Nature's chief masterpiece is writing well.
>
> SHEFFIELD.

All that mankind has done, thought, gained, or been is lying as in a magic preservation in the pages of books. They are the chosen possession of men.

CARLYLE.

Books should to one of these four ends conduce, —
For wisdom, piety, delight, and use.

SIR JOHN DENHAM.

A good book is the precious life-blood of a master-spirit, embalmed and treasured up on purpose to a life beyond life. — MILTON.

I love to lose myself in other men's minds. When I am not walking, I am reading: I cannot sit and think. Books think for me. — LAMB.

Insist on reading the great books, on marking the great events of the world. Then the little books may take care of themselves, and the trivial incidents of passing politics and diplomacy may perish with the using. — DEAN STANLEY.

WHAT a wonderful thing is Influence! There is a thrill of power in the word itself. Our lives are small and insignificant at best, but our influence is mighty for either good or evil. Though we run our course in a few brief years, our influence goes on, sweeping through the ages, into Eternity. Carlyle says, "The work an unknown good man has done, is like a vein of water flowing hidden underground, secretly making the ground green." Nothing is sweeter or more impressive than silence, and nothing more restful and beautiful than verdure; and if we can only yield such an influence as this, how much better the world will be for our having lived in it!

> Who knows
> What earth needs from earth's lowest creatures? No
>   life
> Can be pure in its purpose and strong in its strife,
> And all life not be purer and stronger thereby.
> The spirits of just men made perfect on high,
> The army of martyrs who stand by the Throne
> And gaze into the face that makes glorious their own,
> Knows this surely at last. Honest love, honest sorrow,
> Honest work for the day, honest hope for the mor-
>   row —
> Are these worth nothing more than the hand they
>   make weary,
> The heart they have sadden'd, the life they leave
>   dreary?
> Hush! the sevenfold heavens to the voice of the
>   spirit
> Echo: He that o'ercometh shall all things inherit.

OWEN MEREDITH.

BEGIN the morning with God. Open your eyes to His glories, and let your tongue echo forth His praises. Let each act be a bit of worship. When you admit to your room the first beams of the early sun, think how He has lighted Life's pathway for you: when you brush your hair, remember how His loving hand has smoothed the tangles of difficulties from before you: when you wash your face, think of His dews of Mercy that are "new every morning"; and when you array yourself for the day, send up a little prayer that your soul may also wear the "robe of Righteousness," and that you may be " clad with zeal, as with a cloak." Begin the morning thus, and your heart enjoys noontide's rest and night's repose.

Mornings are mysteries: the first world's youth,
   Man's resurrection, and the future's bud
Shroud in their birth the crown of life, light, truth ;
   Is styled their star; the stone, and hidden food.
Three blessings wait upon them, one of which
Should move — they make us holy, happy, rich.

When the world's up, and every swarm abroad,
   Keep well thy temper; mix not with each day;
Despatch necessities : life has a load
   Which must be carried on, and safely may.
Yet keep these cares without thee: let the heart
Be God's alone, and choose the better part.

HENRY VAUGHAN.

Lord, I my vows to Thee renew,
Scatter my sins as morning dew,
Guard my first springs of thought and will,
And with Thyself my spirit fill.

THOMAS KEN.

[27]

TRUE Nobility consists in making every act of our lives an honor to our Maker. God's noblemen are men of royal birth; they inherit the charity that smiles on all humanity, the heroism that enables them to conquer self, and the courtesy which is a natural instinct to a heart at peace with God and the world. To be truly noble, we must do only noble deeds, and if our praises are not sung on earth, the recompense shall be ours by and by.

Think truly, and thy thought
  Shall the world's famine feed;
Speak truly, and thy word
  Shall be a fruitful seed;
Live truly, and thy life shall be
  A great and noble creed.

ANONYMOUS.

Be good, sweet maid, and let who will be clever;
  Do noble things, not dream them, all day long;
And so make life, death, and the vast forever
  One grand, sweet song.

CHARLES KINGSLEY.

Better not to be at all
Than not to be noble.

TENNYSON.

The grand old gardener and his wife
  Smile at the claims of long descent;
Howe'er it be, it seems to me,
  'Tis only noble to be good;
True hearts are more than coronets,
  And simple faith than Norman blood.

TENNYSON.

TIME never sleeps, but guards with jealous care the passing years. Bold, resolute, and dauntless, he peers into the mystic future, like an engineer with his swift locomotive, and steers his freighted train of hours, days, and seasons through the mists and shadows of the valleys of Fear; over the vernal heights of Hope; through the wilderness of Doubt; along the by-ways of Progress; into the avenues of Success, and down the deeps of Adversity. Time shall know no rest until he meets his great enemy — Eternity — who shall arrest his footsteps and stay his flight; then shall he drop the burden of the Years, fling down his gleaming scythe, and sink into oblivion. Where Time ends and Eternity begins, it is not ours to know; the Author of the universe, in whom we trust, is All-wise, and to Him alone belong the mysteries of Time and Eternity.

Touch us gently, Time!
We've not proud nor soaring wings;
Our ambition, our content,
Lies in simple things.
Humble voyagers are we,
O'er Life's dim, unsounded sea,
Seeking only some calm clime; —
Touch us gently, gentle Time!
BRYAN WALLER PROCTER.

The best is yet to be,
The last of life, for which the first was made.
ROBERT BROWNING.

SOME one has said, "Fame is a bubble," and so it
is. It holds in its fragile globe the fleeting reflection of the sunlight, and when the sky changes, the
glory fades, the bubble bursts and leaves no trace behind. The goal for which we toil, year by year, is
brighter in anticipation than reality, and by the time
we have reached it we are too weary to enjoy it, or
have grown to realize its nothingness. It is more
noble to seek to do good than to desire to be famous.
The praises of men are but weak after all, and if it is
that which inspires us, the end is not worth striving
for.

> The garlands wither on your brow, —
> Then boast no more your mighty deeds;
> Upon death's altar, now,
> See where the victor victim bleeds!
> All heads must come
> To the cold tomb, —
> Only the actions of the just
> Smell sweet, and blossom in the dust.

JAMES SHIRLEY.

He lives in fame, that died in virtue's cause.

SHAKESPEARE.

> The boast of heraldry, the pomp of power,
> And all that beauty, all that wealth e'er gave,
> Await alike the inevitable hour;—
> The paths of glory lead but to the grave.

GRAY.

> Unblemished let me live, or die unknown;
> Oh, grant an honest fame, or grant me none!

POPE.

[30]

THE greatest thing, after all, is to understand our own hearts; to rid them of their faults, so that their virtues may have room for larger and better growth, and to keep them true and tender, and in sympathy with our brother-man.

Heart-culture is full of surprises; we are amazed at our own selves when we once begin the process. The good and bad within us are continually at war with each other, and as fast as we root out one evil thought, another seed will spring up, so that we have great need of patience and perseverance. From the heart issue the thoughts that make for us our everlasting joy or eternal misery; from the heart our bodies are fed and our souls quickened, and through its influence the world is made better or worse.

It's no in titles nor in rank,
It's no in wealth like Lon'on bank,
    To purchase peace and rest;
It's no in making muckle mair,
It's no in books, it's no lear,
    To make us truly blest:
If happiness has not her seat
    And centre in the brest,
We may be wise, or rich, or great,
    But never can be blest:
Nae treasures, nor pleasures,
    Could make us happy lang;
The *heart* aye's the part aye,
    That makes us right or wrang.

                                    BURNS.

If a good face is a letter of recommendation, a good heart is a letter of credit. — BULWER-LYTTON.

ETERNAL hope! when yonder spheres sublime
　Pealed their first notes to sound the march of
　　time,
Thy joyous youth began.

CAMPBELL.

Know then, whatever cheerful and serene
Supports the mind, supports the body too;
Hence the most vital movement mortals feel
Is Hope, the balm and life-blood of the soul.

JOHN ARMSTRONG.

Work without Hope draws nectar in a sieve,
And Hope without an object cannot live.

S. T. COLERIDGE.

Hope, like the gleaming taper's light,
　Adorns and cheers our way;
And still, as darker grows the night,
　Emits a brighter ray.

GOLDSMITH.

Hope, like a cordial, innocent, though strong,
Man's heart at once inspirits and serenes.

YOUNG.

Through the sunset of Hope,
　Like the shapes of a dream,
What paradise islands of glory gleam!

SHELLEY.

Sweet Hope! celestial influence round me shed,
Waving thy silver pinions o'er my head.

KEATS.

[32]

HOW rare and sweet is the grace of Humility, especially when possessed by those who have attained honors or accumulated wealth! A truly humble man is seldom to be found, — but when we once discover him, he is as refreshing to us as an oasis to the traveller in the desert. Some of our greatest men have been as much distinguished for their modesty and humility as for their greatness. I should say that of all classes of men the "self-made man" is most apt to be boastful; he will probably tell you, the first time you are in his company, that he is a self-made man, and expects you to evince much surprise at his assertion, — little guessing that his manner and conversation have proclaimed the fact to every one present. When we sing our own praises, Humility hides her gentle face in very shame for us. Humanity, under all circumstances, needs to be clothed in the garb of Humility ; meekness is not weakness, but lowly strength; it is the triumph of being in the world, but not of it.

> God hath sworn to lift on high
> Who sinks himself by true humility.
>
> **KEBLE.**

> O be very sure
> That no man will learn anything at all,
> Unless he first will learn humility.
>
> **OWEN MEREDITH.**

> Knowledge is proud that he knows so much ;
> Wisdom is humble that he knows no more.
>
> **COWPER.**

[33]

JANUARY TWENTY-EIGHTH.

REST not ! Life is sweeping by;
Go and dare before you die.

GOETHE.

Life is a short day; but it is a working day.

HANNAH MORE.

Employment is the tonic of body, mind, and soul. An idle existence weakens the body: lack of exercise brings us to a physical standstill. The cheek loses its glow of health, the eye its lustre, and the step its elasticity and firmness. Every muscle and sinew expands and responds with life and strength, with proper physical exercise. The mind lies dormant, and all her natural powers become dulled by disuse; to become healthy and vigorous, the mind should have proper nourishment and exercise every day. So, too, with the soul; spiritual ill-health is often caused by neglect.

All Nature works; why not we? The hills, valleys, plains, and mountains know no rest, but each bear an active part to enrich and beautify the earth. Let us not be idle, but while it is To-day, let us take our place among life's toilers, and make its duties ours.

Rise ! — for the day is passing,
And you lie dreaming on;
The others have buckled their armour,
And forth to fight have gone;
A place in the rank awaits you,
Each has some part to play;
The past and the future are looking
In the face of the stern To-day.

ADELAIDE A. PROCTER.

ALL mankind enjoys being appreciated: if we have always been accustomed to it, we expect it, and are disappointed if we fail to receive it. If unaccustomed to it, we are both surprised and pleased, and are made happy that some one is kind enough and frank enough to show their approval of anything we do. If you think an appreciative thought, speak it — you may have but this one chance ; do not fail to improve the opportunity.

Sweet is the breath of praise when given by those whose own high merit claims the praise they give.

HANNAH MORE.

Some hearts go hungering through the world,
   And never find the love they seek ;
Some lips with pride or scorn are curled,
   To hide the pain they may not speak ;
The eye may flash, the mouth may smile,
   The voice in gladdest music thrill,
And yet beneath them all the while,
   The hungry heart be pining still.

O eager eyes which gaze afar !
   O arms which clasp the empty air !
Not all unmarked your sorrows are,
   Not all unpitied your despair.
Smile, patient lips, so proudly dumb ;
   When life's frail tent at last is furled,
Your glorious recompense shall come,
   O hearts that hunger through the world !

ANONYMOUS.

THE lesson of submission is one of the hardest we have to learn. It is so pleasant to have our own way about things, and so hard for us to yield our will to others. Yet submission must come, sooner or later, to us all. You may resolve to do just as you please in this world, but if you find it possible to do this — and very few do — you will be selfish and unhappy. "For even Christ pleased not Himself," we are told, and is not He our example? To live for self alone, when all humanity is crying out to us, — who would call it real living? Let us learn the sweetness of self-sacrifice; to do for God as He shall choose, and be submissive to His choice; to yield our will to His, and follow where He leads us.

My God, my Father, while I stray,
Far from my home, in life's rough way,
Oh! teach me from my heart to say, —
    "Thy will be done."

Renew my will from day to day;
Blend it with Thine and take away
All that now makes it hard to say, —
    "Thy will be done."

CHARLOTTE ELLIOT.

I want a sober mind,
    A self-renouncing will,
That tramples down and casts behind
    The baits of pleasing ill;
A spirit still prepared,
    And armed with zealous care,
Forever standing on its guard,
    And watching unto prayer.

CHARLES WESLEY.

WHATEVER else we may be, let us be charitable. Think what a happy world this would be if we all exercised a spirit of charity towards each other! How quick we are to judge our fellow-men — how often we *misjudge* them; we put a wrong construction on their words and misunderstand their actions and motives. Often we complain of faithless friends, and exclaim mournfully, "There is no one to be trusted: life itself is but a mockery!" when it is only because we have misjudged our friends, and put a wrong construction on their actions. If life is no more to us than a mockery, we should be ashamed to say it. Life is a garden of opportunities, and if we do not cull from it what God has placed there for us, it is no wonder our existence seems useless. There is a sweetness in giving that makes life worth living: to be generous with our charity will not impoverish us; it enriches both ourselves and our neighbors.

> Judge not; the workings of his brain
>   And of his heart thou canst not see;
> What looks to thy dim eyes a stain,
>   In God's pure light may only be
> A scar, brought from some well-won field,
> Where thou wouldst only faint and yield.
>
> ADELAIDE A. PROCTER.

The charities that soothe, and heal, and bless, are scattered at the feet of men like flowers.

WORDSWORTH.

> Charity, decent, easy, modest, kind,
> Softens the high, and rears the abject mind.
>
> MATTHEW PRIOR.

[37]

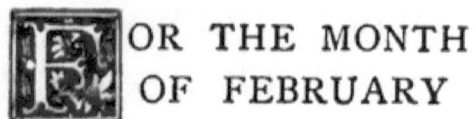

FOR THE MONTH OF FEBRUARY

FEBRUARY FIRST.

I SING, O Year, of melting snows,
   Of thawing icebergs out at sea ;
I sing of Winters past and gone, —
I look before and see the dawn
   Of glorious Springtimes yet to be !

'Twixt two bright realms my lot is cast,
   One where the white world lies at rest ;
The other, waking out of night,
Is upward striving for the light,
   With flowers upon its breast.

I look, I wait ; I sing again —
   O worlds, ye both are dear !
Farewell, white shores just drifting by :
Behold, the vernal land draws nigh —
   And February's here !

I. S. T.

A day of "betweens." After all, it is the betweens
that make up our daily lives, — the little things that
creep in among our duties and divide our thoughts for
a time, giving us sometimes a backward glance, and
sometimes a forward glimpse into the future. Like
February, we, too, are between the snows of the past
and the blossoms of the dawning future : let us find
something sweet to remember, and something bright
to hope for.

LORD BYRON
1788-1824

TAKE a little time to-day for self-examination. What are you doing with your life? Has it been what you intended it should be? Are you going backward or forward? Have you turned its shadows into sunshine with your happy-heartedness, or have you invited the clouds in life's sky to hang a little lower by showing them the clouds in your heart? Clouds usually attract each other: they drift in the same direction, and are swept by the same breeze; and the small ones are often caught up and borne away by the larger ones. Trouble makes trouble; if you do not meet it bravely, you must battle with weakness and cowardice, in addition to your other burdens. If you are not careful, you will have all your little troubles hanging over you in a great overwhelming mass. Better scatter them every day, and let the winds of Good-nature blow them away. Look on the bright side, and make your life a bit of sunshine.

So take Joy home,
And make a place in thy great heart for her,
And give her time to grow, and cherish her;
Then will she come, and oft will sing to thee,
When thou art working in the furrows; ay,
Or weeding in the sacred hour of dawn.
It is a comely fashion to be glad, —
Joy is the grace we say to God.

JEAN INGELOW.

Serene will be our days and bright,
And happy will our nature be,
When love is an unerring light,
And joy its own security.

WORDSWORTH.

[39]

THANK God for sympathy ! It is the firelight of
the soul. How it warms our hearts and brightens
our faces, and enkindles within us a flame of gratitude
and love ! Nothing appeals to the heart more than a
sympathizing word, when we are crushed by sorrow, or
weighed down by perplexing cares. A tear of sympathy is like healing balm to a broken spirit, and it
lessens our grief to know that others share it and make
it their own. Our joys, too, are sweeter when others
share them. A man cannot well keep a good laugh to
himself; it is contagious, and will spread, and broaden
over many faces besides his own.

Sympathy is an electric current with batteries all
over the world ; and blessed be God, that He has put
one in every human heart !

> The look of sympathy, the gentle word,
> Spoken so low that only angels heard ;
> The secret act of pure self-sacrifice,
> Unseen by man, but marked by angels' eyes —
> These are not lost.
>
> ANONYMOUS.

> Yet, taught by time, my heart has learned to glow
> For others' good, and melt at others' woe.
>
> POPE.

> Pity and need
> Make all flesh kin. There is no caste in blood,
> Which runneth of one hue, nor caste in tears,
> Which trickle salt with all.
>
> EDWIN ARNOLD.

[40]

T HY Word is a lamp unto my feet, and a light unto
my path. — PSALM 119: 105.

If we would learn patience, charity, kindness, humility, and forbearance, let us study the Bible. In it
are helps for all our needs, balms for all our ills, and
comforts for all our distresses. It teaches us how to
walk, that our steps may go in the right direction; it
tells us how to order our conversation aright; it edu-
cates our souls for the sacred school of Eternity, and
on its grand, strong promises we may rest our hopes of
Heaven. It is a comfort when other comforts fail, a
stronghold in danger and temptation, and a light in
darkness. If we live by the teachings of the Bible, our
lives will be full of quiet content and true happiness,
and our inheritance shall be a crown of rejoicing.

The Bible ! that's the Book, the Book indeed,
  The Book of books,
  On which who looks,
As he should do, aright, shall never need
  Wish for a better light
  To guide him in the night.

 . . . .

It is the index to Eternity;
  He cannot miss
  Of endless bliss
That takes this chart to steer his voyage by,
  Nor can he be mistook
  That speaketh by this Book.
      GEORGE HERBERT.

A TRAVELLER through a dusty road strewed
  acorns on the lea;
And one took root and sprouted up, and grew into a
  tree.
Love sought its shade, at evening-time, to breathe its
  early vows,
And age was pleased, in heats of noon, to bask beneath
  its boughs;
The dormouse loved its dangling twigs, the birds
  sweet music bore;
It stood a glory in its place, a blessing evermore.

A little spring had lost its way amid the grass and fern,
A passing stranger scooped a well, where weary man
  might turn;
He walled it in, and hung with care a ladle at the
  brink;
He thought not of the deed he did, but judged that
  toil might drink.
He passed again, and lo! the well, by summers never
  dried,
Had cooled ten thousand parching tongues, and saved
  a life beside.

A dreamer dropped a random thought; 'twas old, and
  yet 'twas new;
A simple fancy of the brain, but strong in being true:
It shone upon a genial mind, and lo! its light became
A lamp of life, a beacon ray, a monitory flame.
The thought was small, its issue great; a watch-fire
  on the hill,
It sheds its radiance far adown, and cheers the valley
  still!

CHARLES MACKAY.

FEBRUARY SIXTH.

WELL, and don't we all have burdens? Have you any one's share but your own? You may think yours heavier than your neighbor's, but your neighbor, very likely, wouldn't agree with you. We all complain of our crosses, and tell other people about them, when they have their own to carry, and imagine ours small in comparison. Cheerfulness is a great burden-bearer. Drink in a draught of it with the first breath of fresh air in the morning, and you've no idea how it will exhilarate and refresh you. It lifts you above the everyday trials and annoyances, and fills your heart with sunshine, and your lips with a song. Burdens are a part of our discipline; they belong to our fate. And who could govern all our fate, save God?

Let those deplore their doom
Whose hope still grovels in this dark sojourn;
But lofty souls, who look beyond the tomb,
Can smile at Fate, and wonder how they mourn.

BEATTIE.

Thus would I double my life's fading space,
For he that runs it well, twice runs his race.
    And in this true delight,
These unbought sports, that happy state,
I would not fear nor wish my fate,
    But boldly say each night,
To-morrow let my sun his beams display,
Or in clouds hide them; I have lived to-day.

ABRAHAM COWLEY.

To bear is to conquer our fate.

CAMPBELL.

[43]

FEBRUARY SEVENTH.

Behold!
How short a span
Was long enough of old
To measure out the life of man!
In those well-tempered days his time was then
Survey'd, cast up, and found but threescore years and
ten.

Our days
Begun, we lend
To sleep, to antic plays
And toys, until the first stage end:
Twelve waning moons, twice five times told, we
give
To unrecover'd loss — we rather breathe than live.

How soon
Our new-born light
Attains to full-aged noon !
And this, how soon to grey-haired night!
We spring, we bud, we blossom, and we blast,
Ere we can count our days, our days they flee so fast.

They end
When scarce begun,
And ere we apprehend
That we begin to live, our life is done.
Man! count thy days; and if they fly too fast
For thy dull thoughts to count, count every day thy
last.

FRANCIS QUARLES. (1592.)

[44]

FEBRUARY EIGHTH.

ISN'T it sweet to think of the recompense that shall be ours in God's beautiful Hereafter? In doing our best, we are scattering seed for His great Harvest; and though sometimes we water them with tears, He sends down the sunlight of His love, and quickens them into springing fields of grain. God never forgets nor loses sight of His own, nor will He be satisfied with work half done. He expects us to do our best, and nothing short of that will meet with His acceptance.

A child's kiss
Set on thy sighing lips shall make thee glad;
A poor man served by thee, shall make thee rich;
A sick man helped by thee, shall make thee strong;
Thou shalt be served thyself by every sense
Of service which thou renderest.

E. B. BROWNING.

May I reach
That purest heaven, be to other souls
The cup of strength in some great agony,
Enkindle generous ardour, feed pure love,
Be the sweet presence of a good diffused,
And in diffusion ever more intense!
So shall I join the choir invisible,
Whose music is the gladness of the world.

GEORGE ELIOT.

Oh, dream no more of quiet life;
Care finds the careless out; more wise to vow
Thy heart entire to faith's pure strife;
So peace will come, thou knowest not when or how.

LYRA APOSTOLICA.

[45]

IF we can only keep our hearts young, we shall never really grow old. Let the forehead wear its wrinkles, if it must, but keep them out of the heart. Smooth away all the unkind thoughts and feelings, and do not allow the worries to rankle and drive out all the good there is in you. Live in the sunlight of love — it keeps you young and sweet-tempered. Soar above annoyances; if you continually carry them with you, you will grow old before your time — yes, old and tired and disagreeable. We don't mind an old face ; wrinkles and white hair are beautiful if there is a young heart back of them. It is a grand thing to be able to grow old graciously, and the way to do it is to keep the heart young.

When Victor Hugo was past eighty years of age he gave expression to his religious faith in these sublime sentences : " I feel in myself the future life. I am like a forest which has been more than once cut down. The new shoots are livelier than ever. I am rising toward the sky. The sunshine is on my head. The earth gives me its generous sap, but Heaven lights me with its unknown worlds. You say the soul is nothing but the resultant of the bodily powers. Why, then, is my soul the more luminous when my bodily powers begin to fail? Winter is on my head and eternal spring is in my heart."

> The stars shall fade away, the sun himself
> Grow dim with age, and nature sink in years;
> But thou shalt flourish in immortal youth,
> Unhurt amidst the war of elements,
> The wreck of matter, and the crush of worlds.
>
> ADDISON.

MY Conscience is my crown,
  Contented thoughts my rest;
My heart is happy in itself,
  My bliss is in my breast.

I feel no care of coin,
  Well-doing is my wealth;
My mind to me an empire is,
  While grace affordeth health.

SOUTHWELL.

What a song of Content, Southwell sings! It leads
to a kingdom which money or birth could not purchase.
To wear the crown of a good conscience, and to
possess a mind broader and richer than an empire, is
enough to inspire one to write a song which shall echo
down the ages, and sing itself into the hearts of all
nations. Oh, to be satisfied with our lot in life is a
rare, sweet thing.

My house a cottage, more
Than palace, and should fitted be
For all my use, no luxury.
  My garden painted o'er
With Nature's hand, not Art's; and pleasures yield,
Horace might envy in his Sabine field.

ABRAHAM COWLEY.

It conduces much to our content, if we pass by those
things which happen to our trouble, and consider that
which is pleasing and prosperous; that, by the repre-
sentation of the better, the worse may be blotted out.

JEREMY TAYLOR.

OUR To-morrows ! What heart would be without them ? In childhood, they are as rosy-hued as the dawn, and we run to meet them — our glad young feet as swift as though on soaring wings. Care-free and happy, we close our sleepy eyes at night, our last fond thought of the coming day, our golden dreams made bright, by that one sweet hope — to-morrow !

In life's grave prime, we look forward with less eagerness to the dawn of our to-morrows. Time has become a reality, and the earnestness of living and being fill us with an awed curiosity, as we think of each coming day.

Contact with the world has robbed us of some of our childish faith, I grieve to say, but a calm courage possesses us, and we go forth with resolution to meet to-morrow bravely, be it what it may.

And when the years have gathered on our heads, and left their silver threads above our brows, the eager hopes of youth, the courage of our older years, and all that made us long for bright to-morrows, shall merge into a restful peace — the waiting-time of life — when we shall listen for our Lord to softly call, " Dear tired Heart, look up and see the dawn — 'tis God's To-morrow."

How oft my guardian angel gently cried,
  "Soul, from thy casement look, and thou shalt see
How he persists to knock and wait for thee!"
And oh! how often to that voice of sorrow,
  "To-morrow we will open," I replied,
And when to-morrow came I answered still,
      "To-morrow."

TR. FROM LOPE DE VEGA.

[48]

PERHAPS the reason we make so many mistakes is because we do not fully understand ourselves, and each other. We are more intent on fathoming God's great mysteries, and searching out His plans, than on studying man and man's needs. Had the Author of our being thought best, He would have revealed to us His heavenly secrets, but in His all-wisdom He bids us leave the future in His keeping, and have faith in Him. He has given us life — His grandest creation; He has given us our brother-man to encourage, to help, and to uplift, so that we may travel together the Upward Way and find pleasant companionship. Let us therefore make it our object to find the best that is in our neighbor, learn how to make our pilgrimage a happy one, and render ourselves as congenial as possible. We must understand ourselves first, and as all humanity has kindred feelings, we will then be better able to understand our fellow-men.

Man is his own star, and that soul that can
Be honest, is the only perfect man.
BEAUMONT AND FLETCHER.

Without our hopes, without our fears,
Without our home that plighted love endears,
Without the smile from partial beauty won,
Oh! what were man? — a world without a sun.
CAMPBELL.

Man stands in the centre of Nature; his fraction of Time encircled by Eternity; his handbreadth of Space encircled by Infinitude. — CARLYLE.

[49]

O "MARINERS of England," how loyal and how brave you are ! As over the bright blue ocean you speed and speed away, you ever keep floating above you the flag of your own native land. With jealous care you guard the shores you love, and turn your longing eyes to catch a lingering glimpse of home, the England of the world. You could not brave the stormy wind with half the courage which you do, had you not such principles of love and loyalty as beat with every bounding pulse, and strengthen with each breath you draw. For the sake of dear old England you brave danger, risk life, and, leaving behind the sweet delights of home, go forth to buffet with the perils of the mighty deep. Oh, long live the British mariners, and may they face the waves of Life with as brave hearts and true as any waves that rise at sea !

> Ye mariners of England,
> That guard our native seas ;
> Whose flag has braved a thousand years
> The battle and the breeze !
> Your glorious standard launch again
> To match another foe !
> And sweep through the deep,
> While the stormy winds do blow ;
> While the battle rages loud and long,
> And the stormy winds do blow.
>
> . . . .
>
> Britannia needs no bulwarks,
> No towers along the steep ;
> Her march is o'er the mountain-waves,
> Her home is on the deep.

THOMAS CAMPBELL.

[50]

FEBRUARY FOURTEENTH.

HAIL to thy returning festival, old Bishop Valentine! Great is thy name in the rubric. Like unto thee, assuredly, there is no other mitred father in the calendar. — LAMB.

Apollo has peeped through the shutter,
And waken'd the witty and fair;
The boarding-school belle's in a flutter,
The twopenny post's in despair;
The breath of the morning is flinging
A magic on blossom and spray,
And cockneys and sparrows are singing
In chorus on Valentine's day.

PRAED.

On paper curiously shaped,
Scribblers to-day of every sort,
In verses Valentine's y'clep'd,
To Venus chime their annual court.
I, too, will swell the motley throng,
And greet the all-auspicious day,
Whose privilege permits my song,
My love thus secret to convey.

HENRY C. BOHN.

I give you greeting! for this is St. Valentine's day. Let your heart open a little wider; make room for a few more who need loving; give out more light and heat — you've plenty to spare. Hearts that are bright and warm are royal fireplaces for cold humanity. This is the sort of a Valentine we all want to be, — a Valentine of love and happiness.

[51]

FEBRUARY FIFTEENTH.

THERE are so many ways in which we can make others happy. If we are willing to practise a little self-denial, we will find plenty of opportunity to speak a kindly word, or do a friendly deed. Don't be so absorbed in your business affairs that you fail to say " good morning " to a friend when you pass him on the street. The man who goes about with his head too high to see common humanity, will sometime find himself wondering why he has so few real friends. And the man who passes to and fro with his eyes bent on the ground, will some day discover that he has missed a great deal, because he failed to look any higher than the sidewalk. If you want to be alone, select a retired street, where you can meditate undisturbed, but don't pass your neighbor by without seeing him — you can't afford to be discourteous. Come out of yourself; and don't creep like a snail, if you are a preacher or a professor; on the other hand, don't flash along like a meteor, if you are a business man. You cannot carry your church or school in your head, neither can you bear your warehouse or bank on your shoulders. When on the street, you are only a man among men. People don't care half as much who you are, as *what* you are: if you are cordial in your greeting, and friendly in your manner, it will do the world good if you look it squarely in the face and say " good morning."

Oh, if the selfish knew how much they lost,
What would they not endeavor, not endure,
To imitate, as far as in them lay,
Him, who His wisdom and His power employs
In making others happy!

SAMUEL ROGERS.

[52]

"LEAD us not into temptation." Every day has its own temptations, without and within. If, like our Redeemer when He was tempted, we can put them behind us, we shall be able to go on our way rejoicing. Oh, the little temptations swarm like bees about us, and when we rob them of their honey they always leave a sting. It is only when we keep busy with our appointed tasks, and are doing our best in the hive where God has placed us, that we can escape being stung by the temptations that come to us from unfriendly hives. Armed with the shield of Prayer, the stings shall glance off, and leave no scar, and ours shall be the victory of overcoming.

In the hour of dread temptation
 When the serpent's voice shall call,
Lest we list to its allurements, —
 Lest we weakly faint or fall;
Be Thou near, O gracious Father,
 Lead the feet that fain would stray
Into some forbidden pathway,
 Back to safety's narrow way.

Even as the little children
 Fly, when aught their fears alarm,
To the often tried protection
 Of an earthly parent's arm —
So Thy children call upon Thee,
 When life's shadows darkly fall,
Who alone can keep us scathless, —
 Gracious Father of us all!

HELEN MARION BURNSIDE.

THE Lord watch between me and thee when we are absent one from another. — GENESIS 31 : 49.

How thankful must the Israelites have been for the guidance of the pillar of fire! We can imagine that mighty throng moving on and on in their pilgrimage, sometimes murmuring and complaining, sometimes singing and praising God, yet marching ever nearer to the Promised Land, beneath the radiance of that fiery symbol. And when, at night, they pitched their tents, it must have been a magnificent spectacle — the great army grouped about in tented silence, with that wondrous sign — God's loving "Mizpah" — set, like a seal, in the midst of the starry heavens. We, too, are treading homeward to the Canaan-Land: in the desert and wilderness of life, like the Israelites of old, we have our Mizpah-light to lead us onward and upward to the "rest that remaineth for the people of God."

In absence, when the day-star shineth,
Tho' far apart our paths may be,
I ask His daily presence with us —
The Lord keep watch 'tween me and thee.

At night-fall, when the sun declineth,
And shadows fall on earth and sea,
Oh, may He hide us 'neath His refuge,
And still keep watch 'tween me and thee!

Forever with us! tho' we sever;
His shelt'ring love shall be my plea —
Until we meet again, beseeching,
The Lord keep watch 'tween me and thee!

IDA SCOTT TAYLOR.

WE can put our own interpretation on the word Duty; it means just what we want it to. It is either a hard, stern task-master, or a gentle leader, whose kind approval is always awaiting us,—a sure reward for everything cheerfully and willingly done. There is no task which may not be finished, no burden which shall not be lifted, no cloud that shall not be dispersed, and no night that hath not its glorious dawn. Sometime, sometime, we shall be able to fully realize this, and understand that there is " an end to all things under the sun." Let us go on then, doing the duty nearest, sweetening each task with a smile, and doing with our might what our hands find to do. If we make Duty a pleasure, it will be far easier for us. Each person is a hero in the eyes of God if he is actively engaged in doing his best. Go bravely forward, meet and surmount every difficulty: put your hand into the hand of God.

> Long though my task may be,
>   Cometh the end.
> God 'tis that helpeth me,
> His is the work, and He
>   New strength will lend.
>
> ANONYMOUS.

> Time is indeed a precious boon,
>   But with the boon a task is given;
> The heart must learn its duty well,
>   To man on earth and God in Heaven.
>
> ELIZA COOK.

In common things the law of sacrifice takes the form of positive duty. — FROUDE.

[55]

THE firefly only shines when on the wing;
So with the mind; when once we rest, we darken.

BAILEY.

The world is the school-room of the mind: in it are gathered classified volumes in poetry and prose, where we read and study to our heart's content. The sea is a nautical library: the beat of its waves is a lyric poem, and the thunder of its mighty breakers is a sermon of majestic sweetness. The sky is rich in its collection of songs and sonnets, and in its deep, thoughtful, astronomical works. The woods and hills, and valleys and plains, are Nature's own books, written out by the hand of God. The mines of silver and gold are volumes of hidden love, which need to be brought to the light if we would read their meaning. Man is the speaking book of God, his mind and soul the voice of God, his life a reflection of God, and his only salvation the Son of God.

Creator! Yes! Thy wisdom and Thy word
Created me. Thou source of life and good;
Thou Spirit of my spirit, and my Lord;
Thy light, Thy love, in their bright plenitude,
Filled me with an immortal soul to spring
O'er the abyss of death, and bade it wear
The garments of eternal day, and wing
Its heavenly flight beyond this little sphere —
Even to its source — to Thee, its Author — there.

JOHN BOWRING (Tr. from the Russian).

A little philosophy inclineth a man's mind to atheism, but depth in philosophy bringeth men's minds about to religion. — BACON.

[56]

CHOOSE your author as you choose your friend. —
ROSCOMMON.

Reading is to the mind what exercise is to the body.
As by the one, health is preserved, strengthened, and
invigorated, by the other, virtue (which is the health
of the mind) is kept alive, cherished, and confirmed. —
ADDISON.

The mind, relaxing into needful sport,
Should turn to writers of an abler sort,
Whose wit well managed, and whose classic style,
Give truth a lustre, and make wisdom smile.

COWPER.

Read not to contradict and confute, nor to believe
and take for granted, not to talk and discourse, but to
weigh and consider. . . . Some books are to be read
only in parts; others to be read, but not curiously;
and some few to be read wholly, and with diligence and
attention. — BACON.

All rests with those who read, a work or thought
Is what makes it to himself, and may
Be full of great dark meanings, like the sea,
With shoals of life rushing.

BAILEY.

Learn to read slow; all other graces
Will follow in their proper places.

WM. WALKER.

[57]

FEBRUARY TWENTY-FIRST.

A Day among the Clouds.

OH, it is pleasant, with a heart at ease,
  Just after sunset, or by moonlight skies,
To make the shifting clouds be what you please,
  Or let the easily-persuaded eyes
Own each quaint likeness issuing from the world
  Of a friend's fancy.

COLERIDGE.

What beautiful things we behold in the clouds!
Ever shifting and changing, and drifting about in the
great blue sea of the sky, they float above us — these
fair, white mysteries — spreading their airy wings and
bearing away our sweetest dreams to be lost in the
silence of some unknown world.

Oh, many gilded palaces and stately castles have we
erected in the sunny skies, builded only of the frail,
inconstant clouds. With every breeze our structures
have tumbled from their dizzy heights and been wrecked
before our eyes, but then we only smile and build again.
Our sweetest, purest thoughts take wing among the
clouds, for God is in their midst, and angels round
aboat.

I bring fresh showers for the thirsty flowers,
  From the seas and the streams;
I bear light shade for the leaves when laid
  In their noonday dreams.
From my wings are shaken the dews that waken
  The sweet birds every one,
When rocked to rest on their mother's breast,
  As she dances about the sun.

SHELLEY.

[58]

THERE is a great deal said nowadays about "color-blindness"; this, however, refers to the physical vision, but mental color-blindness is even worse than that. It is a far greater calamity to be unable to distinguish any color but one — and that the hue to our own imaginary loveliness; for loveliness is always imaginary when only one person is aware of it. If you are a true artist, you will find the shadow as well as the light. Train your mental vision to detect both; bring them into better harmony. Soften your shadows a little; get your background ready for the bright tints, then leave God to add the high lights.

There are no shadows where there is no sun;
There is no beauty where there is no shade;
And all things in two lines of glory run,
Darkness and light, ebon and gold inlaid.

F. W. FABER.

I know the Hand that is guiding me through the
    shadow to the light,
And I know that all betiding me is meted out aright;
I know that the thorny path I tread is ruled by a
    golden line,
And I know that the darker life's tangled thread, the
    richer the deep design.

BRITISH EVANGELIST.

Our little systems have their day:
    They have their day and cease to be;
    They are but broken lights of Thee,
And Thou, O Lord, art more than they.

TENNYSON.

THOU camest not to thy place by accident,
It is the very place God meant for thee.

R. C. TRENCH.

Adapt yourselves to circumstances; get into harmony with your surroundings, or you will be miserable. If your circumstances are above you, work up to them; educate your mind and tastes up to a higher plane: keep rising, it is a positive disgrace to go downward or backward in this progressive world of ours. If your circumstances are beneath you, lift them up: this is not asking too much of you — it has been done often. I have seen such dignity and refinement in the midst of abject poverty as lends itself to every faded object in a room. There is nothing in an atmosphere of true gentility and nobleness, but what catches a bit of the spirit of its surroundings. The touch of refinement stamps itself on all with which it comes in contact. If you are gracious yourself, your belongings, no matter how poor they are, will unconsciously become a part of you. Dignify your surroundings and they will honor you, and make you more beautiful by contrast.

The thing which must be, must be for the best;
God helps us do our duty and not shrink,
And trust His mercy humbly for the rest.

OWEN MEREDITH.

Instead of saying that man is the creature of circumstances, it would be nearer the mark to say that man is the architect of circumstances. It is character which builds an existence out of circumstances. Our strength is measured by our plastic power. — GEORGE H. LEWES.

SOME writer describes beauty thus : " All along the isles of earth, all over the arches of Heaven, all through the expanses of the universe, are scattered in rich and infinite profusion the life-germs of beauty. All natural motion is beauty in action. From the mote that plays its little frolic in the sunbeam, to the world that blazes along the sapphire of the firmament, are visible the ever-varying features of the enrapturing spirit of beauty."

Who doth not feel, until his failing sight
Faints into dimness with its own delight,
His changing cheek, his sinking heart confess,
The might, the majesty of Loveliness?

BYRON.

The beauty that addresses itself to the eyes is only the spell of the moment; the eye of the body is not always that of the soul. — GEORGE SAND.

A thing of beauty is a joy forever ;
Its loveliness increases ; it will never
Pass into nothingness ; but still will keep
A bower of quiet for us, and a sleep
Full of sweet dreams, and health, and quiet breathing.

KEATS.

For when with beauty we can virtue join,
We paint the semblance of a point divine.

PRIOR.

Beauty is truth, truth beauty.

KEATS.

FEBRUARY TWENTY-FIFTH.

WE are builders, and each one
    Should cut and carve as best he can.
Every life is but a stone,
Every one shall hew his own.
    Make or mar shall every man.

ANONYMOUS.

Character-building requires patience, perseverance,
and care. To build well, select the Firm Foundation
—Christ. Let no day pass without some progress.

Master! to do great work for Thee, my hand
    Is far too weak. Thou givest what may suit —
Some little chips to cut with care minute,
Or tint, or grave, or polish. Others stand
Before their quarried marble, fair and grand,
    And make a life-work of the great design
    Which Thou hast traced; or, many-skilled, combine
To build vast temples, gloriously planned,
Yet take the tiny stones which I have wrought,
    Just one by one, as they were given by Thee,
Not knowing what came next in Thy wise thought.
Set each stone by Thy master-hand of grace,
    For the mosaic as Thou wilt, for me,
And in Thy temple-pavement give it place.

FRANCES RIDLEY HAVERGAL.

Fling wide the portals of your heart,
Make it a temple set apart
From earthly use for Heaven's employ,
Adorned with prayer, and love, and joy.
So shall your Sovereign enter in,
And new and nobler life begin.

WEISZEL.

A DAY by the fireside! Draw the blind a little, and shut out the outside world: only leave a faint glimmer, to light the weary passer-by. How cozy it is! How you love to watch the flames leap up, and cast a weird flickering radiance on the walls and ceiling! How you enjoy making pictures in the fire, and what sweet, hallowed memories they suggest! Winter is passing away, and soon shall dawn another spring. Take a backward sweep over the years; how many sweet, beautiful things you have to remember: did you ever think of that? How many good gifts have fallen to your share, how many dear friendships have been given you. What choice blessings have been yours, and what royal good cheer. Why, sitting here in the glow of the firelight, you can look back over your life and wonder why you never realized before how well-favored you have been. "Surely the lines have fallen," to you, "in pleasant places." How the hallowed memories come thronging around you to-day: old faces look out of the dancing flames to greet you, and you hear familiar tones speaking out of the silent past. Oh, what a blessed thing it is that our missing ones can all come back to us, back through the Memory of the Past, and thank God, that is not all — we shall see them by and by on the echoless shores of Eternity.

When I remember something which I had,
    But which is gone, and I must do without,
I sometimes wonder how I can be glad,
    Even in cowslip-time, when hedges sprout;
It makes me sigh to think on it — but yet
My days will not be better days, should I forget.

JEAN INGELOW.

WE then that are strong ought to bear the infirmities of the weak, and not to please ourselves.
—ROMANS 15 : 1.

Isn't it a blessed thing to be helpful? Isn't it a
comfort to feel that we are needed and wanted in the
world — to know that there is a place for us, and to be
in our place, ready, willing, aye, and even *anxious* to
do our part, and help some one weaker than ourselves?
Let this be a day of helpfulness : be on the look out for
the needs of others. Isn't there a home that you could
brighten, a burden that you could lighten, a heart that
you could comfort, if you try? The poor little pale-
faced invalid who sits at the window when you pass
by, haven't you a smile to spare her? The ragged
street urchin you were unkind to yesterday, can't you
make it up to him to-day with a pleasant word? You
were cross to some one in your own household yesterday, perhaps, but you have been sorry for it ever since ;
be patient to-day, and help — not hinder the happiness
of those you love.

Be useful where thou livest, that they may
Both want and wish thy pleasing presence still.
    Find out men's wants and will,
And meet them there. All worldly joys go less
To the one joy of doing kindnesses.
G. HERBERT.

Oh, might we all our lineage prove,
Give and forgive, do good and love ;
By soft endearments, in kind strife
Lightening the load of daily life.
J. KEBLE.

WE are all too apt to find fault: it is characteristic of humanity. We cannot expect to have things just as we want them in this world, so why should we grumble and complain ? What if our breakfast is not cooked exactly as we like it; will it taste any better if seasoned with murmurings ? What if the weather doesn't suit our convenience or plans ? Perhaps the sun shines too hotly for a sail on the lake; or the rain is falling, and we must give up a shopping expedition, or a pleasure-trip; will it do any good to find fault ? And then, we see too many flaws in our neighbors. None of us are perfect: are you ? am I ? That is about the only kind of blindness God will tolerate — that which shuts out defects in the dispositions of those around us. Or, if they are too glaring to be hidden, let us not speak of them to others. My grandmother's motto was, "If you cannot say something good about people, say nothing at all." A quick tongue and a complaining spirit stir up strife; let us therefore learn to control both our words and actions.

Back then, complainer; loath thy life no more,
Nor deem thyself upon a desert shore,
    Because the rocks the nearer prospect close.
Yet in fallen Israel are there hearts and eyes
That day by day in prayer like thine arise;
    Thou know'st them not, but their Creator knows.

J. KEBLE.

When thou hast thanked thy God
    For every blessing sent,
What time will then remain
    For murmurs or lament ?

R. C. TRENCH.

FEBRUARY TWENTY-NINTH.

A Day of Gladness.

I OPENED the doors of my heart,
             And behold
There was music within and a song,
And echoes did feed on the sweetness, repeating it long.

JEAN INGELOW.

Let us open the doors of our hearts to-day and see how much gladness we can throw into the world. What is the use to hoard up sunshine and joy ? We cannot leave it to our friends when we die. The only way to be benevolent with gladness, is to keep on giving it out : let it radiate from us every day, and then its sweet influence will be a precious legacy to our friends and loved ones.

O, whatever our lot, let us be glad !
Glad for the toil and the tears,
Glad for the hopes and the fears,
Glad for the gathering years,
        Joyous or sad ;
Ours but to do our best,
Matters not what the test —
God's part to do the rest,
        Let us be glad !

I. S. T.

I praise Thee while my days go on ;
I love Thee while my days go on :
Through dark and dearth, through fire and frost,
With emptied arms and treasures lost,
I thank Thee while my days go on.

E. B. BROWNING.

FELICIA HEMANS
1793–1835

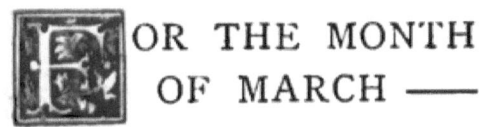# OR THE MONTH OF MARCH ——

MARCH FIRST.

MARCH. Its tree, Juniper. Its stone, Bloodstone. Its motto, "Courage and strength in time of danger." — OLD SAYING.

Look and listen ! All the earth is awakening. For this is Spring's resurrection, and March, with his dauntless courage and strength, has heralded its coming to the world. The Juniper trees are trembling with happiness, and as the cool, crisp breath of March sways their branches, they wave their palms of rejoicing and seem to say, "this is *our* day, for we belong to March ! O world, look up to us, and be strong !" Let us therefore be sturdy and resolute, like March, and putting on our juniper strength, go forth to search for God's truths in all things. Let our souls awake, like the Spring, and seek out God's glories.

> Say not the struggle naught availeth,
>   The labor and the wounds are vain,
> The enemy faints, nor faileth,
>   And as things have been they remain.
>
> . . . .
>
> For while the tired waves, vainly breaking,
>   Seem here no painful inch to gain,
> Far back, through creeks and inlets making,
>   Comes silent, flooding in, the main.
>
> ARTHUR HUGH CLOUGH.

[67]

MARCH SECOND.

LET us take time to consider. We are so hurried in our earth-life, and so burdened with our cares and pleasures, that we have little leisure for reflection. We are so busy clothing our bodies, that we have not time to consider how we may clothe our souls. We are so engrossed with the accumulation of riches that we forget to consider how we may best enrich our minds. We are so taken up with self and self-interests, that we neglect to consider the grand proofs of God's love for us, and to reflect upon His wisdom and might. Oh that we could learn to think more about God, and trust more fully in His loving protection, and grow daily more dependent upon His mercies !

Consider
The lilies of the field whose bloom is brief,
We are as they,
Like them we fade away,
As doth a leaf.

Consider
The sparrows of the air of small account ;
Our God doth view
Whether they fall or mount —
He guards us too.

Consider
The birds that have no barn nor harvest weeks
God gives them food ;
Much more our Father seeks
To do us good.

ROSSETTI.

[68]

THIS lovely world, the hills, the sward —
　　They all look fresh, as if our Lord
　　　　But yesterday had finished them.

JEAN INGELOW.

For winter's rain and ruins are over,
　　And all the season of snows and sins;
The days dividing lover and lover,
　　The light that loses, the night that wins;
And time remembered is grief forgotten,
And frosts are slain and flowers begotten,
And in green underwood and cover
　　Blossom by blossom the spring begins.

ALGERNON CHARLES SWINBURNE.

The heart that loves God rejoices in His works. He has set His seal on the hills and mountains, and breathed His breath into the birds and flowers. A quiet hour of sweet communion with Nature lifts us a little nearer Heaven. You may have read a great many books, but where is there a book that can teach such wisdom as the book of Creation? It is a master work of theology and philosophy, and yet it has all the grace, sweetness, and rhythm of a lyric poem. The book of Nature may be said to be a divine pastoral.

I grant to the king his reign;
　　Let us yield him homage due.
　　.　.　.　.　.　.　.
I grant to the wise his meed,
　　But his yoke I will not brook,
For God taught *me* to read, —
　　He lent me the world for a book.

JEAN INGELOW.

MARCH FOURTH.

VERSE, *a breeze 'mid blossoms straying,*
   *Where **hope** clung feeding like **a bee** —*
Both were mine ! Life went a-Maying
With Nature, Hope, and Poetry,
      When I was young!

When I was young? Ah, woful *when!*
Ah, for the change 'twixt now and then!
   . . . .

Naught cared **this body** for wind or weather,
When Youth and I lived in't together.
Flowers are lovely : **Love is flower-like :**
Friendship is a sheltering tree ;
O the joys that came down shower-like,
Of Friendship, Love, and Liberty,
      Ere I was old !

Ere I was old? Ah, woful *ere!*
Which tells me Youth's no longer here !
O Youth ! for years so many and sweet,
'Tis known that thou and I were one ;
I'll think it but a fond deceit —
It cannot be that thou art gone !

   . . . .

I see these locks in silvery slips,
This drooping gait, this altered size ;
But Springtide blossoms on thy lips,
And tears take sunshine from thine eyes !
Life is but thought ; so think I will,
That Youth and I are house-mates still.

COLERIDGE.

[70]

NOW faith is the substance of things hoped for, the evidence of things not seen. — HEBREWS II : I.

There are times when some graces may be out of use, but there is no time wherein faith can be said to be so : wherefore faith must be always in exercise. . . . Faith is the eye, is the mouth, is the hand, and one of these is of use all day long. Faith is to see, to receive, to work, or to eat : and a Christian should be seeing, or receiving, or working, or feeding all day long. — JOHN BUNYAN.

> If faith produce no works, I see
> That faith is not a living tree.
> Thus faith and works together grow,
> No separate life they e'er can know :
> They've soul and body, hand and heart :
> What God hath joined let no man part.
>
> HANNAH MORE.

We shall be made truly wise if we be made content ; content, too, not only with what we can understand, but content with what we do not understand — the habit of mind which theologians call — and rightly — faith in God. — CHARLES KINGSLEY.

> In such righteousness
> To them by faith imputed, they may find
> Justification towards God, and peace
> Of conscience.
>
> MILTON.

Faith builds a bridge across the gulf of death.

YOUNG.

LET us be careful when, and how, we speak. "To everything there is a season, and a time to every purpose under the Heaven. . . . A time to keep silence and a time to speak." It requires wisdom, delicacy, and discretion to use our words aright; and if using them at all will bring discord, or strife, we should better leave them unsaid. Better to appear dull and stupid, better to sit with closed lips and unuttered thoughts, than say aught that will wound or offend a fellow-being. The silvery tongues are not always the most eloquent to the ear of God. Those whose lips are mute, and who have learned the sweet lesson of silence, are often more pleasing to Him.

> Words are like leaves: when they most abound,
> Much fruit of sense beneath is rarely found.
>
> POPE.

We should be as careful of our words as of our actions, and as far from speaking ill as from doing ill. — CICERO.

Such as thy words are, such will thy affections be esteemed; and such will thy deeds as thy affections, and such thy life as thy deeds. — SOCRATES.

> We know not what we do
> When we speak words.
>
> SHELLEY.

> My words fly up, my thoughts remain below:
> Words without thoughts, never to Heaven go.
>
> SHAKESPEARE.

EVIL communications corrupt good manners.
I CORINTHIANS 15 : 34.

We always judge strangers by their manners: their dress may give us some idea of their worldly possessions, but it is to their manners we look for good or ill breeding. Quietness of movement, and gentleness of speech and action, are marks of true refinement. Though the face may lack beauty, and the form symmetry, if there is a grace of manner and charm of mind, these will atone for the absence of attractions that only please the eye and strike the fancy. Gracious manners may be cultivated to a certain extent, and with innate refinement, are more beautiful still.

> A moral, sensible, and well-bred man
> Will not affront me ; and no other can.
>> COWPER.

What a rare gift, by the by, is that of manners! how difficult to define, how much more difficult to impart! Better for a man to possess them than wealth, beauty, or talents; they will more than supply all. — BULWER-LYTTON.

Manners must adorn knowledge and smooth its way through the world. — CHESTERFIELD.

Good qualities are the substantial riches of the mind ; but it is good breeding that sets them off to advantage. — LOCKE.

[73]

NOTHING so touches the human heart as the word *home*. It is the beginning of life, the centre of life, and its true perfection lies at the *end* of life. No place has such hallowed memories, no faces are so dear, no counsels so wise, and no voices so sweet as those that cluster about the home. It is a beacon in the darkness, when clouds obscure our way, and a haven of rest when the day's long toil is done. With what longing do our hearts turn towards home when distance rolls between us! Truly, "absence makes the heart grow fonder"—the heart that is loyal and loving and to whom home is "the dearest spot on earth."

God pity the homeless! yet even they are not so much to be pitied as those who have a place they call home, but in which there is no sympathy of congeniality. Such are but abiding-places. Where the heart is, there is home!

Sweet is the smile of home, the mutual look
   When hearts are of each other sure;
Sweet all the joys that crowd the household nook,
   The haunts of all affections pure.

J. KEBLE.

O happy house! and happy servitude!
   Where all alike one Master own;
Where daily duty, in Thy strength pursued,
   Is never hard or toilsome known;
Where each one serves Thee, meek and lowly,
   Whatever Thine appointment be,
Till common tasks seem great and holy,
   When they are done as unto Thee.

C. J. P. SPITTA.

A LITTLE thought about Self-control! "Self-conquest," says Plato, "is the greatest of victories."

There are real heroes around us every day, but we do not call them such. They are fighting the enemy Self, and it is a mighty combat. The man who governs a hasty temper, subdues a proud spirit, and masters a stubborn will, deserves a laurel-wreath more than he who dies on the battle-field. It is easier to meet the enemy in one great conflict, when your whole strength is armed for it, than to wage a daily warfare with self and sin. "He that overcometh shall inherit all things."

> Within ! within, oh, turn
> Thy spirit's eyes, and learn
> Thy wandering senses gently to control;
> Thy dearest Friend dwells deep within thy soul,
> And asks thyself of thee,
> That heart, and mind, and sense, He may make whole
> In perfect harmony.
>
> G. TERSTEEGEN.

I will be lord over myself. No one who cannot master himself is worthy to rule, and only he can rule.
— GOETHE.

> Lord of himself, though not of lands;
> And having nothing, yet hath all.
>
> SIR HENRY WOTTON.

THERE is an individuality in voices that we can hardly understand or explain. The tone, the inflection, the accent, marks them with a sweetness or harshness, that rings in our ears when only Memory can call them back. O Voices, Voices! how much joy and sorrow you bring into our lives! When, long ago, God spake and the world sprang into space, the sun and moon were illumined, and the stars blossomed in the blue garden of the sky, in the grand, majestic stillness and out of chaos and darkness, think how powerful must have been the sound of that holy Voice! Then, when He walked in the Garden of Eden at the close of the day, and spake His first reproving word to man, how sorrowful must have been the Voice of the Lord! Again, with what infinite tenderness He must have said of Christ, " This is my beloved Son, in whom I am well pleased." When He calls to you and me, in the silence and in the hour of sacred communion, how softly and lovingly falls "the still small Voice" on our ears! Oh, the ineffable sweetness of the Voice of the Lord! let us listen to its warnings, and follow its guidance all through our earthly pilgrimage.

My heart is resting, O my God!
  My heart is in Thy care;
I hear Thy voice of joy and health
  Resounding everywhere.
" Thou art my portion," saith my soul,
  Ten thousand voices say,
The music of their glad Amen
  Will never die away.

ANNE L. WARING.

HE that speaks ill of another, commonly before he is aware, makes himself such a one as he speaks against; for if he had civility or breeding, he would forbear such kind of language. — ANONYMOUS.

A gallant man is above ill words. Speak no ill of a great enemy, but rather give him good words, that he may use you better if you chance to fall into his hands. — JOHN SELDEN.

> Evil is wrought by want of Thought,
> As well as want of Heart!
>
> HOOD.

> Duly advis'd, the coming evil shun:
> Better not do the deed, than weep it done.
>
> PRIOR.

> But then I sigh, and, with a piece of Scripture,
> Tell them, that God bids us do good for evil.
>
> SHAKESPEARE.

> O! many a shaft, at random sent,
> Find mark the archer little meant!
> And many a word, at random spoken,
> May soothe or wound a heart that's broken!
>
> SCOTT.

Shakespeare says, "Ill deeds are doubled with an evil word." How true this is! Unkind acts are magnified by the power of the tongue. Evil-speaking leaves its own sting: sharp, cruel words are like a stab to a sensitive heart. Oh, the harm they have done! the friendships they have broken, the households they have blighted, the scars they have left! Let this not be a day of evil-speaking, but a day of gentle words.

IT is the little rift within the lute,
That by and by will make the music mute,
And ever widening, silence all.

TENNYSON.

Byron says, "Doubt and Discord step 'twixt thine
and thee." How little misunderstandings separate
friends; how little unkind thoughts will creep into our
hearts and gnaw at them until our whole nature
changes, and our dispositions become fretful and
peevish. We grow suspicious and distrustful; we
wonder at the change in ourselves, and are at a loss to
understand it. Whenever you are conscious that a
weed of doubt is springing up in the soil of your heart,
root it up, and cast it out. Rid yourself of unkind
thoughts — don't harbor them. Be at peace with all
men. Don't let Doubt get the better of you; mend
the " little rift within the lute " before the music of love
and faith is silenced forever.

An old affront will stir the heart
Through years of rankling pain.

JEAN INGELOW.

Doubt indulged soon becomes doubt realized.

FRANCES R. HAVERGAL.

Our doubts are traitors,
And make us lose the good we oft might win,
By fearing to attempt.

SHAKESPEARE.

MARCH THIRTEENTH.

TELL me, where is fancy bred;
  Or in the heart, or in the head?

SHAKESPEARE.

Sweet dreams and fancies — waking or sleeping, they leave their impression upon our minds and hearts. Our hopes, our longings, our aspirations — all come to us, borne on the wings of Fancy. We dream with our eyes wide open, and with the daylight about us — dream as softly as if it were in the stillness of night, and the stars were in the sky. Day-dreams are the longings within us; like little tendrils from the vine, reaching out for something strong to cling to, they shoot out of the heart-soil and twine themselves about us, strengthening each day, until they grow to be a part of our being. If our dreams and fancies are pure and elevating, they will help mould our characters aright; if our longings are noble and good, they will make us better. Then let us dream to a purpose, and let our dreams develop into realities.

Dreams are but interludes, which fancy makes;
When monarch Reason sleeps, this mimic wakes.

DRYDEN.

I believe it to be true that dreams are the true inter-preters of our inclinations; but there is art required to sort and understand them. — MONTAIGNE.

And yet, as angels in some brighter dreams
Call to the soul when man doth sleep,
So some strange thoughts transcend our wonted
    dreams,
And into glory peep.

VAUGHAN.

[79]

SWIFT kindnesses are best; a long delay
In kindness takes the kindness all away.

GREEK ANTHOLOGY.

God bless the man whose law is the law of Kindness, and whose heart throbs warmly towards all humanity! The man who has a kind word for the oppressed, a kind look for the erring, and a kind smile for all of God's creatures. Blessings are in his path, and happiness blossoms around him like flowers in early spring.

That best portion of a good man's life,
His little, nameless, unremembered acts
Of kindness and of love.

WORDSWORTH.

Fraternity is the reciprocal affection, the sentiment which inclines man to do unto others as he would that others should do to him. — MAZZINI.

Never elated, while one man's oppressed;
Never dejected, while another's blest.

POPE.

Good words make friends; bad words make enemies. It is great prudence to gain as many friends as we honestly can, especially when it may be done at so easy a rate as a good word. . . . You will find that silence, or very gentle words, are the most exquisite revenge for reproaches. . . . Be kind and loving to one another. — SIR MATTHEW HALE.

A Day of Good Wishes.

THE wind is sweeping along the highways and blowing open the first young flowers of the year. Nature is stirring and pushing, and pulsing up, and out, into light, and joy, and liberty. What a sweet privilege it is to live and to grow; to breathe, to expand, to progress, and to go on progressing throughout eternity! My wish for you is that your heart may be like the spring highways; and that the winds of opportunity may not pass you by, but that they may blow open the buds of purity and gentleness that lie folded within you and carry their fragrance into all the world.

My wish for you, is a forgiving spirit. May the breath of Heaven scatter all clouds in your sky, and blow away all unpleasant thoughts. Forgive as you wish to be forgiven.

Again, I wish for you a useful life! Let head, hands, heart, and feet be engaged in active service: allow no part of your being to grow old and rusty through neglect. Polish the gold and silver of your character, and it will shine so brightly as to throw its lustre into the lives of others. I wish for you God's blessing!

May no sorrow distress thy days;
May no griefs disturb thy nights;
May the pillow of peace kiss thy cheek,
And the pleasure of realization attend
    Thy beautiful dreams.

May the Angel of God attend thy bed and
Take care that the expiring lamp of life
Shall not receive one rude blast to hasten on
    Its extinction.

ANONYMOUS.

[81]

THE Lord is good to all; and His tender mercies are over all His works. — PSALM 145 : 9.

Maker of earth and sea and sky,
   Creation's sovereign Lord and King
Who hung the starry worlds on high,
   And formed alike the sparrow's wing;
Bless the dumb creatures of Thy care,
And listen to their voiceless prayer.

ANONYMOUS.

The Lord of all, Himself through all diffused,
Sustains, and is the life of all that lives;
Nature is but a name for an effect,
Whose cause is God. . . .
        . . . Not a flower
But shows some touch in freckle, streak, or stain,
Of His unrivalled pencil. He inspires
Their balmy odours, and imparts their hues,
And bathes their eyes with nectar, and includes,
In grains as countless as the seaside sands,
The forms in which He sprinkles all the earth.
Happy who walks with Him! whom what he finds,
Of flavour or of scent, in fruit or flower,
Of what he views of beautiful or grand
In Nature, from the broad majestic oak
To the green blade that twinkles in the sun,
Prompts with remembrance of a present God.

WILLIAM COWPER.

O Heart, look up and praise Him! He who hath made earth so beautiful for thee accounts thy soul of far more value than all earth's richest treasures. Acquaint thyself with Him through His works.

[82]

L OVING and serving, serving and loving ! nothing
else can bring true happiness. Love is the key
that unlocks the heart of stone, and melts the coldest
natures. It softens and subdues, sweetens and ennobles our lives, and brings us into sympathy and harmony with the whole created world. Loving eyes ever
seek for the good, the true, and the beautiful; loving
hands soothe the aching head, and smooth the rum-
pled pillow, and never weary of tender ministrations;
loving feet are swift to bear good tidings, and from
morning until night are walking in ways of kindness.
Loving voices speak comforting words and sing songs
of gladness; and loving hearts blossom into beautiful
thoughts. It is the unselfish spirit that loves the most;
acts of self-denial prove the strength and depth of our
love. Daily sacrifice becomes pleasure, if made for
those who are dear to us. Let us learn to renounce
self; each act of self-denial is a round of the ladder by
which we climb nearer to Heaven.

Sublimest joy is won through fiery trial,
And sweetest rest by toil and self-denial.
ANONYMOUS.

The trivial round, the common task,
Would furnish all we ought to ask;
Room to deny ourselves; a road
To bring us, daily, nearer God.
J. KEBLE.

All the doors that lead inward to the secret place of
the Most High are doors outward — out of self, out of
smallness, out of wrong. — GEORGE MACDONALD.

MARCH EIGHTEENTH.

A YEAR! A life! What are they? The telling of a tale, the passing of a meteor, a dim speck seen for a moment on Time's horizon dropping into eternity. — THOMASON.

The sands in God's great hour-glass are falling, one by one. Silently and steadily the little golden moments are measuring their brief span, and Time is marching on. His footprints are on the valleys and hills, his touch is on the forest-trees, and the giant rocks wear his impress. May Time whisper to you of Eternity, and as you walk with him through life's pathway, fret not because you are growing older, but let this, the rather, be your anxiety: "Am I growing better?"

I sometimes feel the thread of life is slender,
And soon with me the labor will be wrought;
Then grows my heart to other hearts more tender.
                        The time is short.

There are no fragments so precious as those of time, and none are so heedlessly lost by people who cannot make a moment, and yet can waste years. — MONT-GOMERY.

Oh, let us carry hence, each one,
    Some kindly word, some look, some tone,
Into his after life, to be
    Treasured heart-deep and carried home —
An echo from the distant sea,
A thing of joy to memory,
    In all the years to come!
                        ANONYMOUS.

MARCH NINETEENTH.

A Song of the Olden Time.

LET us give it a place in our hearts, and a page in our book! We catch the tender music winged to us from Memory's busy hive, and once again gather from the meadows of the past the honied sweets of half-forgotten strains. Oh, sometime, I think all the music of our lives shall come back to us, — not a note missing, — and the unwritten songs of our hearts shall find words and tune our tongues to harmonies divine.

There's a song of the olden time,
    Falling sad o'er the ear,
Like the dream of some village chime,
    Which in youth we lov'd to hear.
And ev'n amidst the grand and gay,
    When music tries her gentlest art,
I never hear so sweet a lay,
    Or one that hangs so round my heart.

.   .   .   .   .   .

And when all of this life is gone, —
    Ev'n the hope, ling'ring now,
Like the last of the leaves left on
    Autumn's sere and faded bough, —
'Twill seem as still those friends were near,
    Who loved me in youth's early day,
If in that parting hour I hear
    The same sweet notes, and die away, —
To that song of the olden time,
    Breath'd, like Hope's farewell strain,
To say, in some brighter clime,
    Life and youth will shine again.

MOORE.

[85]

ONE of our writers has said, " The art of conversation is not to be taught in books; it can be acquired only by constant intercourse with society, acting upon a well-stocked mind. Both conditions are essential to success — experience and information. We must know not only *what* to say, but how to say it. And, remember, if the faculty of talking well be one indispensable accomplishment in a successful conversationalist, another is the faculty of listening patiently. The man who always talks and never listens, is a bore of the greatest magnitude; so is the man who listens, and never talks. For conversation must be neither monologue nor duologue; but the harmonious combination of many voices and many minds."

> Discourse may want an animated "No,"
> To brush the surface, and to make it flow;
> But still remember, if you mean to please,
> To press your point with modesty and ease.
>
> COWPER.

Equality is the life of Conversation; and he is as much out who assumes to himself any part above another, as he who considers himself below the rest of the society. — SIR RICHARD STEELE.

The power to converse well is a very great charm. You think anybody can talk? How mistaken you are. Anybody can chatter. Anybody can exchange idle gossip. . . . But to talk wisely, instructively, freshly, and delightfully, is an immense accomplishment. It implies exertion, observation, study of books and people, and receptivity of impression. — RUSKIN.

DESPISE not the chastening of the Lord, neither be weary of His correction; for whom the Lord loveth He correcteth, even as the father the son in whom he delighteth. — PROVERBS 3 : 11, 12.

Well-pruned hedges put forth fresh life and vigor, and take on a new and thrifty growth. But underneath still lie the thorns. When God prunes His children with the discipline of sorrow and adversity, some of us only put on an outward show of sweetness and submission, while underneath lie the thorns of complainings and rebellion. No one but God, who sees beyond the surface-growth, can know the unyielding force of a human heart: it often requires repeated chastisings to rid us of the undergrowth of rebellious thoughts and feelings, and bring us into a state of calm resignation to His will.

My God, my Father, while I stray
Far from my home, in life's rough way,
Oh, teach me from my heart to say,
　" Thy will be done."

If Thou shouldst call me to resign
What most I prize, it ne'er was mine :
I only yield Thee what was Thine ;
　" Thy will be done."

Renew my will from day to day ;
Blend it with Thine, and take away
All that now makes it hard to say,
　" Thy will be done."

CHARLOTTE ELLIOTT.

L ET us drink from the chalice of Joy, for the winter
is over, and God hath waked the world into new-
ness of life !

How natural is joy, my heart !
JEAN INGELOW.

Joy is the mainspring in the whole round of everlasting Nature; Joy moves the wheels of the great
timepiece of the world; she it is that loosens flowers
from their buds, suns from their firmaments, rolling
spheres in distant space seen not by the glass of the
astronomer. — SCHILLER.

I was only then
Contented, when with bliss ineffable
I felt the sentiment of Being spread
O'er all that moves and all that seemeth still ;
O'er all that, lost beyond the reach of thought
And human knowledge, to the human eye
Invisible, yet liveth to the heart ;
O'er all that leaps and runs, and shouts and sings,
Or beats the gladsome air ; o'er all that glides
Beneath the wave, yea in the wave itself,
And mighty depth of waters.   Wonder not
If high the transport, great the joy I felt
Communing in this sort through earth and Heaven
With every form of creature, as it looked
Towards the Uncreated with a countenance
Of adoration, with an eye of love.
WORDSWORTH.

THE surest, as the shortest, way to make yourself beloved and honoured, is to be indeed the very man you wish to appear. Set yourself, therefore, diligently to the attaining of every virtue, and you will find on experience, that no one of them whatsoever but will flourish and gain strength when properly exercised. — SOCRATES.

So Virtue blooms, brought forth amid the storms
Of chill adversity; in some lone walk
          Of life she rears her head,
          Obscure and unobserved;
While every bleaching breeze that on her blows,
Chastens her spotless purity of breast,
          And hardens her to bear
          Serene the ills of life.
                              HENRY KIRK WHITE.

Salt of the earth, ye virtuous few,
    Who season human kind;
Light of the world, whose cheering ray
    Illumes the realms of mind:
Where Misery spreads her deepest shade,
    Your strong compassion glows:
From your blessed lips the balm distils,
    That softens mortal woes.
                              ANNE L. BARBAULD.

The virtuous and truly wise man distinguishes himself, not by a peculiar dress, not by singular actions, words, and gestures, but by his whole conduct. One view must appear in all his actions — the view to do as much good by his existence as possible. — FEDER.

[89]

HAVE high aims and aspirations; be constantly travelling upward, and keep Heaven always in sight. No matter where your lot may be cast, nor how lowly your surroundings, lift your hopes above you. Let your mind and soul keep steadily mounting Godward. Spread your spirit-wings up into the pure atmosphere of Infinite love, and let your whole life be an uplifting of your soul and the souls of fellow-men.

> Fasten your souls so high, that constantly
> The smile of your heroic cheer may float
> Above all floods of earthly agonies,
> Purification being the joy of pain.
>
> E. B. BROWNING.

> Raise me above the vulgar's breath,
> Pursuit of fortune, fear of death,
>   And all in life that's mean;
> Still true to reason be my plan,
> Still let my actions speak the man,
>   Through every various scene.
>
> MARK AKENSIDE.

> Let each man think himself an act of God,
> His mind a thought, his life a breath of God;
> And let each try, by great thoughts and good deeds,
> To show the most of Heaven he hath in him.
>
> BAILEY.

> I hold in truth, with him who sings
>   To one clear harp in divers tones,
>   That men may rise on stepping-stones
> Of their dead selves to higher things.
>
> TENNYSON.

THE voice of the Lord is upon the waters. — PSALM 29:3.

What is more majestic than the sweep of the ocean as it lashes against its shores! In a storm, its tones are like muffled thunder, as the huge breakers dash and plunge, and rear their crested heads high in the air, like tossing manes on white battle-horses. Can you not hear the powerful voice of God speaking through the waters? Does it not bring to mind those familiar lines, by Cowper?

> God moves in a mysterious way,
> His wonders to perform;
> He plants His footsteps on the sea,
> And rides upon the storm.

Not only on troublous seas, and amid angry billows, is heard the grandeur and sublimity of the voice of God, but beneath fair, cloudless skies, when soft, calm winds are blowing — then it sings in our ears a tender Song of Peace. It is heard in the ceaseless flow of the rushing river, reaching ever towards the sea; and even the bright mountain stream hath a bit of God in it, and is a symbol of His wonderful love, whose fountain shall flow on through eternity.

Christ and His love shall be thy blessed all
    Forevermore!
Christ and His light shall shine on all thy ways
    Forevermore!
Christ and His peace shall keep thy trembling soul
    Forevermore!

BONAR.

I WISH this may be to you a day of true contentment!

Down the windings, lanes, and among the sprouting hedges you can hear the clear, ringing call of early birds, whistling and piping as they go. The air is full of whispers and odors of Spring; the damp earth steams in the sunlight, and from the very moisture of its sodden mould new seeds take root, new blossoms burst, and everywhere is something fresh and green. Life and Progress sing a daily song of content. When we are busy growing and thriving, and reaching up towards Heaven, we have no time for repining; like the birds, our songs of gladness will burst forth, and go ringing down the lanes of life, and fill other hearts with joy. We are content when doing our duty, and helping some one else to do theirs. True contentment is in the heart, and not in the surroundings.

Sweet are the thoughts that savour of content;
The quiet mind is richer than a crown;
Sweet are the nights in careless slumber spent;
The poor estate scorns fortune's angry frown;
Such sweet content, such minds, such sleep, such bliss,
Beggars enjoy, when princes oft do miss.

ROBERT GREENE.

We'll therefore relish with content,
Whate'er kind Providence has sent,
   Nor aim beyond our power;
For, if our stock be very small,
'Tis prudent to enjoy it all,
   Nor lose the present hour.

NATHANIEL COTTON.

MARCH TWENTY-SEVENTH.

WE cannot be half thankful enough. God has bestowed so many gifts upon us, is bestowing them now, and will continue to do so as long as we live. Last year's acorns lie half-buried beneath the dead leaves, and though cast aside and trodden under foot of man, they still hold their shapely cups open to the sky ready to gather the dews of Heaven. It may be a tiny germ is sleeping there, and nourished and watered by those refreshing drops; sometime a mighty tree shall spring up, and spread its leaves and lend shelter to the passer-by. Oh, let us make the most of our daily blessings, showered down upon us, as the crystal drops of dew that fill the little brown acorn's cup! Isn't your cup, and mine, running over? Let us plant a germ of thankfulness in our heart-soil every day that shall take root and grow towards God. If our cups are always ready to catch God's blessings, it will not be long before the world shall be able to sit under the shadow of our wide-spreading oaks of thankfulness; for like the chalice the acorn holds, there will always be heavenly dews to fill them.

Enough that He who made can fill the soul
Here and hereafter till its deeps o'erflow;
Enough that love and tenderness control
Our fate where'er in joy or doubt we go.
ANONYMOUS.

My heart for gladness springs,
It cannot more be sad,
For very joy it laughs and sings,
Sees nought but sunshine glad.
P. GERHARDT.

[93]

LITTLE things
  On little wings
Bear little souls to Heaven.

FABER.

Love's secret is to be always doing things for God,
and not to mind because they are such very little
ones. — FABER.

We miss so much in this life, because we often pass
by the little things. We are ever looking forward to
great achievements, instead of making the most of
trifles.

Why do we heap huge mounds of years
  Before us and behind,
And scorn the little days that pass
  Like angels on the wind?

Each turning round a small, sweet face
  As beautiful as near;
Because it is so small a face
  We will not see it clear:

And as it turns from us, and goes
  Away in sad disdain:
Though we would give our lives for it,
  It never comes again.

DINAH MULOCH CRAIK.

Wiser it were to welcome and make ours
Whate'er of good, though small, the Present brings, —
Kind greetings, sunshine, song of birds, and flowers,
With a child's pure delight in little things.

R. C. TRENCH.

AN able writer has said, "The path of duty in this world is not all gloom or sadness, or darkness. Like the roads of the South, it is hedged with ever-bloom, pure and white as snow. It is only when we turn to the right hand or the left that we are lacerated by piercing thorns and concealed dangers."

Hark, hark, a voice amid the quiet intense!
It is thy Duty waiting thee without.
Rise from thy knees, in hope, the half of doubt:
A hand doth pull thee — it is Providence;
Open thy door straightway and get thee hence;
Go forth into the tumult and the shout;
Work, love, with workers, lovers, all about:
Of noise alone is born the inward sense
Of silence; and from action springs alone
The inward knowledge of true love and faith.

GEORGE MACDONALD.

"What shall I do to gain eternal life?"
    "Discharge aright
The simple dues with which each day is rife,
    Yea, with thy might."

E. VON SCHILLER.

Our thoughts, good or bad, are not in our command, but every one of us has at all hours duties to do, and these he can do negligently like a slave, or faithfully, like a true servant. "Do the duty that is nearest thee" — that first, and that well; all the rest will disclose themselves with increasing clearness, and make their successive demand. Were your duties never so small, . . . set yourself with double and treble energy and punctuality, to do them. — T. CARLYLE.

[95]

" LEAD us not into temptation." . . . Perhaps
you will find this a day of temptations. It may
be you will want to do the very things that you know
you ought not to do. God's grace can sustain you, His
love can uphold you, His strength can support you.
Don't trust to yourself to meet temptations; we are all
so frail, and so weak by nature, that we cannot with-
stand them; God alone is able to save us.

Thus everywhere we find our suffering God,
    And where He trod
May set our steps; the Cross on Calvary
    Uplifted high
Beams on the martyr host, a beacon light
    In open fight.

Mortal, if life smile on thee, and thou find
    All to thy mind,
Think, who did once from Heaven to Hell descend
    Thee to befriend;
So, shalt thou dare forego at His dear call,
    Thy best, thine all.

J. KEBLE.

Oh, deliver us from evil,
    Our Father — that at last
When our pilgrimage is ended,
    And its perils safely past;
We may see the morning breaking
    On our promised Canaan's shore,
Where Thou reign'st in pow'r and glory
    Evermore — and evermore !
        Amen.

HELEN MARION BURNSIDE.

IF thou hast learned *why* thou livest, thou wilt surely learn *how* to love. Why did God place thee in the world? Was it merely for thine own pleasure and satisfaction? Was it that thou mightest reach the heights of wisdom and look down from an exalted position on all humanity? If thou art a true believer in Christianity, thou wilt say this was not His purpose, but that thou shouldst glorify and enjoy Him forever, and that thou shouldst, while having a care for thine intellectual advancement, take even greater thought for thy soul's welfare. Suffer not pleasure to keep thee enchained within its narrow bounds, for pleasure in itself is but vanity; it soars no higher than thine own head, but dies in languid indolence, and so is lost forever. Thou wert made in the image of God, therefore do not lose thy resemblance to Him. Let thy soul reflect His purity, goodness, and truth. If thou dost care for naught but the things of this world, thou wilt soon find thy spirit growing more like the world, and less like God. It is right that thou shouldst be joyful and happy; but it is not expedient for thee to be absorbed in mere pleasures and frivolities. Let God and thy duty lead thee, then shalt thou walk aright.

Oh, righteous doom, that they who make
   Pleasure their only end,
Ordering the world for its sake,
   Miss that whereto they tend;
While they who bid stern Duty lead,
   Content to follow, they
Of duty only taking heed,
   Find pleasure by the way.

R. C. TRENCH.

[97]

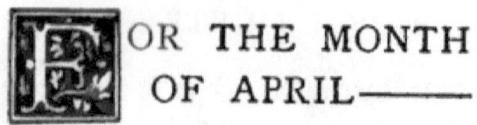
OR THE MONTH
OF APRIL———

APRIL FIRST.

SHE comes, she comes, the April-child; now bid her welcome one and all!

God smiles through the Spring's dear eyes, and speaks through Spring's dear voice: and man looks up in thankfulness to listen, and rejoice. A thousand echoes wake the grove, all glad and strong, and full of praise. Oh, hear! 'tis our Creator's voice that speaks in love and tenderness.

> Dip down upon the northern shore,
>   O sweet new year, delaying long:
>   Thou doest expectant Nature wrong;
> Delaying long, delay no more.
>
> Who stays thee from the clouded noons,
>   Thy sweetness from its proper place?
>   Can trouble live with April days,
> Or sadness in the summer noons?
>
> Where now the seamew pipes, or dives
>   In yonder greening gleam, and fly
>   The happy birds, that change their sky
> To build and brood, that live their lives
>
> From land to land; and in my breast
>   Spring wakens too; and my regret
>   Becomes an April violet,
> And buds and blossoms like the rest.

ALFRED TENNYSON.

JOHN KEATS
1795–1821

APRIL SECOND.

A Day of Violets.

DEEP violets, you liken to
  The kindest eyes that look on you,
  Without a thought disloyal.

E. B. BROWNING.

May their sweetness pervade your lives; and may
you, like them, be adorned with the grace of humility,
that your good deeds may shed their fragrance, and
make glad the earth! Hold up your hearts for the
truth, and God will fill them with drops of love, as the
cup of the violet is filled with the dews of Heaven. So
shall you grow like an April violet, blossoming in the
garden of God's world, refreshing the highways of life's
beautiful Spring.

Violets! deep-blue violets!
April's loveliest coronets!
There are no flowers grow in the vale
Kiss'd by the dew, woo'd by the gale, —
None by the dew of the twilight wet,
So sweet as the deep-blue violet.

LETITIA E. LANDON.

We are violets blue,
  For our sweetness found
Careless in the mossy shades,
  Looking on the ground.
Love dropp'd eyelids and a kiss, —
Such our breath and blueness is.

LEIGH HUNT.

"WHEN I consider the heavens the work of Thy fingers, the moon and the stars which Thou hast ordained, what is man that Thou art mindful of him, and the son of man that Thou regardest him?"

Addison, who was once surveying the heavens, said, . . . "When I considered the infinite hosts of stars, or to speak more philosophically, of suns, which were then shining upon me, with those innumerable sets of planets or worlds which were moving around their respective suns, . . . I could but reflect on that little insignificant figure which I myself bore amidst the immensity of God's works."

> Thou art, O God, the life and light
>   Of all this wondrous world we see;
> Its glow by day, its smile by night,
>   Are but reflections caught from Thee.
> Where'er we turn Thy glories shine,
> And all things bright and fair are Thine!
>
> When youthful Spring around us breathes,
>   Thy spirit warms her fragrant sigh;
> And every flower the summer wreathes
>   Is born beneath that kindling eye:
> Where'er we turn, Thy glories shine,
> And all things fair and bright are Thine!

THOMAS MOORE.

> Thou that hast given so much to me,
> Give one thing more, a grateful heart.
> Not thankful when it pleaseth me,
> As if Thy blessings had spare days;
> But such a heart, whose pulse may be
>   Thy praise.

G. HERBERT.

APRIL FOURTH.

HE who dares not, fail he must !
  Only let the cause be just,
Then have courage, thou shalt win —
Let thy task at once begin.

Does life's pilgrimage seem long? Did yesterday's
trials discourage you for to-day? Trials fall to the lot
of all mankind, therefore you will have your share.
Meet them bravely, bear them cheerfully, and do not let
them dishearten you. Arm yourself with Courage, and
you will ride over difficulties ; a spirit of valor is needed
every day to overcome the evil in your nature, and it is
only by continued warfare that you may hope to be
victorious.

Brave spirits are a balsam to themselves.
CARTWRIGHT.

True valor, friends, on virtue founded strong,
Meets all events alike.
MALLET.

The intent and not the deed
Is in our power ; and therefore who dares greatly,
Does greatly.
BROWN.

True fortitude is seen in great exploits
That justice warrants, and that wisdom guides.
ADDISON.

The brave man is not he who feels no fear,
For that were stupid and irrational ;
But he whose noble soul its fear subdues,
And bravely dares the danger nature shrinks from.
JOANNA BAILLIE.

[101]

APRIL FIFTH.

MAY this day end in a peaceful evening, when the tumults of your heart, and mine, shall be hushed to rest, and discords steal away amid the gloom! The close of each day will be welcome indeed, if we but will it so. Even though our sun sets in shadow, and our spirits are sorrowing, an inward calm shall lend tranquillity to our minds, and soothe them into sweet repose. Let us then possess this peace within, whose presence shall make every storm a calm.

The twilight star to Heaven,
  And the summer dew to flowers,
And the rest to us is given
  By the cool, soft, evening hours.

FELICIA HEMANS.

God who madest earth and heaven,
  Darkness and light,
Who the day for toil hast given,
  For rest the night,
May Thine angel-guards defend us,
Slumber sweet Thy mercy send us,
Holy dreams and hopes attend us,
  This livelong night.

Guard us waking, guard us sleeping,
  And when we die,
May we in Thy mighty keeping
  All peaceful lie;
When the last dread call shall wake us,
Do not Thou our God forsake us,
But to reign in glory take us
  With Thee on high.

REGINALD HEBER.

THE hours are flying! Change sets her seal on all
about us, and we, with all the world, are changing
too. But why complain? Would we sit idly down,
nor soil our hands, nor tire our feet, nor take no part in
the affairs of life? Would we rather not bear the signs
of labor on our brows, than have them smooth and
fair, too fair alas, to win the toiler's crown? Would
we not far rather show our Lord brown, withered, weary
hands that have their noble work done, in loving, faithful servitude, than lift to Him a useless pair, though
white and beautiful they look to human eyes? Methinks the hand best skilled to patient labor here, shall
sweeter play the harps above. The feet, though falter-
ing, tired, and worn, whose pilgrimage ends nearest
Heaven, methinks with gladdest steps shall tread the
golden streets of God. Oh, then let Change and Time
sweep on; it matters little, so we change to ripe fruition,
and our souls are ready for His aftermath.

Well, — give the little Years their way;
    Think, speak, and act the while;
Lift up the bare front to the day,
    And make their wrinkles smile.
They mould the noblest living head;
They carve the best tomb for the dead.
                                    ANONYMOUS.

Lord, we have wandered forth through doubt and
        sorrow,
    And thou hast made each step an onward one;
And we will ever trust each unknown morrow, —
    Thou wilt sustain us till its work is done.
                                    S. JOHNSON.

APRIL SEVENTH.

L IGHT is our sorrow, for it ends to-morrow,
      Light is our death which cannot hold us fast;
So brief a sorrow can be scarcely sorrow,
Or death be death so quickly past.

One night, no more, of pain that turns to pleasure,
One night, no more, of weeping, weeping sore;
And then the heaped-up measure beyond measure,
In quietness forevermore.

Our sails are set to cross the tossing river,
Our face is set to reach Jerusalem;
We toil awhile but then we rest forever,
Sing with all saints and rest above with them.

CHRISTINA ROSSETTI.

Joy will be sweet indeed that follows sorrow, and
rest will be welcome that follows toil. How gladly
shall we lay down our burdens, and, ever keeping in
view the New Jerusalem, journey on to find our promised rest. The river will not be dark or troublous if
lighted by the Divine Presence; the way will not be
long if He bears us company; our hearts shall not faint
nor shrink if He is near to cheer and comfort us. Then
shall all earthly sorrows vanish, and our faces reflect
the sunlight of His gladness, and the beauty of His
smile.

There's no way to make sorrow light
But in the noble bearing; be content;
Blows given from Heaven are our due punishment;
All shipwrecks are not drowning; you see buildings
Made fairer from their ruins.

WILLIAM ROWLEY.

COME, let us spend a day with the birds! Nature's jubilee-choir has begun to chant the glad hallelujahs of the year. The vales are trills of rapture, the brooks are symphonies of joy, and the rocks are harmonies of sound. What a grand orchestra! How everything vibrates to the rhythmical measure! Learn a lesson to-day; take the birds for your text; every song is tuned to the key-note of praise; this gush of gladness is the overflowing of joyous hearts in thankfulness to God. Ye human hearts, like them unite your songs in adoration sweet!

And the blackbirds helped us with the story, for they
    knew it well.
Piping, fluting, " Bees are humming,
April's here, and summer's coming."

JEAN INGELOW.

The welcome guest of settled Spring,
    The swallow too is come at last ;
Just at sunset, when thrushes sing,
I saw her dash with rapid wing,
    And hailed her as she passed.

CHARLOTTE SMITH.

Hark, hark ! the lark at Heaven's gate sings!

SHAKESPEARE.

See yon robin on the spray,
    Look ye how his tiny form
Swells, as when his merry lay
    Gushes forth amid the storm.

HARRISON WEIR.

[105]

APRIL NINTH.

THE Time hath laid his mantle by
　　Of wind and rain and icy chill,
And dons a rich embroidery
　　Of sunlight poured on lake and hill.

No beast or bird in earth or sky,
　　Whose voice doth not with gladness thrill,
For Time hath laid his mantle by
　　Of rain and wind and icy chill.

CHARLES OF ORLEANS.

You who have longed and waited for the Spring, behold how gently and how blithely she comes! All in the silence her glad feet come tripping over the hills, and each day she has a sweet surprise in store for us: she sings a rhythmical song in the echoing woods, and spreads a beautiful mosaic over all the wide corridors of the created world — a mosaic of richest design and color, fashioned and formed by the hand of God.

This magnificent tapestry of flowers, and leaves, and velvety moss is spread for the feet of man. It is free as the air we breathe, — ours to enjoy, to appropriate, and to be thankful for, and ours to give to others who may not see its loveliness or smell its fragrance.

Gather the primroses,
Make handfuls into posies;
Take them to the little girls who are at work in the
　　mills;
Pluck the violets blue, —
Ah, pluck not a few!
Knowest thou what good thoughts from Heaven the
　　violet instills?

EDWARD YOUL.

SOME one has said, "There is sacredness in tears. They are not the mark of weakness, but of power. They speak more eloquently than ten thousand tongues. They are the messengers of overwhelming grief, of deep contrition, and of unspeakable love."

No radiant pearl which crested fortune wears,
No gem that, twinkling, hung from beauty's ears,
Not the bright stars, which night's blue arch adorn,
Nor rising sun that gilds the vernal morn,
Shines with such lustre as the tear that flows
Down virtue's manly cheek for others' woes.

DARWIN.

The rose is fairest when 'tis budding new,
And hope is brightest when it dawns from fears;
The rose is sweetest wash'd with morning dew,
And love is loveliest when embalm'd in tears.

SCOTT.

All the rarest hues of human life take radiance and are rainbowed out in tears. — GERALD MASSEY.

Sooner mayest thou trust thy pocket to a pickpocket than give loyal friendship to a man who boasts of eyes to which the heart never mounts in dew! Only when man weeps he should be alone, not because tears are weak, but they should be secret. Tears are akin to prayer; Pharisees parade prayers, imposters parade tears. — BULWER.

THE temple of God is holy, which temple ye are. —
I CORINTHIANS 3 : 17.

We are building for Eternity — what a responsibility
is ours! Each day your temple and mine counts an
added stone; let us make them such that the great
Builder will not reject; and let us choose only the best
material, and build on the Sure Foundation — which is
Jesus Christ. There are no perfect spiritual temples in
this life; each stone must first be polished by the hand
of God before it can reach perfection. But we may do
our part, and chisel off the rough corners as best we
can, leaving the rest to Him. Let our aim be to build
as near Heaven as we can, and to make ourselves worthy to be called "temples of the Living God."

Whereas on earth
Temples and palaces are formed of parts
Costly and rare, but all material,
So in the world of spirits nought is found,
To mould withal and form into a whole,
But what is immaterial; and thus
The smallest portion of this edifice,
Cornice, or frieze, or balustrade, or stair,
The very pavement is made up of life —
Of holy, blessed, and immortal beings,
Who hymn their Maker's praise continually.

J. H. NEWMAN.

Now shed Thy mighty influence abroad
On souls that would their Father's image bear;
Make us as holy temples of our God,
Where dwells forever calm, adoring prayer.

C. J. P. SPITTA.

APRIL TWELFTH.

WHEN gratitude o'erflows the swelling heart,
   And breathes in free and uncorrupted praise
For benefits receiv'd, propitious **Heaven**
Takes such acknowledgment as fragrant incense,
And doubles all his blessings.

GEORGE LILLO.

Learn to be grateful; don't take blessings and favors as a matter of course: you have done nothing to merit them, and why should you receive them as if they were your right? You owe God everything. What have you done for Him? To begin with, He has given you life, and instead of being thankful for every breath you draw, you murmur and complain that your lot was not cast in a different place, that you must have trials, that you must suffer pain, that you must shed tears, and bear sorrow, and have disappointments, and lose friends, and oh, basest ingratitude! you often grieve Him by wishing that He had never given you life at all. Get all you can out of this gift; be glad that you are alive, and make yourself a part of creation and God; look up to Him and be thankful. And when loving favors are showered upon you by earthly friends, receive them with loving gratitude; often they have been extended to you through some act of self-denial, the meaning of which you may never understand. Let your whole life be one of gratitude, and take the opportunity to show it whenever you can.

A grateful mind
By owing owes not, but still pays, at once,
Indebted and discharg'd.

MILTON.

TO the pure mind alone hath solitude
Its charms.

An hour of solitude, passed in sincere and earnest prayer or conflict with, and conquest over, a single passion or subtle bosom sin, will teach us more of thought, will more effectually awaken the faculty and form the habit of reflection than a year's study in the schools without them. — COLERIDGE.

'Tis sweet to be alone and turn our thoughts inward; to muse on what we are — how wonderfully made, how mightily endowed; to meditate on God's eternal wisdom, goodness, love. No human sculptor can perfectly imitate man; he may chisel a beautiful work of art so exquisitely that the world shall hold him in remembrance as long as it lasts, but even then his masterpiece is but cold marble and will crumble to dust. There is no light in the eyes, no breath in the nostrils, no smile on the lips, and no blood in the heart. God's masterpiece lives, and moves, and sees, and hears, and feels: and yet he is but a thought of God, His great, immortal thought — a living soul. In the solitude man was created, when light, and darkness, and sea, and sky, and land were new, and when no life, save the Divine Life, had existence. In the solitude of the beginning of time man's career began, before the cycles past and gone had started on their pilgrimage. What marvel then that man should wish to turn aside for silent meditation, when Solitude cries out to him to look within and hear the voices of his soul, and Nature's speech, in gentle tone, beseeches him to look without and see what God has wrought!

APRIL FOURTEENTH.

LET this be to you a day of resurrection! Now when all Nature is waking out of its long winter sleep, and donning robes of freshness and brightness, shake off the gloom that envelops your spirit, and like the chrysalis, let your soul mount up on gladsome wing and soar to greater heights of love and joy. Leave behind your dull, dark self, your load of care, and all that frets or weighs you down. Feast on Nature's freshness and bloom, drink in her sunshine and dew, and let your soul look up to God and be glad. It is a time to think of Christ and His resurrection, a time to remember His glorious awakening — His triumph over the cross, His victory over death. It is the fair Easter-tide of the year; when the dark brown bulbs are stirring and swelling under the silent earth, and making sweet preparation to burst into lilies of beauty and fragrance. So, too, may your soul blossom into deeds of purity and peace!

Awake, thou wintry earth!
  Fling off thy sadness!
Fair vernal flowers, laugh forth
  Your ancient gladness:
      Christ is risen!

All is fresh and new,
  Full of spring and light:
Wintry heart, why wear'st the hue
  Of sleep and night?
      Christ is risen!

THOMAS BLACKBURN.

APRIL FIFTEENTH.

THE word of the Lord came unto me, saying,
    Jeremiah, what seest thou?
And I said, I see a rod of an Almond-tree.

JEREMIAH I: II.

Blossom of the almond-trees,
April's gift to April's bees,
Birthday ornament of spring,
Flora's fairest daughterling;
Coming when no flowerets dare
Trust the cruel outer air,
When the royal king-cup bold
Dares not don his coat of gold,
And the sturdy blackthorn spray
Keeps his silver for the May; —
Coming when no flowerets would,
Save thy lowly sisterhood —
Early violets, blue and white,
Dying for their love of light.

Almond blossoms, sent to teach us
That the spring days soon will reach us,
Lest, with longing over-tried,
We die as the violets died, —
Blossom clouding all the tree
With thy crimson broidery,
Long before a leaf of green
On the bravest bough is seen, —
Ah! when winter winds are swinging
All the red bells into ringing,
With a bee in every bell,
Almond bloom, we greet thee well.

EDWIN ARNOLD.

WE read of Jacob's ladder; Christ is Jacob's ladder that reacheth up to Heaven, and he that refuses to go by this ladder thither, will scarce by any other means get up so high. There is none other name given under Heaven among men whereby we must be saved. — BUNYAN.

Aye, and Christ sends down to us His angel messengers, to whisper tender words from Heaven; and silently they come and go upon the ladder of His love, which we, too, may ascend if Faith illumes our way and points us through the skies.

Ah! many a time we look on starlit nights
　Up to the sky as Jacob did of old;
Look longing up to the eternal lights,
　To spell their lives of gold.

.　.　.　.　.　.　.　.

Yet, to pure eyes the ladder still is set,
　And Angel visitants still come and go;
Many bright messengers are moving yet,
　From the dark world below.

Thoughts, that are surely Faith's outspreading wings—
　Prayers of the church, aye, keeping time and tryst—
Heart-wishes making bee-like murmurings,
　Their flower, the Eucharist.

These are the messengers, forever wending
　From earth to Heaven, that faith alone may scan;
These are the Angels of our God, descending
　Upon the Son of Man.

W. ALEXANDER.

BE careful how you make a promise; look ahead first, and see that you will be able to keep it. A " man of his word," if unpopular otherways, possesses at least one admirable quality. It is easy enough to make a promise, but not always so easy to fulfil it, therefore count the cost before your word is pledged. Sometimes circumstances make it necessary for us to break a promise, and if such is the case, let us frankly state the reason, and ask to be released from our obligation. It is more honorable even to break one's word, than to commit an unpardonable wrong simply for the sake of keeping it. It is well to make few promises, and then there will be few to break, but if we *do* make them let us fulfil them, if we can possibly do so. The world always has a place for the man who can be depended upon, and whose word is as good as his bond.

Promising is the very air of the
Time; it opens the eyes of expectation.
Performance is ever the duller for
His act; and, but in the plainer and simpler
Kind of people, the deed is quite of
Use. To promise is most courtly and fashionable;
Performance is a kind of will or testament,
Which argues a great sickness in his judgment
That makes it.

SHAKESPEARE.

Promises were the ready money that was first coined and made current by the law of nature, to support that society and commerce that was necessary for the comfort and security of mankind. — CLARENDON.

Behold a sower went forth to sow:

" AND when he sowed, some seeds fell by the way-
side :
Some fell upon stony places :
And some fell among thorns ;
But other fell into good ground, and brought forth
fruit."

Prepare your ground before you sow ; let it be rich
and fertile ; turn up the sod to the sunlight, dews, and
showers of Heaven : scatter your seed, and — wait.
Likewise, make ready your heart-soil : baptize it with
tears, and warm it with smiles, and while the summer
winds are blowing soft and sweet, and while the summer moons in silence wax and wane, be patient, Heart,
and — wait. God guards the smallest seed ; His Harvest-time is sure to come ; your ripened wheat shall be
His care, your tares His loving heart shall grieve.

Sow with a generous hand ;
    Pause not for toil or pain ;
Weary not through the heat of summer,
    Weary not through the cold spring rain :
But wait till the autumn comes,
    For the sheaves of golden grain.

Then sow, — for the hours are fleeting,
    And the seed must fall to-day,
And care not what hands shall reap it,
    Or if you shall have passed away
Before the waving cornfields
    Shall gladden the sunny day.

ADELAIDE A. PROCTER.

HOW many mistakes we make, and how much we have to regret! We can sit down for a few moments and think of these things until they almost overwhelm us. We can look back on our past lives, and see, as in a glass, the reflection of so much that we would give almost anything to recall. There are so many ways in which to make mistakes; sometimes they can hardly be avoided, and we are not responsible for them, but oftentimes they are made through ignorance, — ignorance through neglected opportunities, — and through carelessness and indifference: we *might* have avoided them had we only tried. Shall we not endeavor to be less heedless hereafter? Regretting is such sorrow, let us give it no cause to shadow our lives and the lives of others.

Lifelong our stumbles, lifelong our regret,
　Lifelong our efforts failing and renewed,
　　While lifelong is our witness, "God is good."
Who bore with us till now, bears with us yet,
Who still remembers and will not forget,
　Who gives us light and warmth and daily food,
　And gracious promises half understood,

And glories half revealed, whereon to set
Our heart of hearts and eyes of our desire;
　Uplifting us to longing and to love,
Luring us upward from this world of mire,
　Urging us to press on and mount above
　Ourselves and all we have had experience of,
Mounting to Him in love's perpetual fire.

CHRISTINA ROSSETTI.

SPEECH is silver, silence is gold. — GERMAN PROVERB.

Silence is the perfectest herald joy :
I were but little happy, if I could say how much.
SHAKESPEARE.

It is the silent influence, after all, that makes or mars our lives. It is the look or action, often, that carries the greatest weight, and that speaks more eloquently than the tongue. A man's real life is the life that the world never knows or understands : you may think you can read it like a book, but I think the best, as well as the worst, that is in him is only revealed to his God. If he is modest, he is often chary of giving of his best ; if he is proud, he carefully guards his worst, so that only in the silent chambers of his soul do these two antagonists have their abode, sending forth an occasional thought or look or action to give the world a hint that they are there. O friend, make your silent influence pure and holy ; let your fellow-men feel that your inner life means something. Retire to the silence of yourself, and commune with God, and make the result of that communion a benefit to mankind.

The silence often of pure innocence
Persuades, when speaking fails.
SHAKESPEARE.

O Breath from out the Eternal Silence ! blow
Softly upon our spirits' barren ground ;
The precious fulness of our God bestow,
That fruits of faith, love, reverence may abound.
G. TERSTEEGEN.

APRIL TWENTY-FIRST.

WHEN we gather all our blossoms of hope before they reach fruition, they wither in their fresh, sweet youth, and leave but empty nothingness. Watch them, one by one, guard them tenderly — the budding apple-blossoms of joy and hope that hang heavy from life's green tree : let them grow sweeter, fuller every day, until, at God's great Harvest-time, they shall drop ripened to the ground, in deeds of richest gold.

Our wants, our wishes, — yea, our hopes and fears,
  Lie folded like the apple-blooms;
With modesty flushing,
Like them are they blushing,
    And white in their purity
    Are waiting futurity;
Thus in their silken cells they lie
  Our heart's own cherished apple-blooms
That thrive and grow, and ripen with the years.

What inexpressible joy for me to look up through the apple-blossoms and the fluttering leaves, and to see God's love there ; to listen to the thrush that has built his nest among them, and to feel God's love, who cares for the birds, in every note that swells their little throats; to look beyond to the bright blue depths of the sky, and feel they are a canopy of blessing; . . . and to know that if I could unwrap fold after fold of God's universe, I should only unfold more and more blessing, and see deeper and deeper into the love which is at the heart of all. — ELIZABETH CHARLES.

THE Homes of England! God bless them, and
may they all be happy ones!

The stately Homes of England,
How beautiful they stand!
Amidst their tall ancestral trees,
O'er all the pleasant land;

. . . .

The blessed Homes of England!
How softly on their bowers
Is laid the holy quietness
That breathes from Sabbath hours!
Solemn, yet sweet, the church-bell's chime
Floats through their woods at morn;
All other sounds, in that still time,
Of breeze and leaf are born.

The cottage Homes of England!
By thousands on her plains,
They are smiling o'er the silvery brooks,
And round the hamlet-fanes.
Through glowing orchards forth they peep,
Each from its nook of leaves;
And fearless there the lowly sleep,
As the birds beneath their eaves.

The free, fair Homes of England!
Long, long in hut and hall,
May hearts of native proof be reared
To guard each hallowed wall!
And green forever be the groves,
And bright the flowery sod,
Where first the child's glad spirit loves
Its country and its God.

FELICIA HEMANS.

[119]

LIFE — let it be to you a reality; remember it is the breath of God; if you do not realize this, you have never learned to value it. God has given it to you pure and innocent; let it be your business to keep it so. He has placed within its reach possibilities; make it your aim to be all that He intended you to be, and let no opportunity pass unimproved. In the very humblest lives, and amid the poorest surroundings, there is always a chance to climb, if you will watch for it, and take it when it comes. It may be at a time when least expected, it may be in a way you would not choose, but if it is God's opportunity for you, why question the time or way? Make your life a reflection of His life, and it will breathe out some of His sweetness, and gladden the lives of others.

Be not amazed at life. 'Tis still
　The mode of God with His elect,
Their hopes exactly to fulfil,
　In times and ways they least expect.

DEAN ALFORD.

Didst fancy life one Summer holiday,
With lessons none to learn, and naught but play?
Go, get thee to thy task. Conquer or die!
It must be learned; learn it then patiently.

No help! nay, 'tis not so;
Though human help be far, thy God is nigh,
Who feeds the ravens, hears His children's cry;
He's near thee wheresoe'er thy footsteps roam,
And He will guide thee, light thee, help thee Home.

ANONYMOUS.

A DAY of noble activity, — God help you to do your best in it!

There is no action so slight nor so mean but it may be done to a great purpose, and ennobled therefore; nor is any purpose so great but that slight actions may help it, and may be so done as to help it much, most especially, that chief of all purposes — the pleasing of God. — RUSKIN.

One secret act of self-denial, one sacrifice of inclination to duty, is worth all the mere good thoughts, warm feelings, passionate prayers in which idle people indulge themselves. — J. H. NEWMAN.

When first thy eyes unveil, give thy soul leave
    To do the like; our bodies but forerun
The spirit's duty; true hearts spread and heave
    Unto their God, as flowers do to the sun.
                      H. VAUGHAN.

        Get leave to work;
  In this world 'tis the best you get at all:
For God, in cursing, gives us better gifts
Than man in benediction.
                    E. B. BROWNING.

    Worship God by doing good;
    Help the suffering in their needs.
    He who loves God as he should,
    Makes his heart's love understood
        By his deeds.
                ANONYMOUS.

[121]

DO you wonder how you shall ever endure to the end? Did you not live yesterday, and last week and last year? To-day will soon be another yesterday, and the longest day has but twenty-four hours. The trouble is you are adding to your burden, instead of lightening it: don't you know complainings and murmurings will weigh more heavily than anything else? Throw out a little ballast and you will rise higher; you are carrying too much to make much progress upward. Weighted wings cannot soar. Rid yourself of anxieties and complaints, and you will find the journey easier. It is only a little while until your pilgrimage shall be ended; take heart and think what lies above and beyond you. Life is short, and it will soon be over, but God's Eternity knows no little while.

Up, my drowsing eyes!
Up, my sinking heart!
Up to Jesus Christ arise!
Claim your part
In all the rapture of the skies.

Yet a little while,
Yet a little way,
Saints shall reap and rest and smile
All the day: —
Up! let's trudge another mile.

CHRISTINA ROSSETTI.

A little longer still — patience, beloved:
A little longer still, ere Heaven unroll
The glory, and the brightness, and the wonder,
Eternal and divine, that waits thy soul.

HYMNS OF THE AGES.

APRIL TWENTY-SIXTH.

AS the Alpine heights tower above the world in their grandeur and sublimity, so the heights of God's love tower above us. We can only reach them by an upward flight, yet the ascent is easy because He makes it so. All He requires is a simple, childlike faith and trust in Him, and a heart ready to love and obey Him. Hold out your hand to Him, and He will uplift you, and you shall one day stand with Him on the Alpine heights of His wonderful love.

On Alpine heights the love of God is shed;
   He paints the morning red,
   The flowerets white and blue,
   And feeds them with His dew.
On Alpine heights a loving Father dwells.

On Alpine heights, o'er many a fragrant heath,
   The loveliest breezes breathe;
   So free and pure the air,
   His breath seems floating there.
On Alpine heights a loving Father dwells.

On Alpine heights, in troops all white as snow,
   The sheep and wild goats go;
   There in the solitude,
   He fills their hearts with food.
On Alpine heights a loving Father dwells.

On Alpine heights the herdsman tends his herd;
   His Shepherd is the Lord;
   For He who feeds the sheep
   Will sure His offspring keep.
On Alpine heights a loving Father dwells.

KRUMMACHER.

NOW is the constant syllable ticking from the clock of time. *Now* is the watchword of the wise. *Now* is the banner of the prudent. Let us keep this little word always in our minds, and whenever anything presents itself to us in the shape of work, whether mental or physical, we should do it with all our might, remembering that *Now* is the only time for us — that *Now* is ours; that *Then* may never be. — ANONYMOUS.

> Time past, and time to come, are not —
> Time present is our only lot;
> O God, henceforth our hearts incline
> To seek no other love than thine!
>
> MONTGOMERY.

The Present is *our* time — yours and mine; the Past is with death, the Future is with God. The Present is a princely guest; let us give him a royal welcome, and make glad his stay; if well entertained, he will leave us a precious legacy in his will; but if ignored and slighted, he will rob us of our peace, and send the ghost of Regrets to haunt us in after years.

> Time flows from instants, and of these, each one
> Should be esteem'd, as if it were alone:
> The shortest space, which we so highly prize
> When it is coming, and before our eyes,
> Let it but slide into th' eternal main,
> No realms, no worlds can purchase it again:
> Remembrance only makes the footsteps last,
> When winged time, which fix'd the prints, is past.
>
> SIR JOHN BEAUMONT.

APRIL TWENTY-EIGHTH.

A Day with the Wind!

WIND! thou art lovelike, everywhere; o'er earth,
O'er ocean triumphing, and aye with clouds,
That like the ghost of ocean's billows roll.

BAILEY.

Thou wind!
Which art the unseen similitude of God
The Spirit; His most meet and mightiest sign!

BAILEY.

The wind hath a language, I would I could learn;
Sometimes 'tis soothing, and sometimes 'tis stern;
Sometimes it comes like a low, sweet song,
And all things grow calm, as the sound floats along,
And the forest is lull'd by the dreamy strain,
And slumber sinks down on the wandering main,
And its crystal arms are folded in rest,
And the tall ship sleeps on its heaving breast.

. . . .

And the billows leap up when the summons they hear,
And the ship flies away, as if winged with fear,

. . . .

And when the moon rises, the ship is no more,
Its joys and its sorrows are vanish'd and o'er,
And the fierce storm that slew it has faded away,
Like the dark dream that flies from the light of the day.

LETITIA E. LANDON.

May the winds of Heaven blow away all your feuds,
until they are lost forever; and may they sow the seed
of your good influence all over the world, until it shall
spring up and blossom for eternity!

[125]

FRIEND is a word of royal tone;
  Friend is a poem all alone.

ANONYMOUS.

We can never replace a friend. When a man is fortunate enough to have several, he finds that they are all different, no one has a double in friendship. — SCHILLER.

Friendship hath the skill and observation of the best physician; the diligence and vigilance of the best nurse; and the tenderness and patience of the best mother. — LORD CLARENDON.

Who knows the joys of friendship?
The trust, security, and mutual tenderness,
The double joys, where each is glad for both?
Friendship our only wealth, our last retreat and
    strength,
Secure against ill-fortune and the world.

NICHOLAS ROWE.

Lay this into your breast:
Old friends, like old swords, still are truest best.

JOHN WEBSTER.

It is the friendship that flows from the heart which is the only true friendship; no other will stand the test of sorrow and adversity, and remain steadfast. That which is assumed for the sake of policy is short-lived; it smiles upon you and wears a semblance of sincerity, but gives you the cold shoulder if you fail in the accomplishment of its hopes and wishes. Keep your heart warm, if you would give out a warm friendship.

APRIL THIRTIETH.

A Day of Sweet Remembrance!

SHE sent him rosemary, to the intent that he should hold her in remembrance. — DRAYTON.

Ah yes, there is a buried April somewhere in your heart and mine : a time half sun, half tears, half hopes, half fears, an April of our vanished years! Don't you remember it? Don't you like to go off alone somewhere and think of it, and smile over it, and — yes, even grieve over it? We take a sorrowful delight, sometimes, in recalling sad things, and when we have lived them over, and come back once more to the reality of the present, we find ourselves smiling through our tears — the dead April rising again in us with a new resurrection.

When shall we come to that delightful day,
  When each can say to each, "*Dost thou remember ?*"
Let us fill urns with rose-leaves in our May,
  And hive the thrifty sweetness for December!

BULWER.

I cannot but remember such things were
That were most precious to me.

SHAKESPEARE.

Many kindly deeds be your rosemary of remembrance in the heart-gardens of your friends!

Sweet Memory, wafted by the gentle gale,
Oft up the stream of time I turn my sail,
To view the fairy haunts of long-lost hours,
Blest with far greener shades, far lovelier flowers.

SAMUEL ROGERS.

[127]

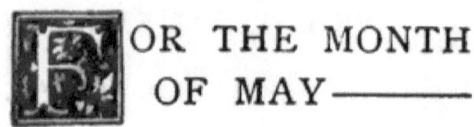

FOR THE MONTH OF MAY——

MAY FIRST.

AH, there is no one like her — bonny May, the rosy, dimpled darling of the year! How light is her step, how silvery her laugh, and how blithe her heart! She hath power to dispel sadness, to banish gloom, and to drive away care. Her young hands are full of blossoms, with which to beautify the earth. God must have put a song in her lips, and a light in her eye for the joy of all mankind. Oh, that you may be akin to her in sunshine and gladness, scattering sweetness wherever you go, and making your influence a perpetual May!

Now the bright morning-star, day's harbinger,
Comes dancing from the east, and leads with her
The flowery May, who from her green lap throws
The yellow cowslip and the pale primrose. ‹
MILTON.

Little brings the May breeze
  Beside pure scent of flowers,
While all things wax and nothing wanes
  In lengthening daylight hours.
Across the hyacinth beds
  The wind lags warm and sweet,
Across the hawthorn tops,
  Across the blades of wheat.
CHRISTINA ROSSETTI.

THOMAS CARLYLE
1795–1881

MAY SECOND.

O SWEET English primroses! May you be like them, carrying gladness in your face, and God's vernal Springtime in your heart. Like them, may you grow and thrive in the light of God.

My soul lies out like a basking hound —
A hound that dreams and dozes;
Along my life my length I lay,
I fill to-morrow and yesterday,
I am warm with the suns that have long since set,
I am warm with the summers that are not yet,
And like one who dreams and dozes,
Softly afloat on a sunny sea,
Two worlds are whispering over me,
And there blows a wind of roses
From the backward shore to the shore before,
From the shore before to the backward shore,
And like two clouds that meet and pour
Each through each, till core in core
A single self reposes,
The nevermore with the evermore
Above me mingles and closes;
As my soul lies out like the basking hound,
And wherever it lies seems happy ground;
And when, awakened by some sweet sound,
A dreamy eye uncloses,
I see a blooming world around,
And I lie amid primroses, —
Years of sweet primroses,
Springs of fresh primroses,
Springs to be, and springs for me,
Of distant, dim primroses.

SIDNEY DOBELL.

MAY THIRD.

LET your heart beat in unison with God's, and He will stand revealed in His marvellous works.

My God, what is a heart,
That Thou should'st it so eye and woo,
Pouring upon it all Thy art,
As if Thou had'st nothing else to do?

Indeed, man's whole estate
Amounts — and richly — to serve Thee;
He did not Heaven and earth create,
Yet studies them, not Him by whom they be.

Teach me Thy love to know;
That this new light which now I see
May both the work and Workman show;
Then by a sunbeam I will climb to Thee.

GEORGE HERBERT.

The Psalms of David show forth God's continual goodness and love, as manifested in His works. Oh, that our hearts may unite in this glad melody and sing with thanksgiving, "O Lord, how manifold are Thy works! in wisdom hast Thou made them all: the earth is full of Thy riches."

The spacious firmament on high;
    With all the blue ethereal sky,
And spangled heavens, a shining frame,
    Their great Original proclaim;
The unwearied sun, from day to day,
    Does his Creator's power display,
And publishes to every land
    The work of an Almighty hand.

ADDISON.

BEST things are obtainable, but they do not come to us of themselves. Ambition, energy, and perseverance are the levers that remove many obstacles in our path, and leave the way clear to the attainment of our end. Ambition beckons, energy pushes, and perseverance keeps us continually toiling and delving, so that, if we unite the three, we cannot help but succeed. Perseverance will do more for us than mere talent. Science owes her wonderful progress to perseverance; art and invention are indebted to her for their marvellous discoveries; and, through her mighty influence, the world is growing wiser every day.

Perseverance is a Roman virtue,
That wins each god-like act, and plucks success
E'en from the spear-proof crest of rugged danger.
HAVARD.

Attempt an end, and never stand to doubt;
Nothing's so hard, but search will find it out.
HERRICK.

He who flies,
In war or peace, who his great purpose yields,
He is the only villain in this world:
But he who labours firm and gains his point,
Be what it will, which crowns him with success,
He is the son of fortune and of fame.
THOMSON.

Perseverance, dear my lord,
Keeps honour bright. To have none, is to hang
Quite out of fashion
SHAKESPEARE.

[131]

GOD knows what is best for you. Why should you doubt Him? You think you can choose for yourself, but the choice is always a poor one, if made in opposition to His will. If things look unusually dark and gloomy to-day, there is a reason for it. Why should they look gloomier and darker to-day than yesterday? God is the same, the world is the same, and you — are *you* the same, or are you tormented with doubts and fears, and are you shrinking from the future, because of your poor, weak faith? Let God carry your burdens; take as your text for to-day,

NOT WHAT I WILL! BUT WHAT THOU WILT.

Send what thou wilt: or beating shower,
  Soft dew or brilliant sun;
Alike in still or stormy hour,
  My Lord, Thy will be done.

FRANCES R. HAVERGAL.

I have no cares, O blessed Will!
  For all my cares are Thine!
I live in triumph, Lord, for Thou
  Hast made Thy triumphs mine.

He always wins who sides with God,
  To him no chance is lost;
God's will is sweeter to him, when
  It triumphs at his cost.

Ill that He blesses is our good,
  And unblessed good is ill;
And all is right that seems most wrong,
  If it be His sweet will.

F. W. FABER.

NOTHING can live well without proper nourishment. A half-starved body soon loses its health and vigor; muscle, blood, and nerves need wholesome food if they would perfectly perform their part of God's great plan. If we refuse to eat, we are neglecting our bodies, and are therefore dishonoring our Creator. The mind needs quickening and enlightening, lest it should lie dormant, and lose the strength of its faculties: without thought and study the intellect becomes starved — it has nothing to feed upon. The soul, too, the spiritual part of our being, must likewise be nourished, or it also shrinks and shrivels into a dull, lifeless thing, and fails to fulfil the mission for which God intended it. Every part of our being should be industrious; the body, if well fed, will give strength to the intellect, and a bright, active mind *ought* to give us broader and deeper spiritual growth. If the mind is alive to earth's beauty, the soul should be alive to God's goodness. Let us be careful and watchful of all three of these treasures, — body, mind, and soul, — that each may be active and industrious, and able to grow and thrive. Riches of health, riches of intellect, and riches of soul are all the result of constant diligence.

Industry . . .
To meditate, to plan, resolve, perform,
Which in itself is good — as surely brings
Reward of good, no matter what be done.

POLLOCK.

If little labour, little are our gains:
Man's fortunes are according to his pains.

HERRICK.

MAY SEVENTH.

THERE is no true rest outside of Christ. It is sweet to go apart with Him for a little season of rest, during the busy hours of the day. His Presence strengthens and refreshes us, and His sweet peace calms our troubled spirits, and fills us with inward repose.

> Silken rest,
> Tie all my cares up.
>
> BEAUMONT AND FLETCHER.

The camel, at the close of day,
    Kneels down upon the sandy plain,
To have his burden lifted off,
    And rest to gain.

My soul, thou, too, shouldst to thy knees
    When daylight draweth to a close,
And let thy Master lift the load,
    And grant repose.

Else how couldst thou to-morrow meet,
    With all to-morrow's work to do,
If thou thy burden all the night
    Dost carry through?

The camel kneels at break of day
    To have his guide replace his load,
Then rises up anew to take
    The desert road.

So thou shouldst kneel at morning's dawn,
    That God may give thee daily care.
Assured that He no load too great
    Will make thee bear.

ANONYMOUS.

[134]

READING maketh a full man, conference a ready man, and writing an exact man. . . . Histories make men wise; poets, witty; the mathematics, subtle; natural philosophy, deep; moral, grave; logic and rhetoric, able to contend. — BACON.

Read, mark, learn, and inwardly digest. — COLLECT FOR THE SECOND SUNDAY IN ADVENT.

Books, we know,
Are a substantial world, both pure and good;
Round these, with tendrils strong as flesh and blood,
Our pastime and our happiness will grow.

WORDSWORTH.

Books are men of higher stature,
And the only man who speaks aloud for future time to
hear.

E. B. BROWNING.

As good almost kill a man as kill a good book; who kills a man kills a reasonable creature, God's image; but he who destroys a good book kills reason itself. — MILTON.

Read the Bible, the precious "Book of books," whose Great Author is the Divine Poet of Heaven and earth. He is the Historian of every age of man; the Astronomer of all created suns, moons, and stars; the Philosopher of deepest thought and reason; the most eminent Scientist, the best Mathematician, and the truest Theologian, — in that He alone is the God from whence Theology had its rise; His Book is our safest guide, and our sweetest comfort.

[135]

MAY NINTH.

WITH God there is no night, and they that walk with Him are never in darkness. He is the Sun of Righteousness, and in His presence is always light. Is your life overshadowed? If poverty, sickness, trouble, disgrace, or sorrow hang darkly above you, let in the Light. It will warm and brighten and cheer you. God's glorious Light can disperse the gloom, and scatter the clouds in your sky. He comforts in sorrow, soothes in distress, and sweetens the bitter draught in every cup. Oh, may the Light of God illumine your being, and be the Day-star to guide you Home at last!

Shine, my only Day-star, shine:
So mine eyes shall wake by Thine;
So the dreams I grope in now
To clear visions all shall grow;
So my day shall measured be
By Thy Grace's clarity;
So shall I discern the Path
Thy sweet Law prescribed hath;
For Thine ways cannot be shown
By any light but Thine own.

BEAUMONT.

A blind man, being led one day
Where fragrant roses blossomed gay,
Said to his guide: "Here roses bloom;
I know them by their sweet perfume."
Oh! when blind souls around us go,
Led by the eyes that watch us so,
Blessed the Christian life that throws
The sweet perfume of Sharon's rose.

ANONYMOUS.

MAY TENTH.

THE only worthy end of all learning, of all science, of all life, in fact, is that human beings should love one another better. Culture merely for culture's sake can never be anything but a sapless root, capable of producing, at best, a shrivelled branch. — GEORGE ELIOT.

Learn that to love is the one way to know
Or God or Man; it is not love received
That maketh man to know the inner life
Of them that love him; his own love bestowed
Shall do it.

JEAN INGELOW.

There is a power to bless
In hillside loneliness,
    In tarns and dreary places;
A virtue in the brook,
A freshness in the look
    Of mountain's joyless faces.

And I would have my heart
From littleness apart,
    A love-anointed thing;
Be set above my kind,
In my unfettered mind
    A veritable king.

F. W. FABER.

A simple tolerance is not enough: our hearts must be bound by the cords of sympathy and love. We must share each other's burdens, and they will be lighter; we must bask in each other's sunshine, and it will be brighter.

OH, the mystery of to-morrow!
Ambitious man is ever looking forward with
eager curiosity to to-morrow. He dreams, and plans,
and hopes for it, and is often bitterly disappointed
when it comes. God has veiled the face of the Future,
so that we may not know what is in store for us. Is
not this kind? How miserable we would be if we knew
what tears our eyes would shed. It is well also that
we do not know of all the brightness to come. Did
you ever look through the window out into the mistiness and murkiness of a rainy day, when, suddenly,
the clouds were rifted, and like a smile from Heaven
the sunlight came pouring down upon the earth in a
flood of gold? Ah, what a sweet unexpected joy! Had
you known of its coming, you might have fretted and
worried that it did not come sooner, and been wearied
with long waiting. So it is with the future; our to-
morrows will open their windows to us, and God's
folded sunshine will stream into our hearts, while we,
perchance, stand doubting beneath a dismal sky.

Heaven from all creatures hides the book of fate, .
All but the page prescribed, their present state.
.   .   .   .
O blindness to the future! kindly given,
That each may fill the circle mark'd by Heaven;
Who sees with equal eye, as God of all,
A hero perish, or a sparrow fall,
Atoms or systems into ruin hurl'd,
And now a bubble burst, and now a world.

POPE.

Live so that your yesterdays may be blessings, your
to-days, opportunities, and your to-morrows, rewards.

MAY TWELFTH.

GOD'S mercy, how boundless it is! It is like a great sea without a shore, whereon we are sailing, safe from danger and alarm. How He holds us; how He guides us! Oh, let us trust Him completely, and sail on in calm assurance, for on His sea of Mercy, when life and time are ended, we shall be borne,—cast anchor, and reach Home at last.

> Man may dismiss compassion from his heart,
> But God will never.
>
> COWPER.

> There's a wideness in God's mercy,
>   Like the wideness of the sea;
> There's a kindness in His justice
>   Which is more than liberty.
>
> For the love of God is broader
>   Than the measure of man's mind;
> And the heart of the Eternal
>   Is most wonderfully kind.
>
> F. W. FABER.

> O'er friendless grief Compassion shall awake,
> And smile on innocence, for Mercy's sake!
>
> CAMPBELL.

> Oh, think! think upward on the thrones above:
> Disdain not mercy, since they mercy love;
> If mercy were not mingled with their pow'r,
> This wretched world could not subsist an hour.
>
> DAVENANT.

> But mercy first and last shall brightest shine.
>
> MILTON.

[139]

THIS is such a beautiful time of the year to say and do beautiful things. With God's fresh, sweet May-time adorning the earth, and carrying into our hearts a sense of His goodness and love, you surely cannot harbor an evil thought towards any one. You should be ready to breathe out kind and gentle thoughts to the whole world. No matter how fast the years are heaping on your head, so that they are not gathering on your *heart*. Do not grow old in false judgments, and unkind words and deeds. They shrivel the heart until it becomes as dry and wrinkled as a sour apple — eaten up by its own acidity. Do not grow old in false judgments and deeds. Let the May-time start within you a new growth of kindly words and deeds, and when the Autumn days come you will not be able to gather half of the abundant harvest they will yield.

Before the birth of love, many fearful things took place through the empire of necessity; but when this god was born, all things arose to man. — SOCRATES.

Man is dear to man ; the poorest poor
Long for some moments in a dreary life,
When they can know and feel that they have been
Themselves the fathers and the dealers-out
Of some small blessings ; have been such
As needed kindness, for the single cause,
That we have all of us one human heart.
                                        WORDSWORTH.

Gently to hear, kindly to judge.
                                        SHAKESPEARE.

LEARN to be as the angel, who could descend among the miseries of Bethesda without losing his heavenly purity or his perfect happiness. Gain healing from troubled waters. Make up your mind to the prospect of sustaining a certain measure of pain and trouble in your passage through life. By the blessing of God this will prepare you for it. — J. H. NEWMAN.

Is it raining, little flower?
    Be glad of rain !
Too much sun would wither thee ;
    'Twill shine again.
The sky is very black, 'tis true ;
But just behind it shines the blue.

Art thou weary, tender heart?
    Be glad of pain !
In sorrow sweetest things will grow,
    As flowers in rain.
God watches ; and thou wilt have sun,
When clouds their perfect work have done.

Rejoice, O grieving heart !
    The hours fly fast ;
With each some sorrow dies,
With each some shadow flies,
    Until at last
The red dawn in the east
Bids weary night depart,
    And pain is past.
Rejoice, then, grieving heart,
    The hours fly fast !

ADELAIDE A. PROCTER.

[141]

MAY FIFTEENTH.

A DAY AMONG THE TREES.

I HEARD a Seer cry, — "The wilderness,
        The solitary place,
Shall yet be glad for Him, and He shall bless

. . . .

The forests; they shall drop their precious gum,
And shed for Him their balm; and He shall yield
The grandeur of His speech to charm the field."

JEAN INGELOW.

Trees are the exquisite workmanship of God. The
seed, the root, the sap, the vein, the leaf, the bough,
the branch,—all make a magnificent whole. Yet how
soon a tree becomes dead and useless, unless there is
life in the heart. God remembers this; He feeds the
roots that lie in darkness hidden from the eye of man.
And now, behold, the May is here, and overhead the
leaves are spread, and each with each in gladness joins,
to make a canopy of green to shelter *man*, of all God's
creatures, dearest, best. O monarch trees! O tossing
leaves! may we have power, like you, to shelter some
one weary grown, who longs to hide from life's oppres-
sive heat, or fierce, descending storms!

The Laurel, meed of mighty conquerors,
And poets sage, the Fir that weepeth still,
The Yew, obedient to the bender's will,
The Birch for shafts, the Sallow for the mill,
The Myrrh sweet bleeding in the bitter wound,
The warlike Beech, the Ash for nothing ill,
The sailing Pine, the Cedar proud and tall,
The builder Oak, sole king of forests all.

EDMUND SPENSER.

EVERY kindness done to others in our daily walk, every attempt to make others happy, every prejudice overcome, every truth more clearly perceived, every difficulty subdued, every sin left behind, every temptation trampled under foot, every step forward in the cause of what is good, is a step nearer the cause of Christ, through which only death can really be a gain to us. — DEAN STANLEY.

If thou art blest,
Then let the sunshine of thy gladness rest
On the dark edges of each cloud that lies
Black in thy brother's skies.
If thou art sad,
Still be thou in thy brother's gladness glad.
ANONYMOUS.

The kindly plans devised for other's good,
So seldom guessed, so little understood.
The quiet, steadfast love that strove to win
Some weary wanderer from the ways of sin —
These are not lost.
ANONYMOUS.

All sweet, pure thoughts that bloom into deeds, and send forth a fragrance into the hearts of others, are never lost. You shall find them blooming in the garden of Eternity.

The greatest pleasure I know is to do a good action by stealth, and to have it found out by accident. — CHARLES LAMB.

MAY SEVENTEENTH.

REAL friendship is of slow growth. It seldom arises at first sight. Nothing but our vanity will make us think so. It never thrives unless engrafted upon a stock of known and reciprocal merit. — CHESTERFIELD.

There is a vast difference between humanity and friendship. If you are ill or in trouble people will aid and sympathize with you, who would perhaps utterly ignore you in health and in the midst of your daily activities. Don't mistake this for friendship: it is only common humanity reaching out to you in a time of need. A man may sometimes lend a helping hand, too, to satisfy his conscience; he may do a kind act and get the credit of it, and yet have no warm or generous impulses — this is not friendship. True friendship hath its rise in the heart; it is fed from a hidden source, and its springs never run dry.

> Every one that flatters thee
> Is no friend in misery.
> Words are easy, like the wind;
> Faithful friends are hard to find.
>
> .   .   .   .
>
> He that is thy friend indeed,
> He will keep thee in thy need;
> If thou sorrow, he will weep,
> If thou wake, he cannot sleep.
> Thus of every grief in heart,
> He with thee doth bear a part.
> These are certain signs to know
> Faithful friend from flattering foe.

RICHARD BARNFIELD.

[144]

MAY EIGHTEENTH.

THERE'S not a cheaper thing on earth,
　　Nor yet one half so dear;
'Tis worth more than distinguish'd birth,
　　Or thousands gain'd a year:

　·　　·　　·　　·　　·　　·　　·　　·

It maketh poverty content,
　　To sorrow whispers peace;
It is a gift from Heaven sent
　　For mortals to increase.
It meets you with a smile at morn,
　　It lulls you to repose;
A flower for peer and peasant born,
　　An everlasting rose.

As smiles the rainbow through the cloud
　　When threat'ning storm begins —
As music 'mid the tempest loud,
　　That still its sweet way wins.
As springs an arch across the tide,
　　Where waves conflicting foam,
So comes this seraph to our side,
　　This angel of our home.

What may this wondrous spirit be,
　　With power unheard before —
This charm, this bright divinity?
　　Good temper! — nothing more!
Good temper! — 'tis the choicest gift
　　That woman homeward brings;
And can the poorest peasant lift
　　To bliss unknown to kings.

CHARLES SWAIN.

MAY NINETEENTH.

MAKE yourselves nests of pleasant thoughts. None of us yet know, for none of us have been taught in early youth, what fairy palaces we may build of beautiful thoughts — proof against all adversity. Bright fancies, satisfied memories, noble histories, faithful sayings, treasure-houses of precious and restful thoughts, which care cannot disturb, nor pain make gloomy, nor poverty take away from us, — houses built without hands, for our souls to live in. — RUSKIN.

I pray you hear my song of a nest,
    For it is not long.

.   .   .   .

Once, awhile ago, I peered
In the nest where Spring was reared.
There, she quivering her fair wings,
Flattered March with chirrupings;
And they fed her; nights and days,
Fed her mouth with much sweet food,
And her heart with love and praise,
Till the wild thing rose and flew
Over woods and water-springs,
Shaking off the morning dew
In a rainbow from her wings.

JEAN INGELOW.

In the home-nests of our souls let us, like the March, feed upon the food of praise from out our Father's hand. Then shall sweet messengers of gladness take wing therefrom, and fly into the waiting world about us, to help make vocal life's blossoming May. Let us feed upon God's goodness, and drink in His sunshine and dews of grace, then shall we make happy nests.

MAY TWENTIETH.

HE is waiting, waiting, waiting,
   He is waiting through the night;
He has looked with wondrous patience
      For the hour of dawning light,
When the oft-mistaken spirit
      Shall observe Him at the door,
And shall cry, Come in, my Saviour,
      Come, and leave me nevermore.

. . . .

Did you hear Him gently knocking
      When you played among the flowers?
Did you notice how He waited
      In the hush of evening hours?

He is waiting, waiting, waiting,
      You have let all others in.
Some odd guests are in your temple,
      Sad with sorrow, dark with sin.
There is only One can bless you
      In your times of grief and doubt,
There is only One can save you —
      But you strangely keep Him out!

He is waiting, waiting, waiting;
      Surely He may enter now:
Haste to throw your heart's door open,
      And before the Master bow.
Bid Him come, no more to leave you
      Till you dwell with Him above.
Oh, receive the waiting Saviour,
      And return Him love for love!

                    MARIANNE FARNINGHAM.

GOOD common-sense will take a man through the world a great deal easier than talent, genius, or wealth. Talented people are often without tact; the true genius is generally self-absorbed and absent-minded, and the man of wealth cannot always count on his pocketbook to carry him through. There are things that mere money cannot buy; a man with more in his pocket than in his head is to be pitied, for when his riches take flight he is helpless indeed, unless he has a good round measure of common-sense. Common-sense is equal to any emergency; it is wide awake and swings in a steady balance. The man who possesses a goodly share of it, though he may be an Englishman or an American, will find himself rich in his own right. His judgment is strong and impartial, his counsel wise, and his character is usually as straight as a plumb-line. If he is modest, and not inclined to boast of his gift (for it *is* a gift), he is indeed blest; William Penn once said, "Sense shines with a double lustre when it is set in humility."

Sense is our helmet, wit is but the plume;
The plume exposes, 'tis our helmet saves.
Sense is the diamond, weighty, solid, sound;
When cut by wit, it casts a brighter beam;
Yet, wit apart, it is a diamond still.

YOUNG.

Something there is more needful than expense,
And something previous e'en to taste — 'tis sense;
Good sense which only is the gift of Heaven,
And though no science, fairly worth the seven.

POPE.

HE is the richest who is content with the least, for content is the wealth of nature. — SOCRATES.

> Stone walls do not a prison make,
> Nor iron bars a cage,
> Minds innocent and quiet, take
> That for a heritage.
>
> LOVELACE.

> There is a jewel which no Indian mine can buy,
> No chemic art can counterfeit;
> It makes men rich in greatest poverty,
> Makes water wine, turns wooden cups to gold,
> The homely music to sweet music's strain;
> Seldom it comes — to few from Heaven sent —
> That much in little — all in naught — content.
>
> WILBYE.

> 'Tis better to be lowly born,
> And range with humbler lives in content,
> Than to be perk'd up in a glittering grief,
> And wear a golden sorrow.
>
> SHAKESPEARE.

> Such is the force of each created thing,
> That it no soiled happiness can bring,
> Which to our minds may give contentment sound;
> For, like as Noah's dove no succour found,
> Till she returned to him that sent her out,
> Just so the soul in vain may seek about
> For rest or satisfaction anywhere,
> Save in His presence who hath sent her here.
>
> ANNE COLLINS.

[149]

GOD is our Light; let us therefore continually reach up to Him for sunshine. There is no mine so far underground, no prison-cell so dark, no dwelling-place so obscure, but His presence can enter and His glory illumine.

Shadows to-day, while shadows show God's Will.
  Light were not good except He send us light.
  Shadows to-day, because this day is night
Whose marvels and whose mysteries fulfil
Their course and deep in darkness serve Him still.
  Thou dim aurora, on the extremest height
  Of airy summits wax not over bright;
Refrain thy rose, refrain thy daffodil.
Until God's Word go forth to kindle thee
  And garland thee and bid thee stoop to us,
  Blush in the heavenly choirs and glance not down:
To-day we race in darkness for a crown,
In darkness for beatitude to be,
  In darkness for the city luminous.

CHRISTINA ROSSETTI.

A root set in the finest soil, in the best climate, and blessed with all that sun and air and rain can do for it, is not in so sure a way of its growth to perfection, as every man may be, whose spirit aspires after all that which God is ready and infinitely desirous to give him. For the sun meets not the springing bud that stretches toward him with half that certainty, as God, the source of all good, communicates Himself to the soul that longs to partake of Him. — WILLIAM LAW.

BE yourself. Bring the best that is in you to light;
do not keep it hidden away, as if there were nothing good about you. Some persons imagine this to be
an evidence of sincerity, and are continually showing
others their worst side. This is a mistake; our faults
and failings should be secrets between ourselves and
God, therefore to Him alone should they be revealed.
It would be well if of each of us it might be said, as
Shakespeare has it,

" His words are bonds, his oaths are oracles :
His love sincere, his thoughts immaculate ;
His tears pure messengers sent from his heart;
His heart so far from fraud, as Heav'n from earth."

Sincerity's my chief delight,
The darling pleasure of the mind :
Oh, that I could to her invite,
All the whole race of human kind ;
Take her, mortals, she's worth more
Than all your glory, all your fame,
Than all your glittering boasted store,
Than all the things that you can name :
She'll with her bring a joy divine,
All that's good, and all that's fine.
                              LADY CHUDLEIGH.

I give thoughts
Words, and words truth, and truth boldness. She
    whose
Honest freeness makes it her virtue to
Speak what she thinks, will make it her necessity
To think what is good.
                              JOHN MARSTON.

MAY TWENTY-FIFTH.

WHO pipes upon the long green hill,
   Where meadow grass is deep?
The white lamb bleats but followeth on —
   Follows the clean white sheep.

   .   .   .   .

   The white lambs feed in tender grass ;
   With them and thee to bide,
How good it were.

JEAN INGELOW.

Kind Shepherd, who Thy little flock dost guide,
   Wisdom Thy rod — Thy staff unceasing love ;
And dost in pastures feed and coverts hide
   The wanderers, till they reach Thy fold above.

Each weakness and each want to Thee are known ;
   All strength is Thine, and every holy joy ;
The people whom Thou choosest for thine own,
   No force can sever, and no power destroy.

Rich is the food Thou givest, bread from heaven,
   Waters of life which from Thy presence flow ;
And fitting guidance all their journey given,
   Thy hand directing every step they go.

When through the vale of death they leave this land —
   That vale where all is dark and chilly night —
Thou wilt conduct them to Thine own right hand,
   And gild the vale of death with light.

JAMES EDMESTON.

   I praise my loving Lord, who maketh me
   His type of harmless sweet simplicity :
   Yet He the Lamb of lambs incomparably.

CHRISTINA ROSSETTI.

LET your thoughts, words, and deeds be worthy of
the Sabbath, any day in the week. James Shirley said,

> " Only the actions of the just
> Smell sweet and blossom in the dust,"

and if your life will bear close inspection, it will be as
beautiful in the midst of a work-a-day world as it will
in the quietude of the Sabbath. Do not carry your
goodness with your Sunday clothes and lay it away
to be worn once a week, but let it become a part of
yourself, your companion in the daily walks of life. If
you only don your good thoughts one day out of seven,
they will become mouldy and ill-fitting from disuse,
and you will wear them awkwardly, because your nature
will shrink away from them, and soon be too small to
wear them at all. Let your life be a Sabbath of rest
to the weary, and a Sabbath of joy to the depressed
and discouraged, and carry about with you a bit of the
Gospel in your smiles and cheery words, all the week.

Sabbath is not a day to feast our bodies, but to feed
our souls. — EMPRESS JOSEPHINE.

The Sabbath is to the rest of the week in spirituals,
what summer is to the rest of the year in temporals;
it is the chief time for gathering knowledge to last you
through the following week, just as summer is the
chief season for the gathering of food to last you
through the following twelvemonth. — A. W. HARE.

I feel as if God had, by giving the Sabbath, given
fifty-two springs in every year. — COLERIDGE.

MAY TWENTY-SEVENTH.

I WANDERED lonely as a cloud
　　That floats on high o'er vales and hills,
When all at once I saw a crowd, —
　　A host of golden daffodils
Beside the lake, beneath the trees,
Fluttering and dancing in the breeze.

Continuous as the stars that shine
　　And twinkle on the Milky Way,
They stretched in never-ending line
　　Along the margin of the bay:
Ten thousand saw I, at a glance,
Tossing their heads in sprightly dance.

The waves beside them danced, but they
　　Outdid the sparkling waves in glee;
A poet could not but be gay
　　In such a jocund company;
I gazed — and gazed — but little thought
What wealth the show to me had brought.

For oft, when on my couch I lie,
　　In vacant or in pensive mood,
They flash upon that inward eye
　　Which is the bliss of solitude;
And then my heart with pleasure fills,
And dances with the daffodils.

WORDSWORTH.

Were I in churchless solitudes remaining,
　　Far from all voice of teachers or divines,
My soul would find, in flowers of God's ordaining,
　　Priests, sermons, shrines!

HORACE SMITH.

[154]

DO not think it wasted time to submit yourself to any influence which may bring upon you any noble feeling. — RUSKIN.

Wouldst thou know thyself, observe the actions of
    others.
Wouldst thou other men know, look thou within thine
    own heart.
                SCHILLER.

Do not forget that the world is hung with mirrors, reflecting you as you really are. Have you never realized this? Perhaps not, and yet it is true. How small you look when you see the image of yourself in the bright eyes of a friend! Yet you occupy just as much room as is possible in so diminutive a space. So with the soul that looks into your soul; you are measured according to space. Be careful of your friends and associates. Remember they measure you by themselves, and imagine you to be as small-minded as they. Their influence will affect your whole life, and you will unconsciously adopt their thoughts and ideas, even if you do not altogether approve of them. Choose only such friends as those whose influence is pure and wholesome.

Thy face
Gives a meaning of all space ;
And thine eyes, with starbeams fraught,
Hold the measure of all thought ;
For of them my soul besought,
And was shown a glimpse of thine.
                JEAN INGELOW.

WE ought to cultivate the friendships of little things. Beauty is one of the surest antidotes to vexation. Often when life looks dreary from some real or fancied injustice, or indignity, has a thought of truth been flashed into my mind from a flower, the frost, a shadow, clouds, rainbows, stars, and sunrises!
— GEORGE MACDONALD.

Was never true love loved in vain,
For truest love is highest gain.
No art can make it; it must spring
Where elements are fostering.
So in Heaven's spot and hour
Springs the little native flower,
Downward root and upward eye,
Shapen by the earth and sky.

GEORGE ELIOT.

Our outward life requires them not;
    Then wherefore had they birth?
To minister delight to man,
    To beautify the earth:

To comfort man, to whisper hope
    Whene'er his faith is dim;
For "Whoso careth for the flowers,
    Will care much more for him!"

MARY HOWITT.

Your voiceless lips, O Flowers! are living preachers,
    Each cup a pulpit, and each leaf a book,
Supplying to my fancy numerous teachers,
    From loneliest nook.

HORACE SMITH.

MAY THIRTIETH.

THE days are slipping softly by, and our sweet May is about to say farewell. How much brightness she has brought with her! How much gladness she brought this year, and last year, and the year before, and all the other years since there was a May-time! She is warm-hearted and sympathetic — see how she caresses the flowers, and how she smiles through their beautiful faces! She is constant and true, for every year she comes back at just the same time, to walk the old paths through the woodlands, and across the meadows, and to gladden our hearts and make us forget our cares. Ah, let us be constant too — true-hearted, pure-hearted, warm-hearted, like the May! Our years roll onward with the flood of time, and when another May shall blossom on the earth, let our friendship be just as deep and true as it is to-day.

Year after year the cowslips fill the meadow,
   Year after year the skylarks thrill the air,
Year after year, in sunshine or in shadow,
   Rolls the world round, love, and finds us as we were.

Year after year, as sure as birds' returning,
   Or field flowers' blossoming above the wintry mould,
Year after year, in work or mirth or mourning,
   Love we with love's own youth, that never can grow
     old.

Sweetheart and lady-love, queen of boyish passions,
   Strong hope of manhood, content of age begun,
Loved in a hundred ways, each in a different fashion,
   Yet loved supremely, solely, as we never love but
     one.

D. M. CRAIK.

A SOUL which sincerely longs after God never considers whether a thing be small or great; it is enough to know that He for whom it is done is infinitely great; that it is His due to have all creation solely devoted to His glory, which can only be fulfilling His will. — FENELON.

Oh, let us not this thought allow!
The heat, the dust upon our brow,
Signs of the contest, we may wear;
Yet thus we might appear more fair
    In our Almighty Master's eye,
Than if in fear to lose the bloom,
Or ruffle the soul's lightest plume,
    We from the strife should fly.

R. C. TRENCH.

Wanted: Deeds.
Not words of winning note,
Not thoughts from life remote,
Not fond religious airs,
Not sweetly languid prayers,
Not love of scent and creeds.
Wanted: Deeds.

DUNCAN MACGREGOR.

This is exactly what God wants every day of your life and mine — deeds. Something to prove our love for Him and for each other.

Let me not leave my space of ground untilled,
Call me not hence with mission unfulfilled.
Let me not die before I've done for Thee
My earthly work, whatever that may be.

ANONYMOUS.

ELIZABETH BARRETT BROWNING
1806–1861

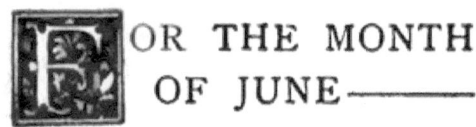

FOR THE MONTH OF JUNE———

JUNE FIRST.

AH, June is here! wake, heart of mine, she hath a message sweet for thee — a message from a mystic land, a Realm of Roses pure and fair, where all day long new joys unfold, and happy winds blow fresh and free. To-day the Summer-tide is born; to-day we leave behind the May, and butterflies and birds and bees begin the roundelay of June, quaint queenly June, with roses crowned, the Rose of all the garden of the year. She hath a message: listen well! a message for each one who hears; for me and mine, for you and yours. 'Tis this: "Behind the roses hid, I smile and smile the livelong day: I breathe in every rose's breath, and sing in every bird's glad throat, and make the earth look fresh and gay; but back of me a Higher Power has showered gifts of love on me; the Heart of June beats large and warm, above the wind, above the storm, and silvery streams and rivers run and sing His praise — His voice obey. The Rose of Sharon is His name, and I have come to bid the earth look up to Him, take heart anew, and, like the rose, exalt His fragrance till it rise in incense to the throne above."

> Woo on, with odour wooing me,
>   Faint rose, with fading core:
> For God's rose thought that blooms in thee
>   Will bloom forevermore.

GEORGE MACDONALD.

[159]

JUNE SECOND.

A Day of Roses.

IN the wind of sunny June
　　Thrives the red rose crop,
Every day fresh blossoms blow
　　While the first leaves drop;
White rose and yellow rose
　　And moss-rose choice to find,
And the cottage cabbage-rose
　　Not one whit behind.

CHRISTINA ROSSETTI.

Jasmine is sweet, and has many lovers,
　　And the broom's betrothed to the bee;—
But I will plight with the dainty rose,
　　For fairest of all is she.

THOMAS HOOD.

Roses, roses, all my song!
　　Roses in a gorgeous feast!
Roses in a royal throng
　　Surging, rosing from the east!

Roses all the rosy way,
　　Roses to the rosier west,
Where the roses of the day
　　Cling to night's unrosy breast.

Out of darkness light is born;
　　Out of weakness make me strong
For the day when every thorn
　　Breaks into a rose of song.

GEORGE MACDONALD.

JUNE THIRD.

AH, we cannot think about it too often — the sweetness of charity! And if we brought it to mind *twice* as often, we should still regret that we thought of it so little. Put a great deal of charity into this June day. Breathe it in with the air and sunshine — God has smiled upon you and given you plenty of it, because you are always an object of His divine charity; — give it out generously to others.

The sun gives over; so the earth —
What it can give so much 'tis worth:
The ocean gives in many ways —
Gives paths, gives fishes, rivers, bays;
So, too, the air, it gives us breath —
When it stops giving comes in death.
  Give, give, be always giving;
  Who gives not is not living.
    The more you give,
    The more you live.

God's love has to us wealth upheaped;
Only by giving it is reaped.
The body withers, and the mind,
If pent in by a selfish rind.
Give strength, give thought, give deeds, give pelf,
Give love, give tears, and give thyself;
  Who gives not is not living.
    The more we give,
    The more we live.

ANONYMOUS.

The truly generous is the truly wise;
And he who loves not others, lives unblest.

JOHN HOME.

JUNE FOURTH.

THOU shalt not bear false witness against thy neighbor. — NINTH COMMANDMENT.

You only repeated innocently what you heard? Yes, that is the way most of us do: we are surprised that such little sayings can ever result in harm; we do not intend to injure any one's good name, or hurt any one's feelings, and yet we sometimes thoughtlessly do that very thing. Oh, let us start afresh this June weather!

> On eagles' wings immortal scandals fly;
> While virtuous actions are but born and die.
>
> > HERVEY.

> Nor do they trust their tongues alone,
> But speak a language of their own:
> Can read a nod, a shrug, a look,
> Far better than a printed book;
> Convey a libel in a frown,
> And wink a reputation down.
>
> > SWIFT.

Beware how you allow words to pass for more than they are worth, and bear in mind what alteration is sometimes produced in their current value by the course of time! — R. SOUTHEY.

God preserve us from the destructive power of words! There are words which can separate hearts sooner than sharp swords; there are words whose sting can remain through a whole life! — MARY HOWITT.

It is busy talking world. — NICHOLAS ROWE.

[162]

JUNE FIFTH.

A SWARM in May
    Is worth a load of hay;
A swarm in June
Is worth a silver spoon;
A swarm in July
Is not worth a fly.

OLD SAYING.

June is our opportunity, and we may as well embrace
it. May has gone, and we have only the present time,
which, if we will improve, will be of more value than a
"silver spoon." We are all God's bees, gathering
honey for His hive, I trust. Oh, how much sweetness
there is around us! Life's meadows are overflowing
with rich and rare perfumes, and flowers are springing
everywhere. Let us store up honey for the future:
loving and gentle words, little unexpected kindnesses,
charitable deeds, and daily sacrifices — these will come
back to us in golden honey for the Hive of Eternity.

So work the Honey Bees:
Creatures that, by a rule in nature, teach
The art of order to a peopled kingdom.
They have a king, and officers of sorts:
Where some, like magistrates, correct at home;
Others, like merchants, venture trade abroad;
Others, like soldiers, armed in their stings,
Make boot upon the Summer's velvet buds;
Which pillage they with merry march bring home
To the tent royal of their emperor.
Who, busied in his majesty, surveys
The singing masons building roofs of gold.

SHAKESPEARE.

JUNE SIXTH.

PATIENCE is the truest sign of courage. Ask old soldiers who have seen real war, and they will tell you that the bravest men, the men who endure best, not in mere fighting, but in standing still for hours to be mowed down by cannon-shot; who were most cheerful and patient in shipwreck and starvation and defeat — all those things ten times worse than fighting; ask old soldiers, I say, and they will tell you that the men who showed best in such miseries were generally the stillest, meekest men in the whole regiment. That is true fortitude; that is Christ's image; the meekest of men, and the bravest, too. — CHARLES KINGSLEY.

Patience! why, 'tis the soul of peace:
Of all the virtues, 'tis nearest kin to Heaven:
It makes men look like gods. The best of men
That e'er wore earth about Him was a sufferer,
A soft, meek, patient, humble, tranquil spirit:
The first true Gentleman that ever breathed.

THOMAS DEKKER.

Therefore wait; be patient. Look at the grain-fields; what are they doing these early June days? Waiting for the harvest. Look at the orchards; they have dropped their blossoms, and they are waiting for ripened fruition. Is this all? Ah, no; they are *growing*, too. Are you growing richer and better?

Whate'er God does is well!
In patience let us wait;
He doth himself our burdens bear,
    He doth for us take care,
And He, our God, knows all our weary days.

B. SCHMOLCKE.

GOD will bring the sweet recompense by and by;
so do not falter by the way, nor look into the
June sunshine blinded by your tears to all the glory
around you. The little unkind word that has rankled
all day long in your heart — forgive it: you love the
dear offender too well to harbor ill-feelings for so small
a thing. Do you not often speak hastily yourself?
Are you not always sorry for it? How much better
you will feel to forgive it!

Now, the sowing and the weeping,
  Working hard and waiting long;
Afterward, the golden reaping,
  Harvest home and grateful song.

Now, the long and toilsome duty,
  Stone by stone to carve and bring;
Afterward, the perfect beauty
  Of the palace of the King.

Now, the tuning and the tension,
  Wailing minors, discord strong;
Afterward, the grand ascension
  Of the Alleluia song.

Now, the spirit conflict-riven,
  Wounded heart, unequal strife;
Afterward, the triumph given,
  And the victor's crown of life.

Now, the training, strange and lowly,
  Unexplained and tedious now;
Afterward, the service holy,
  And the Master's "Enter thou!"

FRANCES RIDLEY HAVERGAL.

JUNE EIGHTH.

THERE are but two paths in life: one leading upward; the other, downward. We are compelled to travel one of them; there is no standing still in this world: we must go forward. We are under marching orders. Be careful how you choose your path in life. Is it the pathway of faith? It will be trodden in difficulties often, but little acts of self-denial will drop their seed by the wayside, and spring up into blossoms of gold, and all the world shall know you are travelling heavenward by the brightness you scatter around you. The downward path is the way of evil and sin: when the heart is so full of Self that it cannot find room for God, weeds of envy and malice and worldliness will choke out the blossoms of gold that might have lighted some darkened soul to Heaven.

There is no pathway man hath ever trod,
By faith or seeking sight, but ends in God.
Yet 'tis in vain ye look without to find
The inner secrets of the eternal mind,
Or meet the King on His eternal throne.
But when ye kneel at heart, and feel so lone,
Perchance behind the veil you get the grip
And spirit-sign of secret fellowship;
Silently as the gathering of a tear
The human want will bring the Helper near;
The very weakness that is utterest need
Of God, will draw Him down with strength indeed.

GERALD MASSEY.

Man should be ever better than he seems, and shape his acts, and discipline his mind, to walk adorning earth, with hope of Heaven. — SIR A. DEVERE.

JUNE NINTH.

" AND God said, I do set my bow in the cloud, and it shall be for a token of a covenant between me and the earth."

One of the grandest sights I ever beheld was a rainbow above the mountains. Arched in perfect grace and symmetry, with every separate color glowing against a misty sky, the great bow of God's promise hung in jewelled radiance over the vernal, pine-clad peaks. The trees, still wet with "the late-fallen showers," glittered with diamond drops, as if bathed in tears, while far down below us the sodden valleys and bosky dells were steaming in the warm summer air. A perfect silence seemed to reign, as we stood with hushed voices, within the circle of the divine radius, and looked upon the heavenly sign of our Almighty Creator. We are ever encircled by the rainbow of His promises: the Bible is full of them; let us bind them about us as a girdle of praise, and wear them as precious jewels in our hearts.

> Meanwhile, reflected from yon eastern cloud,
> Bestriding earth, the grand ethereal cloud,
> Shoots up immense ; and every hue unfolds,
> In fair proportion running from the red
> To where the violet fades into the sky.
>
> JAMES THOMSON.

May all go well with you! May life's short day glide on peaceful and bright, with no more clouds than may glisten in the sunshine, no more rain than may form a rainbow. — RICHTER.

NO earthly kingdom could be to thee what the Kingdom of Heaven shall prove, when thou hast entered into its glories, and obtained the rights of heirship. The higher thou dost lift thy soul while here below, the higher shall be thy place above. Let each day be a step upward; climb by little things. He who could paint with such beauty a butterfly's wing hath made nothing without a purpose. Is there not a lesson for thee hidden under the butterfly's wing? If so, learn thy lesson, for God is thy Teacher, and His teachings are never in vain.

Look high, O soul! for what is earth but dust?
    The fleeting shadow of the better things?
    The heavens are thine if thou wilt use thy wings,
And sighs are songs if thou wilt only trust.

Aim high, O soul! for on the higher forms
    Is always room, while lower ranks are filled;
    Who climbs the heights finds all earth's noises stilled,
And a sweet calm and light above the storms.

Be high, O soul! scorn what is low and base;
    "Child of a King," they call thee; be a king,
    And troops of vassals will their tribute bring,
To crown thee, heir of glory, child of grace.

HENRY BURTON.

Is life a field? Then plough it up — re-sow
With worthier seed. Is life a ship? Oh, heed
The southing of thy stars. Is life a breath?
Breathe deeper; draw life up from hour to hour, —
Ay, from deepest deep of thy soul.

JEAN INGELOW.

MUSIC is the inarticulate speech of the heart, which cannot be compressed into words, because it is infinite. — WAGNER.

Were it not for music we might, in these days, say the beautiful is dead. — DISRAELI.

God grant that your soul may be filled with music! Even if denied the gift of song, you can cultivate a love for the harmonies of Nature, the symphonies of thought, and the songs without words, which are quiet communings with God whispered into your spirit by the Divine Musician. Keep the heart in tune, and let its music draw other hearts to yours, that your gladness may be to them the key-note, which shall be like a sweet chime ringing out the music of a Better Life, whose harp resounds with melodies of Heaven.

The loveliest scenes, e'en harmonies of June,
Seem discord, if the heart be out of tune.
Beneath the veil of pride and outward show
Ariseth many a hidden sigh of woe.
The wish that seems to thee as dear as life,
Granted, may yield but sorrow, care, or strife.
Many a wish may come to thee at will,
And leave thee restless and unhappy still.
ANONYMOUS.

Music dwells
Lingering, and wandering on as loth to die,
Like thoughts whose very sweetness yieldeth proof
That they were born for immortality.
WORDSWORTH.

JUNE TWELFTH.

A S you grow ready for it, somewhere or other you will find what is needful for you in a book, or a friend, or, best of all, in your own thoughts — the eternal thought speaking in your thought. — GEORGE MACDONALD.

It is not always the depth or the novelty of a thought which constitutes its value to ourselves, but the fitness of its application to our circumstances.— SEWELL.

Thoughts must come naturally, like wild flowers; they cannot be forced in a hot-bed — even although aided by the leaf-mould of your past. — ALEXANDER SMITH.

They are never alone that are accompanied with noble thoughts. — SIR PHILIP SIDNEY.

Thought can never be compared with action, but when it awakens in us the image of truth.— MADAME DE STAËL.

Nurture your mind with great thoughts; to believe in the heroic makes heroes.— I. DISRAELI

Learning without thought is labour lost; and thought without learning is perilous. — CONFUCIUS.

Receive your thoughts like guests, to be entertained according to their importance. — AL-MAIDANI.

Thought is the wind, knowledge the sail, and mankind the vessel. — J. C. HARE.

A thoughtful day to you!
[170]

JUNE THIRTEENTH.

LET there be nothing in to-day to regret! Make to-day better than yesterday: you remember, perhaps, when you calmly reviewed the day's events before you went to sleep, you thought of something you did which you were sorry for. Don't let it happen again to-day. Speak guardedly, act deliberately, and then there will be no cause for "repenting at leisure." Regrets are like myriads of little insects that swarm about the light, ever following in its wake, and all together forming a persistent cloud of annoyance. Go where we will, regrets take wing and swarm about us, and even in our dreams they come to haunt us. Oh, for the idle word of yesterday!

Oh, that word Regret!
There have been nights and morns when we have
    sighed,
"Let us alone, Regret! We are content
To throw thee all our past, so thou wilt sleep
For aye." But it is patient, and it wakes;
It hath not learned to cry itself to sleep,
But plaineth on the bed that it is hard.

We did amiss when we did wish it gone
And over; sorrows humanise our race;
Tears are the showers that fertilise this world;
And memory of things precious keepeth warm
The heart that once did hold them.

          They are poor
That hath lost nothing; they are poorer far
Who, losing, have forgotten; they most poor
Of all, who lost and wish they *might* forget.

JEAN INGELOW.

JUNE FOURTEENTH.

PATIENCE and resignation are the pillars
  Of human peace on earth.

YOUNG.

We may always find peace, if we look for it in the
right place: it can be had simply for the asking.

He to the conflict
  Was turning His face,
The cross loomed before Him,
  But He, full of grace,
Looked on the disciples,
  Grown weary with care,
And gave them His blessing,
  And stilled them with prayer.

He the departed One —
  What would He leave
To quiet and comfort
  The hearts that must grieve?
This, that would ever
  Cause sorrow to cease,
His benediction
  Of quiet and peace.

Down through the centuries,
  None of it lost,
Comes the kind legacy
  Won through great cost.
Know, all ye troubled ones,
  Treading life's way,
Peace is the blessing
  Christ gives you to-day.

MARIANNE FARNINGHAM.

JUNE FIFTEENTH.

JUSTICE is a grand thing, and the man who practises it in all affairs of his daily life sits on a higher throne than kings. His throne is Reason, and he has conquered prejudice and policy, and holds in his hand the well-balanced scales with which to weigh the acts and deeds of his fellow-men.

Justice is truth in action.
ANONYMOUS.

Fidelity is the sister of Justice.
HORACE.

Patience and gravity of bearing are an essential part of justice; and an over-speaking judge is no well-tuned cymbal. — LORD BACON.

Justice must be from violence exempt;
But fraud's her only object of contempt:
Fraud in the fox, force in the lion dwells;
But justice both from human hearts expels;
But he's the greatest monster, without doubt,
Who is a wolf within, a sheep without.
SIR JOHN DENHAM.

All are not just because they do no wrong;
But he who will not wrong me when he may,
He is the truly just.
RICHARD CUMBERLAND.

God is the God of Justice; in His hands are the scales of Justice, with which He weighs the deeds of all men. Let us not be "weighed, and found wanting."

JUNE SIXTEENTH.

MAY this day have a bright sunrise and a glorious
sunset! How restful it is, at the close of a
dreamy summer day, to look back over the hours, and
feel that they were well and profitably spent; to know
that you have faithfully tried to do your duty in all
things, and have not murmured or complained; and
that your crosses have been patiently and cheerfully
borne! The glad heart turns sighs into singing, and
tears into smiles. Make the day beautiful, and you shall
have a beautiful sunset. Peace will enfold you with
her white wings, and you shall lie down to pleasant
dreams, with the consciousness that you have spent a
happy, useful day. Oh, that the glory of a Christian's
sunset may illumine for you each dying day, and help
to fit you for the sunrise in Heaven!

How fine has the day been, how bright was the sun,
How lovely and joyful the course that he run,
Though he rose in a mist, when his race he begun,
    And there followed some droppings of rain!
But now the fair traveller's come to the west,
His rays are all gold, and his beauties are best;
He paints the sky gay as he sinks to his rest,
    And foretells a bright rising again.

Just such is the Christian; his course he begins,
Like the sun in a mist, when he mourns for his sins,
And melts into tears; then he breaks out and shines;
    And travels his heavenly way;
But when he comes nearer to finish his race,
Like a fine setting sun, he looks richer in grace,
And gives a sure hope at the end of his days,
    Of rising in brighter array.

ISAAC WATTS.

JUNE SEVENTEENTH.

OUR great trouble is, we are too sure of ourselves.
It is not until we do the wrong thing, at the wrong
time, and in the wrong place, that we find out how little real tact we possess; not until we fail of making a
success in life that we realize we were not so gifted
after all; not until we have planned our future, and
God has decreed it otherwise, that we discover our lack
of judgment; and not until we learn how strong God
is, that we feel our utter weakness. It is when we are
crushed and stricken that we turn our hearts heavenward. Oh, that we could learn to trust God more fully!

Leave all to God,
Forsaken one, and stay thy tears;
For the Highest knows thy pain,
Sees thy sufferings and thy fears;
Thou shalt not wait His help in vain:
Leave all to God.

Be still and trust!
For His strokes are strokes of love
Thou must for thy profit bear;
He thy filial fear would move;
Trust thy Father's loving care.
Be still and trust!

Oh, teach Him not
When and how to hear thy prayers;
Never doth our God forget.
He the cross who longest bears
Finds his sorrows' bounds are set.
Then teach Him not.

ANTON ULRICH, OF BRUNSWICK, 1667.

[175]

LIFE is a restless sea, and man the mariner steer-
ing across from shore to shore. When the sky
is fair, and the waves calm, the voyage will be smooth
and prosperous ; but storms will come and the breakers
dash high, and what then? There is a Divine Hand
guiding the barque of the Christian mariner, which the
eye of faith can discern in the darkest night. The
mariner knows his Captain's powers; calmly and
serenely he sails beneath the terrors of a stormy sky,
flashing with lightning and booming with thunders, assured of the strength of that guiding Hand that rules
the fiercest gale. Be not thou afraid to launch thy
boat, if thou hast chosen God to go with thee across
life's perilous sea : the voyage is not long — a few brief
years, then Home shall rise in sight, and all be well.

Launch thy bark, mariner!
    Christian, God speed thee!
Let loose the rudder-bands —
    Good angels lead thee!
Set thy sails warily,
    Tempests will come ;
Steer thy course steadily;
    Christian, steer home!

Slacken not sail yet
    At inlet or island ;
Straight for the beacon steer,
    Straight for the high land;
Crowd all thy canvas on,
    Cut through the foam —
Christian! cast anchor now —
    Heaven is thy home!

CAROLINE SOUTHEY.

JUNE NINETEENTH.

HOW sweet is the name of Mother! In it is embraced all that is pure and holy, good and beautiful. We linger over it with tenderness, and enshrine it in our heart of hearts, like a precious jewel to be guarded and prized as long as life shall last. About that hallowed name clusters the sacredness of home; and from a mother's loving influence emanates all that is ennobling, and that inspires us with longings after a higher and better life. Who can estimate the value of a mother's influence? Who can measure the depths of a mother's love? They are links between us and Heaven. They who have never known a mother's love have missed half the blessedness of living, and to such as these the love of God must be more tender and sweet. May the influence of the good mothers of England, whether in palace or cot, make her name more and more revered, and her people worthier of all God's goodness!

The mother, in her office, holds the key
Of the soil; and she it is who stamps the coin
Of character, and makes the being who would be a
　　savage,
But for her gentle cares, a Christian man.
Then crown her Queen of the world.

OLD PLAY.

Sweet is the image of the brooding dove!
Holy as Heaven a mother's tender love!
The love of many prayers, and many tears,
Which changes not with dim declining years —
The only love which, on this teeming earth,
Asks no return for passion's wayward birth.

CAROLINE NORTON.

MAY thy heart be as full of music as England's forest minstrel !

Hark! ah, the nightingale —
The tawny-throated!
Hark! from that moonlit cedar what a burst!
What triumph ! hark ! what pain !

MATTHEW ARNOLD.

Sweet bird that sing'st away the early hours
  Of winters past or coming, void of care,
  Well pleased with delights which present are,
Fair seasons, budding sprays, sweet-smelling flowers.

DRUMMOND.

The nightingale's sweet music
Fills the air and leafy bowers.

HEINE.

The nightingale now wanders in the vines :
Her passion is to seek roses.

LADY MARY WORTLEY MONTAGU.

The bird that sings on highest wing,
  Builds on the ground her lowly nest ;
And she that doth most sweetly sing,
  Sings in the shade when all things rest :
In lark and nightingale we see
What honour hath humility.

MONTGOMERY.

Be thou filled with humility, like the lark, and let
thy soul sing in the darkness, like the nightingale!

[178]

THINK not to escape sorrow. Even in the summer days it comes to happy hearts all over God's green earth. Ah, it is pitiful to stand amid the roses, and feel too sorely stricken to see their beauty and scent their perfume; it is sorrowful to be baptized in a flood of sunshine, and yet be not aware of it; to walk knee-deep in clover, and to think your pathway is dark and gloomy and desolate; and to be too blinded by grief to see that the sky is as blue as ever, and that God's dear Hand is outstretched still. Stand not doubting and desponding, but let Him share your heart-aches. He will pour His sunlight into your spirit, until your vision shall no longer be holden from His glories.

Saviour! by Thy sweet compassion,
　So unmeasured, so Divine;
By that bitter, bitter Passion;
　By that crimson Cross of Thine;
By the woes Thy love once tasted
　In this sin-marred world below,
Succour those in tribulation,
　Succour those in sorrow now.

Thou who wast so sorely burdened,
　Help the weak that are oppressed;
Sanctify all earthly crosses,
　For the coming day of rest;

　.　.　.　.　.　.　.　.

Tell them Thou canst see all sorrow
　In this world's rough wilderness;
Tell them Thou art near to succour,
　Near to comfort and to bless.

ADA CAMBRIDGE.

WHATEVER you are, be faithful. Faithful to duty, faithful in little things, faithful in friendships, faithful to God. Do not allow yourself to slight anything that is worth doing. Half-way sewing gives you a garment to do over again; half-way study makes failures in examinations; half-read articles weaken your memory; half-way business loses customers; half-way friendships are not worth having. God bless the loyal man or woman, who will uphold a good cause, and be faithful to it, come what may! "What is worth doing, is worth doing well," and what is worth *being*, is worth our best in faithfulness and steadfastness of purpose. To be loyal to those you love, and to prove your fidelity in time of need, this too is desirable, and shows a heart sincere. Let it be truthfully said of you, that you were

> Faithful found
> Among the faithless. . . .
> His loyalty he kept, his love, his zeal;
> Nor number with example with him wrought
> To swerve from truth, or change his constant mind,
> Though single.
>
> MILTON.

> Thought ye your iron hands of pride
> Could break the knot that hath been tried?
> No:— let the eagle change her plume,
> The leaf its hue, the flow'r its bloom;
> But ties around this heart were spun,
> That could not, would not, be undone!
>
> CAMPBELL.

> Here is my hand for true constancy.
>
> SHAKESPEARE.

THIS is my prayer for thee to-day: that thou mayst have patience, long-suffering, and endurance; that thou mayst forget self and its weakness, and, relying only upon the divine strength, mayst look upward and outward, and rejoice! God is everywhere; "His strength is in the hills," and His song is rippling in gladness from the rivers and seas. He who hath established the rocks and formed the mountains hath not forgotten thee. He will put a new song into thine heart, and strengthen and uphold thee, and give thee courage to endure unto the end.

Be strong to hope, O Heart!
  Though day is bright,
The stars can only shine
  In the dark night.
Be strong, O Heart of mine,
  Look toward the light!

Be strong to bear, O Heart!
  Nothing is vain:
Strive not, for life is care,
  And God sends pain;
Heaven is above, and there
  Rest will remain!

Be strong to love, O Heart!
  Love knows not wrong;
Didst thou love creatures even,
  Life were not long;
Didst thou love God in Heaven,
  Thou wouldst be strong.

ADELAIDE A. PROCTER.

[181]

A WORD of commendation or praise, sincere because it issues from the heart, is always helpful
and encouraging. But flattery is to every earnest,
truthful nature most unwelcome and distasteful. When
you flatter, you commit two wrongs: one against yourself, and one against the person to whom you are
speaking. The man who indulges in oft-repeated
flatteries grows more and more indifferent to truth,
until his conscience becomes calloused to its gentle
teachings. Don't seek to further your ends by speaking what you don't feel; don't allow policy to lead you
away from your better self and to trample truth under
your feet. Encourage, commend, and say a helpful,
kind word, but do not stoop to the level of a flatterer:
it is always easier to fall a little lower, when once you
are down. Let all of your words and actions tend to
elevate and ennoble you.

> Beware of flattery, 'tis a weed
> Which oft offends the very idol — vice,
> Whose shrine it would perfume.
>
> FENTON.

> Minds
> By nature great are conscious of their greatness,
> And hold it mean to borrow aught from flattery.
>
> ROWE.

> Parent of wicked, bane of honest deeds,
> Pernicious flattery! thy malignant seeds,
> In an ill hour, and by a fated hand,
> Sadly diffus'd o'er virtue's gleby land,
> With rising pride amidst the corn appear,
> And choke the hopes and harvests of the year.
>
> PRIOR.

JUNE TWENTY-FIFTH.

SUMMER days, with all their dreamy beauty, often find us filled with restless longings and discontent. We look up into the sky, and follow the fleecy clouds, and our unsatisfied souls grow weary with watching their ever-shifting whiteness; the song of the river lulls us for a time, and again we cry out for rest. When we shall reach the fadeless Summer-land of the world above, and not until then, shall our longing souls be satisfied.

When I shall wake on that fair morn of morns,
After whose dawning never night returns,
And with whose glory day eternal burns,
　　　I shall be satisfied.

When I shall see Thy glory face to face,
When in Thine arms Thou wilt Thy child embrace,
When Thou shalt open all Thy stores of grace,
　　　I shall be satisfied.

When I shall meet with those whom I have loved,
Clasp in my eager arms the long-removed,
And find how faithful Thou hast proved,
　　　I shall be satisfied.

When I shall gaze upon the face of Him
Who for me died, with eyes no longer dim,
And praise Him in the everlasting hymn,
　　　I shall be satisfied.

When I shall call to mind the long, long past,
With clouds and storms and shadows overcast,
And know that I am saved and blest at last,
　　　I shall be satisfied.

HORATIUS BONAR.

HOW often we are mistaken in people! Havard says,

> "Appearances deceive,
> And this one maxim is a standing rule, —
> Men are not what they seem."

It is true we are unable to understand each other in the brief glimpses we have, as we pass back and forth in our daily lives. A man's outer garb may betoken him a gentleman, when he is at heart anything else. A woman's queenly grace and beauty may stamp her as a lady, when she may never have known the true meaning of the word. The dark side of life may have changed a man's nature to such an extent, that when you look into his face you say, "He is a villain," whereas it is only poverty and hunger and despair that are speaking through his hollow-looking eyes and gloomy countenance. Perhaps

> "That gloomy outside, like a rusty chest,
> Contains the shining treasure of a soul
> Resolved and brave,"

as Dryden has it. We are too easily influenced by appearances, and, in consequence, a rough exterior is often undervalued, when beneath lies hidden a heart of purest truth and highest nobility. Yet, on the other hand, some men are outwardly polished and attractive: we can scarcely believe they can be other than they seem. Shakespeare says,

> "Why should the sacred character of virtue
> Shine on a villain's countenance?"

Because perhaps he makes, to quote Churchill's words,

> "Appearances to save his only care;
> So things seem right, no matter what they *are*."

JUNE TWENTY-SEVENTH.

TO pray together, in whatever tongue or ritual, is the most tender brotherhood of hope and sympathy that men can contract in this life. — MADAME DE STAËL.

He who prays without confidence, cannot hope that his prayers will be granted. — FENELON.

In prayer the lips ne'er act the winning part
Without the sweet concurrence of the heart.

HERRICK.

Prayer moves the Hand which moves the world.

JOHN AIKMAN WALLACE.

Serve God before the world; let Him not go
Until thou hast a blessing; then resign
The whole unto Him; and remember who
Prevail'd by wrestling ere the sun did shine.
Pour oyle upon the stones; weep for thy sin;
Then journey on, and have an eye to Heav'n.

VAUGHAN.

They never sought in vain that sought the Lord aright.

BURNS.

More things are wrought by prayer
Than this world dreams of. Wherefore, let thy voice
Rise like a fountain for me night and day.
For what are men better than sheep or goats
That nourish a blind life within the brain,
If, knowing God, they lift not hands of prayer
Both for themselves and those who call them friend?
For so the whole round earth is every way
Bound by gold chains about the feet of God.

TENNYSON.

[185]

JUNE TWENTY-EIGHTH.

WE should learn to be temperate in all things. The thirst for knowledge has led to the utter ruin of many a mind. The appetite of the mind should be held in check, as well as the appetite of the body. Continued pampering will result in disease: overfed minds cannot continue strong and vigorous, any more than overfed bodies. Many a bright, young intellect has been clouded forever, because ambitious teachers, parents, and friends have made a god of knowledge, and sacrificed an innocent victim on its altar. Youthful inventors, musicians, and artists, as well as students of literature and language, are to-day shut up between the walls of our asylums because of intemperate habits in reading and studying. The mind must have exercise, recreation, and rest; it must not be overcrowded, but should unfold slowly, as an opening rose, in the sunny garden of Knowledge.

The mind of man is this world's true dimension;
And knowledge is the measure of the mind:
And as the mind, in her vast comprehension,
Contains more worlds than all the world can find,
So knowledge doth itself far more extend,
Than all the minds of man can comprehend.

LORD BROOKE.

Knowledge is as food, and needs no less
Her temp'rance over appetite, to know
In measure what the mind may well contain,
Oppresses else with surfeit, and soon turns
Wisdom to folly.

MILTON.

A N argument has often been the means of separating friends. With some people arguing is a hobby; they are never really happy until deep in an argument with some one, and are often very unhappy before they get out of it. A constant war of words is unpleasant; it renders one sharp-tongued and fretful, and takes the sweetness out of any disposition. The man who boasts that he always carries his point often imagines he does so, while, on the other hand, his opponent is just as sure that he has been defeated. An argument seldom results in a change of opinion, and is, therefore, in many cases, a mere waste of time and breath, and often ends in a quarrel. Avoid controversies where they create hard feelings; but where you know a friend is in the wrong, endeavor kindly to point out his error and convince him of his mistake. Do not approach him when he is angry, for then he is unfit to reason with you, but let him calmly and deliberately be shown what you conscientiously believe to be the right, and then he will listen quietly.

Be calm in arguing. For fierceness makes
Error a fault, and truth discourtesy.
Why should I feel another man's mistakes
More than his sickness or poverty?
In love I should; but anger is not love,
Nor wisdom neither; therefore gently move:
Calmness is great advantage.

HERBERT.

If truth be with thy friend, be with them both:
Share in the conquest, and confess a troth.

HERBERT.

JUNE THIRTIETH.

FAREWELL, sweet June! thy little race is run, thy first bright roses hang their drooping heads, but one by one new buds have opened in the sun, and not a link of beauty yet is lost. So in the wheaten fields, that wave like golden seas, if one stalk withers through a blighted heart, its fellows closer crowd and hide its early grave, and no one but the Father knows the spot. The strawberries have turned their soft cheeks to the light, and, rich and luscious, ripened into red; and their abundant yield, like rose, like golden wheat, has failed not in the glory of the June. Our deeds, our acts of love, — oh, that they too have been unmarred by fading leaves of sad mistakes, or withered stalks of blighted trust, or stolen fruits that robbed our neighbor's store of joys! Oh, that in some sweet aftermath, our roses, grain, and fruit may make for some tired heart a rest!

Therefore myself is that one only thing
   I hold to use or waste, to keep or give;
   My sole possession every day I live,
And still mine own despite Time's winnowing.
Ever mine own, while moons and seasons bring
   From crudeness ripeness mellow and sanative:
   Ever mine own, till Death shall ply his sieve;
And still mine own, when saints break grave and sing.
And this myself as king unto my King
   I give to Him who gave Himself for me;
Who gives Himself to me, and bids me sing
   A sweet new song of His redeemed set free;
He bids me sing: O death, where is thy sting?
   And sing: O grave, where is thy victory?

CHRISTINA ROSSETTI.

ALFRED TENNYSON

1809–1892

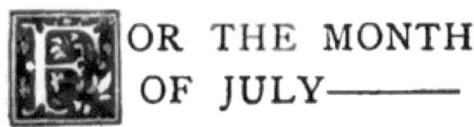 OR THE MONTH
OF JULY——

JULY FIRST.

HOW drowsy and dreamy is July! Bees hum, and flies buzz, and insects chirp in the grasses. The air is still and languid, disturbed now and then by the soft flutter of butterflies' wings, flitting from flower to flower, or the quick whirring of a summer bird. The lark goes, singing, upward from her lowly nest among the grasses, and the cuckoo sends forth happy notes from out the leafy shade. The sea murmurs along the shore, and the dewy freshness of the morning melts into the heart of noon when all is sunshine and drowsiness and stillness. On the valleys rests the midday hush, and man ceases his labor to refresh himself from the cool, sweet waters that lie in the shadow of the wayside well. July is the midsummer season,—the noontide of the year. A beautiful time is it to refresh ourselves from the Fountain of God's Love, and to drink a deep, cooling draught, which, if we drink, we shall never thirst again.

> July has come! the meadow-lands
>   In verdure stretch away;
> In broad-brimmed hat the mower stands
>   Knee-deep amid the hay;
> The scent of clover fills the air,
>   While sunflowers gaily nod,
> And Nature's children sweetly share
>   The joy of praising God.

[189]

JULY SECOND.

MAY your life be an example of sweet humility, and, like the modest daisy, "the eye of the day," may you ever be a white star of purity blooming contentedly for the glory of God.

There is a flower, a little flower
  With silver crest and golden eye,
That welcomes every changing hour,
  And weathers every sky.

.   .   .   .

On waste and woodland, rock and plain,
  Its humble buds unheeded rise;
The rose has but a summer-reign;
  The Daisy never dies!

                   MONTGOMERY.

That well by reason men it call may
The daisie or else the eye of the day.

                   CHAUCER.

The Daisy blossoms on the rocks,
  Amid the purple heath;
It blossoms on the river's banks,
  That thrids the glens beneath;
The eagle, at his pride of place,
  Beholds it by his nest,
And in the mead, it cushions soft
  The lark's descending breast.

                   MOIR.

Daisies infinite
Uplift in praise their little glowing hands,
O'er every hill that under Heaven expands.

           EBENEZER ELLIOTT.

[190]

JULY THIRD.

HIGH Thoughts! They come and go
  Like the soft breathings of a listening maiden,
While round me flow
  The winds, from woods and fields with gladness
      laden :
When the corn's rustle on the earth doth come —
When the eve's beetle sounds its drowsy hum —
When the stars, dewdrops of the summer sky,
Watch over all with soft and loving eye —
      While the leaves quiver by the lone river,
        And the quiet heart
          From depths doth call and garners all —
        Earth grows a shadow
          Forgotten whole,
        And Heaven lives
          In the blessed soul!

High thoughts! They visit us
  In moments when the soul is dim and darkened ;
They come to bless,
  After the vanities to which we hearkened :
When weariness hath come upon the spirit —
(Those hours of darkness which we all inherit) —
Bursts there not through a glint of warm sunshine,
A winged thought, which bids us not repine?
      In joy and gladness, in mirth and sadness,
        Come signs and tokens ;
          Life's angel brings, upon its wings
        Those bright communings
          The soul doth keep —
        Those thoughts of Heaven
          So pure and deep!

ROBERT NICHOLL.

JULY FOURTH.

O sing unto the Lord a new song; sing unto the Lord, all the earth.

Sing unto the Lord, bless his name; shew forth his salvation from day to day.

Declare his wonders among all people. For the Lord is great and greatly to be praised. — PSALM 96: 1–4.

All hail, light of day!
Thy sweet gushing ray
Pours down its soft warmth over pasture and field;
With hues silver-tinged
The meadows are fringed,
And numberless suns in the dewdrop reveal'd.

SCHILLER.

As a bird in meadows fair
Or in lonely forest sings
Till it fills the summer air,
And the greenwood sweetly rings,
So my heart to Thee would raise,
O my God, its song of praise,
That the gloom of night is o'er,
And I see the sun once more.

If Thou, Sun of Love, arise,
All my heart with joy is stirred,
And to greet Thee upward flies,
Gladsome as yon little bird.
Shine Thou in me clear and bright
Till I learn to praise Thee right:
Guide me in the narrow way,
Let me ne'er in darkness stray.

FROM THE GERMAN.

JULY FIFTH.

IT is the secret sympathy,
  The silver link, the silken tie,
Which heart to heart, and mind to mind,
In body and in soul can bind.

SCOTT.

Our Father was very kind when He implanted within us the feeling which we call sympathy. We have need for a great deal of it in this world: not a day goes by but some friend, or passing acquaintance, or stranger, draws upon our fund of sympathy; and I trust we have all a goodly sum in reserve, enough to last us the rest of our natural life. What various appeals there are to us! Sometimes it is poverty, or distress, or sorrow, or disgrace, or affliction, or losses, or severe illness and intense suffering, or cruel injustice, or false accusations, —all of these call forth our sincere sympathy, and fill us with the longing to comfort and relieve those who are troubled and distressed. Let us keep our hearts warm and tender, that they may beat kindly towards all humanity.

The craving for sympathy is the common boundary-line between joy and sorrow. — J. C. AND A. W. HARE.

Sympathy is especially a Christian's duty. — SPURGEON.

As the human countenance smiles on those that smile, so does it sympathise with those that weep. — SMART.

I live not in myself, but I become
Portion of that around me.

BYRON.

JULY SIXTH.

A DAY OF CONSECRATION.

I WOULD rather be what God chose to make me
than the most glorious creature I could think of.
For to have been thought about — born in God's
thoughts, and then made by God, is the dearest,
grandest, most precious thing in all thinking. — GEORGE
MACDONALD.

Take my life, and let it be
Consecrated, Lord, to Thee;

Take my hands, and let them move
At the impulse of Thy love.

Take my voice, and let me sing
Always, only, for my King.

Take my silver and my gold,
Not a mite would I withhold;

Take my moments and my days,
Let them flow in ceaseless praise.

Take my will, and make it Thine,
It shall be no longer mine;

Take my heart, it is Thine own,
It shall be Thy royal throne.

FRANCES RIDLEY HAVERGAL.

Withhold not from God His just due. Talent, time,
wealth, and all that thou hast are His, but given into
thy keeping to improve and use for His glory. See
that thou payest thy debt with interest !

OF all inorganic substances, acting in their own proper nature, and without assistance or combination, water is the most wonderful. If we think of it as the source of all changefulness and beauty which we have seen in clouds; then as the instrument by which the earth we have contemplated was modelled into symmetry, and its crags chiselled into grace; then as, in the form of snow, it robes the mountains it has made with that transcendent light which we could not have conceived if we had not seen; then as it exists in the foam of the torrent, — in the iris which spans it, in the morning mist which rises from it, in the deep crystalline pools which mirror its hanging shore, in the broad lake and glancing river; finally, in that which is to all human minds the best emblem of unwearied, unconquerable power, — the wild, various, fantastic, tameless unity of the sea; what shall we compare to this mighty, this universal element, for glory and for beauty? or how shall we follow its eternal changefulness of feeling? It is like trying to paint a soul. —
RUSKIN.

> Roll on, thou deep and dark blue ocean — roll!
>
> .   .   .   .
>
> Thou glorious mirror, where the Almighty's form
> Glasses itself in tempests; in all time,
> Calm or convuls'd . . .
> . . . boundless, endless, and sublime —
> The image of eternity.
>
> BYRON.

Launch your soul on the ocean of God's love; and in His own time you shall reach His Harbor of Perfect Peace.

JULY EIGHTH.

LET your motto be "Onward and upward," no matter what obstacles you may meet. *Per aspera ad astra.* Keep on climbing higher.

Rest is not quitting
    This busy career;
Rest is the fitting
    Of self to its sphere.

'Tis loving and serving
    The highest and best;
'Tis onward, unswerving,
    And this is true rest.

GOETHE.

Catch, then, O catch the transient hour;
    Improve each moment as it flies;
Life's a short summer, man a flower;
    He dies, — alas! how soon he dies!

SAMUEL JOHNSON.

Seek'st thou the highest, the greatest? In that the
    plant can instruct thee;
What it unwittingly is, be thou of thine own free will!

SCHILLER.

Be like the bird, that, halting in her flight
    Awhile on boughs too slight,
Feels them give way beneath her and yet sings,
    Knowing that she hath wings.

VICTOR HUGO.

Great souls,
By nature half divine, soar to the stars.

NICHOLAS ROWE.

[196]

JULY NINTH.

HOW far the little candle throws its beams!
SHAKESPEARE.

May this be said truly of us! If our light is but small, may its tiny beams shine afar into the paths of others and help them to avoid the pitfalls of temptations and evil. Let us not scorn the little duties and little services, but however humble our place, and small our achievements, let us make it tell for Eternity.

Small service is true service while it lasts:
    Of humblest friends, bright creature, scorn not one;
The Daisy, by the shadow that it casts,
    Protects the lingering dewdrop from the sun.
WORDSWORTH.

To me the meanest flower that blows can give
Thoughts that so often lie too deep for tears.
WORDSWORTH.

What time is little? To the sentinel
That hour is regal when he mounts on guard.
GEORGE ELIOT.

Exactness in little duties is a wonderful source of cheerfulness. — F. W. FABER.

The tasks, the joys of earth, the same in Heaven will
    be;
Only the little brook has widened to a sea.
R. C. TRENCH.

He that is faithful in that which is least, is faithful also in much. — LUKE 16: 10.

[197]

JULY TENTH.

IF the human mind is rich, it will generously give of
its abundance to others; if it is steeped in the
incense of sweet thoughts, it will yield a fragrance to
those around it. The mind enriched by Heaven is
continually getting and giving, absorbing and radiat-
ing, being blessed and blessing others.

> Mind's command o'er mind,
> Spirit o'er spirit, is the clear effect
> And natural action of an inward gift,
> Given by God.
>
> BAILEY.

> Time has small pow'r
> O'er features the mind moulds.   Roses where
> They once have bloom'd, a fragrance leave behind;
> And harmony will linger on the wind;
> And suns continue to light up the air,
> When set; and music from the broken shrine
> Breathes, it is said, around whose altar-stone
> His flower the votary has ceas'd to twine:—
> Types of the beauty, that when youth is gone,
> Breathes from the soul whose brightness mocks decline.
>
> GEORGE HILL.

> Mind, despatch'd upon the busy toil,
> Should range where Providence hast blessed the soil;
> Visiting every flow'r with labour meet,
> And gathering all her treasures, sweet by sweet,
> She should imbue the tongue with what she sips,
> And shed the balmy blessings on the lips,
> That good diffus'd may more abundant grow,
> And speech may praise the pow'r that bids it flow.
>
> COWPER.

WHEN God at first made man,
    Having a glass of blessings standing by,
"Let us," said He, "pour on him all we can ;
  Let the world's riches, which dispersed lie,
    Contract into a span."

So strength first made a way ;
  Then beauty flowed ; then wisdom, honour, pleasure ;
When almost all was out, God made a stay ;
  Perceiving that alone, of all His treasures,
    Rest in the bottom lay.

"For if I should," said He,
  "Bestow this jewel on my creature,
He would adore my gift instead of Me,
  And rest in nature, not the God of nature —
    So both should losers be.

"Yet let him keep the rest —
  But keep them, with repining restlessness —
Let him be rich and weary ; that, at least,
  If goodness lead him not, yet weariness
    May toss him to My breast."

                      GEORGE HERBERT.

There is no perfect rest out of Christ. Sleep but soothes us for a time ; change of scene makes our life less monotonous, perhaps, but we must soon return to the old routine and feel again the old weariness and restlessness. It is the humanity in us seeking a greater Strength to lean upon. When you are most restless and most filled with the realization that earth cannot satisfy you, then, you may depend upon it, you need to get closer to God, and to rest in His sheltering arms.

[199]

TO prove that we have goodness within us, it must blossom into deeds. A tree that yields no bloom and bears no fruit, of what use is it? Even the sturdy pine drops its beautiful, symmetrical cones, and the grand old oak its dainty acorns, — proofs that each not only lends shelter and grace to the world, but that it is showering down its treasures, in token of growth and strength.

It is a kind of good deed to *say* well,
And yet words are not deeds.

SHAKESPEARE.

When the poor and hungry are about you, a kind word will do their hearts good, but it will not feed their bodies. What they need is substantial food, and if you bestow this upon them, and accompany it with kindness, you have given them a noble blessing. The sweetest way to be charitable is to give in such a way that it is not recognized as charity at all. "Not grudgingly or of necessity: for God loveth a cheerful giver."

There is some soul of goodness in things evil,
Would men observingly distil it out.

SHAKESPEARE.

The chamber where the good man meets his fate
Is privileged beyond the common walk
Of virtuous life, quite in the verge of Heaven.

YOUNG.

JULY THIRTEENTH.

IN your occupations try to possess your soul in peace. It is not a good plan to be in haste to perform any action that it may soon be over. On the contrary, you should accustom yourself to do whatever you have to do with tranquillity, in order that you may retain the possession of yourself and of settled peace.
— MADAME GUYON.

One lesson, Nature, let me learn of thee,
One lesson, which in every wind is blown,
One lesson of two duties kept at one,
Though the loud world proclaim their unity —

Of toil unsever'd from tranquillity!
Of labour, that in lasting fruit outgrows
Far noisier schemes, accomplish'd in repose
Too great for haste, too high for rivalry!

Yes, while on earth a thousand discords ring,
Man's senseless uproar mingling with his toil,
Still do they, quiet ministers, move on,
Their glorious tasks in silence perfecting!
Still working, blaming still our vain turmoil,
Labourers that shall not fail, when man is gone.
                              MATTHEW ARNOLD.

In Nature all work is quiet work. The most beautiful flower that ever bloomed unfolded every petal in silence, and yet how many hearts it cheered! The largest grain-field that ever ripened in the sunshine and rain reached perfection without making a sound, and yet how many hungry it fed! God bless the silent workers, and make you one of them!

[201]

JULY FOURTEENTH.

LET us walk among the lilies. "As the Lily is pure and spotless, so may thy life be !" and may thy soul open to the sunshine of God's love, and bloom like the lilies of the field, — clothed in the beauty of humility and the whiteness of peace !

> The Lily is all in white like a saint.
>
> HOOD.

> The lilies say: Behold how we
> Preach, without words, of purity.
>
> CHRISTINA ROSSETTI.

> Very whitely still
> The lilies of our lives may reassure
> Their blossoms from their roots, accessible
> Alone to heavenly dews.
>
> E. B. BROWNING.

> "Look to the lilies how they grow !"
> 'Twas thus the Saviour said, that we,
> Even in the simplest flowers that blow,
> God's ever-watchful care might see.
>
> MOIR.

> "Thou wert not, Solomon ! in all thy glory,
> Array'd," the lilies cry, "in robes like ours ";
> How vain your grandeur ! Ah, how transitory
> Are human flowers !
>
> HORACE SMITH.

> The citron-tree or spicy grove for me would never yield
> A perfume half so grateful as the lilies of the field.
>
> ELIZA COOK.

IT is through a flower-strewn way
   That Thy children walk to-day,
O God, who makest the Summer-time so beautiful to
   see;
   And the sweetly scented air
   Bears upward many a prayer
Of loving, happy gratitude from the sons of men to
   Thee.

   O God, is any sad
   When the world is all so glad,
And Thou hast made the Summer so full of joy and
   love?
   Are there tears in any eyes
   That look upward to Thy skies,
When the earth in beauty vieth with the azure space
   above?

   For all the pain and sadness,
   Thou canst put joy and gladness
In hearts that do not know them though "the corn
   and wine increase."
Hush Thou the care and strife that mar our human life,
And give to every troubled one some share of love and
   peace.

   All things own Thy control;
   Make Summer in the soul,
Whose sobbings spoil with dissonance the season's
   merry chimes;
Thy blessings crowd the sod, — be merciful, O God,
And give to every child of Thine the joy of Summer-
   time.

      MARIANNE FARNINGHAM.

CAST thy bread upon the waters: for thou shalt find it after many days. — ECCLESIASTES II : I.

May you be able to look back upon this day in after years, and remember it as one of the best days of your life ! As one who, sitting on the green shore of some quiet lake, throws a handful of bread to the pure white swans gliding over its tranquil surface, so may you, this July day, feed some sorrowing spirit with crumbs of comfort, or some hungering heart with the manna of Christian love. When life's winter comes, the channels will be all frozen over, and your chances lost forever.

We scatter seeds with careless hand,
And dream we ne'er shall see them more :
But for a thousand years
Their fruit appears,
In weeds that mar the land,
Or healthful store.

The deeds we do, the words we say —
Into still air they seem to fleet,
We count them ever past,
But they shall last ;
In the dead-judgment they
And we shall meet !

I charge thee by the years gone by,
For the love's sake of brethren dear ;
Keep thou the one true way
In work and play,
Lest in the world their cry
Of woe thou hear !

JOHN KEBLE.

JULY SEVENTEENTH.

TO be self-reliant, thoroughly independent, and to possess the knowledge that God has given you a special place in this world, and you feel that you are expected to fill it; this, and to be endowed with the gift of perseverance, is a fortune which is worth more to you than an inherited earthly kingdom. The mere possession of wealth does not always ensure happiness; in fact, it is those who have vast possessions who have greatest responsibilities, and who consequently bear the heaviest burdens. Good health is good fortune. Sound judgment, common sense, a cheerful disposition, and a willingness to be useful, — all of these are things which adverse winds cannot blow away, and which make for its possessors a cause for daily thanksgiving.

> To catch dame Fortune's golden smile,
>   Assiduous wait upon her;
> And gather gear by every wile
>   That's justified by honour.
> Not for to hide it in a hedge
>   Nor for a train attendant;
> But for the glorious privilege
>   Of being *independent*.

BURNS.

> Not always fall of leaf, nor ever spring,
>   Not endless night, yet not eternal day:
> The saddest birds a season find to sing,
>   The roughest storm a calm may soon allay.
> Thus, with succeeding turns, God tempereth all,
> That man may hope to rise, yet fear to fall.

ROBERT SOUTHWELL.

JULY EIGHTEENTH.

GOD said, "Blessed are the merciful: for they shall obtain mercy." One of the sweetest and gentlest virtues is Mercy; patience, charity, love, and compassion are all blended in her, and when she smiles Hatred is melted to tears, and Cruelty hides his face for shame. Be merciful, not only to human beings, but to dumb animals, who look to you for protection and kindness. Without mercy you cannot claim kinship with God, whose great warm Heart is full of tender compassion for all His creatures.

'Tis mercy! mercy!
The mark of Heav'n impress'd on human kind,
Mercy, that glads the world, deals joy around;
Mercy that smooths the dreadful brow of power,
And makes dominion light; mercy that saves,
Binds up the broken heart, and heals despair.

ROWE.

How would you be,
If He, which is the top of judgment, should
But judge as you do? Oh, think on that;
And mercy then will breathe within your lips,
Like man new made!

SHAKESPEARE.

O mercy, heavenly born! Sweet attribute!
Thou great, thou best prerogative of power!
Justice may guard the throne, but joined with thee,
On rocks of adamant, it stands secure,
And braves the storm beneath.

WILLIAM SOMERVILLE.

[206]

JULY NINETEENTH.

CHRIST be with you to-morrow
    In pleasure or in sorrow;
Christ help you in temptation
And every tribulation;
Christ strengthen you for duty,
Give to your spirit beauty,
And comfort you with gladness
For every hour of sadness;
Christ bid His angels serve you
And from all ill preserve you;
Christ make you pure and holy,
Christ keep you meek and lowly,
Until with Him in heaven
His crowning grace be given;
The care of Christ defend you,
The love of Christ befriend you.

MARIANNE FARNINGHAM.

Have nothing apart from Christ. Let Him share all things with you. Plan no to-morrow without Him; include Him in your joys, and ask His sympathy in your sorrows. He knows exactly what you need, and knows far better than you do yourself. Surely with such a Guide and Friend you cannot seek to do your will, and to walk contrary to His choice.

Lead, kindly Light, amid the encircling gloom,
        Lead Thou me on;
The night is dark, and I am far from home,
        Lead Thou me on.
Keep Thou my feet; I do not ask to see
The distant scene; one step enough for me.

J. H. NEWMAN.

[207]

JULY TWENTIETH.

THROUGH the spirit of Divine Love, let the vio-
lent, obstinate powers of thy nature be quieted,
the hardness of thy affections be softened, and thine
intractable self-will be subdued. — G. TERSTEEGEN.

> Only thy restless heart keep still,
>   And wait in cheerful hope ; content
> To take whate'er His gracious will,
>   His all-discerning love, hath sent ;
> Nor doubt our inmost wants are known
>   To Him who chose us for His own.
>
> G. NEUMARK.

> And should the twilight darken into night,
>   And sorrow grow to anguish, be thou strong ;
>   Thou art in God, and nothing can go wrong
> Which a fresh life-pulse cannot set aright.
> That thou dost know the darkness, proves the light.
>   Weep if thou wilt, but weep not all too long ;
>   Or weep and work, for work will lead to song.
>
> GEORGE MACDONALD.

God make thee able to endure the petty trials and
cares that nag and fret and worry thee in thine earthly
pilgrimage. As thou goest, step by step, through the
journey of the year, mayst thou be filled with inward
gentleness and grace of spirit, and with strength to
conquer and subdue the foes without and within.

> Yet still the light of righteousness beams pure,
>   Beams to me from the world of far-off day ;
> Lord who hast called them happy that endure,
>   Lord, make me such as they.
>
> CHRISTINA ROSSETTI.

WE cannot honour our country with too deep a reverence; we cannot love her with an affection too pure and fervent; we cannot serve her with an energy of purpose or a faithfulness of zeal too steadfast and ardent. — GRIMKÉ.

Our country's welfare is our first concern,
And who promotes that best, best proves his duty.

HAVARD.

Give me the death of those
  Who for their country die;
And oh! be mine like their repose,
  When cold and low they lie:
Their loveliest mother earth
  Enshrines the fallen brave;
In their sweet lap who gave them birth,
  They find their tranquil grave.

MONTGOMERY.

A people
Who cannot find in their own proper force
Their own protection, are not worth saving.

THOMSON.

What constitutes a state?

. . . .

Men who their duties know,
But know their rights, and knowing, dare maintain,
  Prevent the long-aimed blow,
And crush the tyrant, while they rend the chain: —
  These constitute a state.

SIR WILLIAM JONES.

JULY TWENTY-SECOND.

A Day in the Hay-Fields.

THE sun had risen, the air was sweet,
 And brightly shone the dew,
And cheerful sounds and busy feet
 Pass'd the lone meadows through;
And waving like a flowery sea
 Of gay and spiry bloom,
The hay-fields rippled merrily
 In beauty and perfume.

I saw the early mowers pass
 Along the pleasant dell,
And rank on rank the shining grass
 Around them quickly fell;
I looked, and far and wide at noon
 The fallen flowers were spread,
And all, as rose the evening moon,
 Beneath the scythe were dead.

" All flesh is grass," the Scriptures say,
 And so we truly find;
Cut down, as in a Summer's day,
 Are all of human kind:
Some, while the morning still is fair,
 Taken in earliest prime;
Some, mid-day's heat and burden bear,
 But all, laid low in time.

JANE TAYLOR.

Whatever life may be to us now, — whether a bright, dreamy day in the hay-fields among ripening grass and blooming flowers, or a weary, heated season of toil and care, — it will end before a great while, and we, like the hay, shall be gathered into God's great Store-house.

[210]

JULY TWENTY-THIRD.

THERE is no virtue the exercise of which, even
momentarily, will not impress a new fairness upon
the features; neither on them only, but on the whole
body, the moral and intellectual faculties have opera-
tion, for all the movements and gestures, however
slight, are different in their modes according to the
mind that governs them — and on the gentleness and
decision of right feeling follows grace of actions, and,
through continuance of this, grace of form. — J. RUSKIN.

Purity of thought and mind leave their impress on
the countenance. A face may be beautiful in outline
and feature, but if it lacks purity and modesty, the
chief charm is wanting. A homely face, in which soul-
beauty is revealed, possesses a loveliness which will
not fade with the youthful bloom, but which will grow
more attractive as the years go by, and in old age will
wear the outward reflection of tranquillity and peace.

May it be said of you that,
              Around her shone
   The light of love, the purity of grace,
   The mind, the music breathing from her face,
   The heart whose softness harmonized the whole,
   And, oh! the eye was in itself a soul!
                                        BYRON.

And that your soul is
              Unstained and pure
   As is the lily, or the mountain snow.
                                        THOMSON.

Blessed are the pure in heart: for they shall see
God. — MATTHEW 5 : 8.

LET us live each day for God; live where He has put us, with an eye single to His glory. We can, perhaps, find it easy to be charitable for God, to be kind for God, to be useful for God, but how do we feel about enduring for God? This is what entire consecration means, — not the willingness to serve Him alone, nor the readiness to die a martyr's death for His cause; but to *live* for Him, to endure trials and persecutions, and to suffer indignities and false accusations; to be misjudged, misrepresented, and to go bravely on climbing nearer to Heaven every day, — this is living for God.

I hold him great who for love's sake,
  Can give with generous, earnest will:
Yet he who takes for love's sweet sake
  I think I hold more generous still.

I bow before the noble mind
  That freely some great wrong forgives;
Yet nobler is the one forgiven
  Who bears the burden well and lives.

.   .   .   .

Great may be he who can command
  And rule with just and tender sway;
Yet is diviner wisdom taught
  Better by him who can obey.

Blessed are they who die for God,
  And earn the martyr's crown of light;
Yet he who lives for God may be
  A greater conqueror in His sight.

ADELAIDE ANNE PROCTER.

WHAT different ideas people have of what *life* is! Some will go through the world careless, bright, and happy, and at its close may still insist it is a beautiful dream, — but these persons are very few. Most of us who have passed through our childhood and earlier years of manhood and womanhood have come to a realization of life's earnestness, its duties, obligations, and responsibilities. But because we have learned to read its prose, we do not lose our appreciation of its poetry; I think, on the contrary, we understand it better and love it all the more. Life would become monotonous if our days were all sunshiny ones. When we have walked for a while in the glare of the light, how welcome and restful is the shadow; and after the darkness, how gladly we step out into the brightness and beauty of sunshine once more. So with life: its smiles are sweeter because of its tears; its joys are purer because of its sorrows. Our individual views of life rest a great deal with ourselves. Look at it through blue glasses, and it will appear gloomy and dismal, but put on rose-colored ones, and immediately all things are tinted with a warm, roseate hue which is beautiful indeed.

When I consider life, 'tis all a cheat.
Yet, fooled with hope, men favour the deceit;
Trust on, and think to-morrow will repay:
To-morrow's falser than the former day.
                              DRYDEN.

Life's but a means unto an end, that end,
Beginning, mean, and all things — God.
                              BAILEY.

[213]

A NEW commandment give I unto you, that ye love one another. — JOHN 13 : 34.

To love is everything; love is God.

LÉON GOZLAN.

Love's holy flame forever burneth;
From Heaven it came, to Heaven returneth,
Too oft on earth a troubled guest,
At times deceived, at times opprest.
It here is tried and purified,
Then hath in Heaven its perfect rest;
It soweth here with toil and care,
But the harvest-time of love is *there*.

SOUTHEY.

True love's the gift which God has given
To man alone beneath the heaven:

.   .   .   .

It is the secret sympathy,
The silver link, the silken tie,
Which heart to heart, and mind to mind,
In body and in soul can bind.

SCOTT.

Love is life's end; an end but never ending;
All joys, all sweets, all happiness awarding;
Love is life's wealth (ne'er spent but ever spending),
More rich by giving, taking by discarding:
Ah! should'st thou live but once love's sweets to
    prove,
Thou wilt not love to live, unless thou live to love.

SPENSER.

" THE life that I now live in the flesh, I live by the faith of the Son of God."

That is not all. Much as my future includes all those elements which go to make the blessed fabric of earthly life, yet, after all, what the summer is compared with all its earthly products — flowers, and leaves, and grass — that is Christ compared with all the products of Christ in my mind and in my soul. All the flowers and leaves of sympathy; all the twining joys that come from my heart as a Christian, — these I take and hold in the future, but they are to me what the flowers and leaves of summer are compared with the sun that makes the summer. Christ is the Alpha and Omega, the beginning and the end of my better life. — PROF. HENRY DRUMMOND.

> I am the end of love; give love to me.
> O thou that sinnest, grace doth more abound
> Than all thy sin! Sit still beneath my rood,
> And count the droppings of my victim-blood,
> And seek none other sound.
>
> E. B. BROWNING.

> Thou hast the words of endless life;
> Thou givest victory in the strife;
> Thou only art the changeless friend,
> On whom for aye we may depend:
> In life, in death, alike we flee,
> O Saviour of the world, to thee.
>
> F. R. HAVERGAL.

Christ, first, last, and always! Let us lift our eyes to Him in our last earthly hours; and in our first glimpse of Heaven, He shall be the first to welcome us Home.

HE who is faithful over a few things is a lord over cities. It does not matter whether you preach in Westminster Abbey, or teach a ragged class, so you be faithful. — GEORGE MACDONALD.

> Never delay
> To do the duty which the hour brings,
> Whether it be in great or smaller things,
> For who doth know
> What he shall do the coming day?
>
> ANONYMOUS.

Example is more forcible than precept. People look at me six days in the week, to see what I mean on the seventh. — CECIL.

Cast forth thy act, thy word, into the ever-living, ever-working universe. It is a seed-grain that cannot die; unnoticed to-day, it will be found flourishing as a banyan-grove, perhaps, alas! as a hemlock-forest after a thousand years. — CARLYLE.

> Lord, with what courage and delight
> I do each thing,
> When Thy least breath sustains my wing!
> I shine and move
> Like those above,
> And with much gladness
> Quitting sadness,
> Make me fair days of every night.
>
> HENRY VAUGHAN.

There is not a moment without some duty. — CICERO.

PERHAPS this is the very day in which you want to be alone. You are in the mood to enjoy a quiet ramble in the woods, or to steal off with a favorite book and shut out the world for a while. Or, it may be, you have a sweet dream-world of your own, where you can build pretty air-castles out of the clouds, and where your ships of thoughts can go sailing about blown by innocent little gales of happiness. Perhaps when you awakened this morning, you planned to spend this warm July day in quiet, peaceful enjoyment, just to your own liking. But it may be God chose otherwise for you, and gave you the better, sweeter opportunity of doing for others. "For even Christ pleased not Himself," though doubtless He needed a season of rest far more than you; but He was ever ministering to those around Him, no matter how weary He was. Thank God that He gave you the chance to do some sweet service for Him.

Be kind to each other !
  The night's coming on ;
When friend and when brother
  Perchance may be gone !
Then 'midst our dejection,
  How sweet to have earned
The blest recollection
  Of kindness returned !

              CHARLES SWAIN.

Kindness by secret sympathy is tied ;
For noble souls in Nature are allied.

              DRYDEN.

L ET envy have no place in your thoughts or feelings. If your neighbor's possessions are greater than yours, rejoice that he has so much, and so great an opportunity of doing good. The more wealth we have, the greater our responsibility will be, and if not used aright we are better off if we have less. Do not envy your neighbor his talent; it may prove his downfall, if not properly valued and improved. Do not envy him his position or fame; doubtless he would willingly surrender it all for your quiet, retired life, and for your sweet, untroubled sleep. He is perhaps uneasy and restless even in his dreams. He belongs to the public, he toils for the public, and the demands of the public have robbed him of the happiness and repose which you have the privilege of enjoying, if you will. Fill your little niche as God intended; if He wants you to be rich or great, you will be, but do not spoil your life by continually envying some one else, and wishing you could have their gifts or goods. If you honor your calling, God will honor you, and in some sweet, unexpected way will overrun your cup with blessings.

For the condition of envy, is

.   .   .   .   .   to have
Our eyes continually fix'd upon another
　　Man's prosperity, that is, his chief happiness,
　　And to grieve at that.

BEN JONSON.

For envy doth invade
Works breathing to eternity, and cast
Upon the fairest piece the greatest shade.

CHARLES ALEYN.

CARRY some message of gladness to-day. Look at the birds; their little throats are swelling with rapture. They are telling God's love, and this is my message.

> Give me some word to say for Thee,
> I pray. The world needs charity,
> Its sorrows are so great to bear,
> And men bow down 'neath loads of care,
> Fain would I bring them some relief
> And comfort for their hours of grief.
> May I not tell them something? "Go,"
> A voice replied, "and let them know
>   Their Father loves them."
>
> His blessing touches every head,
> He knows the path their tired feet tread,
> He pities them when they are sad,
> It is His good-will makes them glad.
> Let no one doubt Him. Every child —
> The good, the bad, the meek, the mild —
> Is to the Father's heart most dear;
> He sent His Son to bring you near
>   Because He loves you.
>
> Receive the good, glad news again,
> O heavy-laden sons of men!
> Our Father will your burdens bear,
> Our Father will your sorrows share,
> Because He loves you. Cold of heart
> Are you to others? Do your part,
> And thank Him thus. To your heart take
> Earth's sad ones, for your Father's sake —
>   Because He loves you.

MARIANNE FARNINGHAM.

[219]

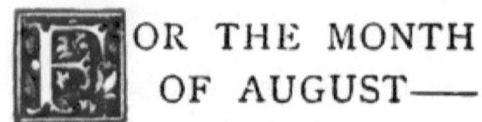

AUGUST FIRST.

AUGUST is like a princess; she wears the royal colors, and moves with stately grace, following close on the steps of daisy-crowned, sunny July. The gold of the wheat, the purple of the grape, and the scarlet of the poppy are woven in the folds of her flowing robe, and emblazoned on her royal crest. When she comes, the corn-fields wave her a welcome.

> A song in a corn-field
>   Where corn begins to fall,
> Where reapers are reaping,
>   Reaping one, reaping all.
> .   .   .   .   .   .
> Out in the fields
>   Summer heat gloweth,
> Out in the fields
>   Summer wind bloweth,
> Out in the fields
>   Summer friend showeth,
> Out in the fields
>   Summer wheat groweth:
> But in the winter
>   When summer heat is dead
> And summer wind has veered
>   And summer friend has fled,
> Only summer wheat remaineth,
>   White cakes and bread.

CHRISTINA ROSSETTI.

[220]

GEORGE ELIOT
1819–1880

ON one side is a field of drooping oats,
  Through which the poppies show their scarlet
  coats.

KEATS.

Find me next a poppy posy.

MOORE.

We are slumbrous poppies,
  Lord of Lethe downs,
Some awake and some asleep,
  Sleeping in our crowns.
What perchance our dreams may know,
Let our serious beauty show.

Central depth of purple,
  Leaves more bright than rose,
Who shall tell what brightest thought
  Out of darkest grows?
Who, through what funereal pain,
Souls to love and peace attain?

LEIGH HUNT.

Let but my scarlet head appear
And I am held in scorn;
Yet juice of subtle virtue lies
Within my cup of curious dyes.

CHRISTINA ROSSETTI.

Gold flashed out of the wheat-ear brown,
And flame from the poppy's leaf.

ELIZA COOK.

Pleasures are like poppies spread,
You seize the flow'r, its bloom is shed!

BURNS.

SOCRATES, accounted by many to have been the wisest man who has ever lived since the time of King Solomon, said : —

"As for me, all I know is that I know nothing."

Spurgeon, one of our ablest divines, said : —

"The doorstep to the temple of Wisdom is a knowledge of our own ignorance."

What a lesson for us! That such great minds as these were so modest and unassuming seems marvellous, when we hear many who are intellectually inferior to them boasting of their fund of knowledge, whenever an occasion presents itself. I believe the more we learn, the deeper realization we have of what yet remains to be learned.

Wisdom does not show itself so much in precept as in life — in a firmness of mind and mastery of appetite. It teaches us to do, as well as to talk; and to make our actions and words all of a colour. — SENECA.

When swelling buds their od'rous foliage shed,
And gently harden into fruit, the wise
Spare not the little offsprings, if they grow
Redundant.
                              JOHN PHILIPS.

Tell (if you can) what it is to be wise?
'Tis but to know how little can be known.
To see all others' faults, and feel our own.
                              POPE.

Knowledge is proud that he has learn'd so much;
Wisdom is humble that he knows no more.
                              COWPER.

AUGUST FOURTH.

THE wish falls often on my heart, that I may learn
nothing here that I cannot continue in the other
world; that I may do nothing here but deeds that will
bear fruit in Heaven. — JEAN PAUL RICHTER.

Up and away, like the dew of the morning,
  Soaring from earth to its home in the sun;
Thus would I pass from the earth and its toiling,
  Only remember'd by what I have done.

Shall I be missed if another succeed me,
  Reaping the fields I in Springtime have sown?
No, for the sower may pass from his labours,
  Only remember'd by what he has done.

Only the truth that in life I have spoken,
  Only the seed that on earth I have sown,
These shall pass onward when I am forgotten,
  Fruits of the harvest, and what I have done.

Oh, when the Saviour shall make up His jewels,
  When the bright crowns of rejoicing are won,
Then will His faithful and weary disciples
  All be remember'd by what they have done!

H. BONAR.

I will go forth 'mong men, not mailed in scorn,
But in the armour of a pure intent;
Great duties are before me, and great songs,
And whether crowned or crownless when I fall,
It matters not, so as God's work is done.

ALEXANDER SMITH.

[223]

AUGUST FIFTH.

LORD of Earth! Thy bounteous hand
Well this glorious frame hath planned;
Woods that wave, and hills that tower,
Ocean rolling in his power,
All that strikes the gaze unsought,
All that charms the lonely thought;
Friendship, gem transcending price;
Love, a flower of Paradise;
Yet, amid this scene so fair,
Should I cease Thy smile to share,
What were all its joys to me!
Whom have I in Heaven but Thee!

Lord of Heaven! beyond our sight
Rolls a world of purer light;

.   .   .   .

Oh, that scene is passing fair!
Yet should'st Thou be absent there,
What were all its joys to me!
Whom have I in Heaven but Thee!

Lord of Earth and Heaven! my breast
Seeks in Thee its only rest!
I was lost: Thy accents mild
Homeward lured Thy wandering child.
I was blind: Thy healing ray
Charmed the long eclipse away.
Source of every joy I know,
Solace of my every woe;
Yet should once Thy smile divine
Cease upon my soul to shine,
What were Heaven or earth to me!
Whom have I in Heaven but Thee!

SIR ROBERT GRANT.

ALL true work is sacred; in all true work, were it but true hand-labour, there is something of divineness. — CARLYLE.

> Strike and struggle; ever strive,
>   Labour with hand, and heart, and brain.
> Work doth more than genius give;
> He who faithfully toils doth live;
>   'Tis labour that doth reign.
>   ANONYMOUS.

Blessed is he who hath found his work; let him ask no other blessedness. He has a work, a life-purpose; he has found it and will follow it. — CARLYLE.

>   Let no one till his death
>   Be called unhappy. Measure not the work
>   Until the day's out and the labour done.
>   E. B. BROWNING.

We enjoy ourselves only in our work, our doing; and our best doing is our best enjoyment. — JACOBI.

> God be thank'd that the dead have left still
>   Good undone for the living to do —
> Still some aim for the heart and the will
>   And the soul for a man to pursue.
>   OWEN MEREDITH.

>   In every rank, or great or small,
>   'Tis industry supports us all.
>   GAY.

Nothing is impossible to industry. — PERIANDER OF CORINTH.

LET us have patience; the way will grow brighter as we press on. Our hearts are discouraged to-day, but they will be lighter to-morrow. Our feet are tired to-day, but they will rest when the night cometh. There are things in store for us worth waiting for; let us, then, not be too eager and impatient, but let us span our sky with the rainbow of hope, and wait God's time for the fulfilment of our heart's desires. For the patient soul, He has in reserve His dearest blessings.

If only we strive to be pure and true,
To each of us all there will come an hour
When the tree of life shall burst into flower,
And rain at our feet the glorious dower
Of something grander than ever we knew.

ANONYMOUS.

For who that leans on His right arm
Was ever yet forsaken?
What righteous cause can suffer harm
If He its part hath taken?
    Though wild and loud
    And dark the cloud,
    Behind its folds
    His hand upholds
The calm sky of to-morrow.

. . . .

    God give us grace
    Each in his place
    To bear his lot
    And murmur not,
Endure and wait and labour.

LUTHER.

DID you ever notice how a child skips and dances
in the summer sunshine? Its feet seem scarce to
touch the ground, they have so much elasticity in them;
its face is a mirror of happiness; its eyes are as bright
as stars, and its sweet little innocent heart seems overflowing with gladness. Life is like a beautiful garden,
—all flowers, and sunshine, and cooling shadows, with
blue sky and sailing clouds overhead; why should not
the child rejoice? More, too, the joy of youth is in the
blithe little spirit, and it trusts in and loves all mankind. It knows it will be cared for, and its heart is
full of childish faith; it sees no clouds in the sky of
the future, so it clasps confidingly the hand of Hope,
and fears no ills to come. Why should we lose our
faith and hope? God cares for us. Why should we
lose our joy in His sunshine when He is overhead?
Why should we leave our youth behind if we love all
mankind? Ah, it is the lack of these things that makes
us grow old. Keep your heart young with trust in
God and man, and your youth will never die.

Blest hour of childhood! then, and then alone,
Dance we the revels close round Pleasure's throne,
Quaff the bright nectar from her fountain-springs,
And laugh beneath the rainbow of her wings.
O time of promise, hope, and innocence,
Of trust, and love, and happy ignorance!
                    THOUGHTS OF A RECLUSE.

Life went a-Maying
With Nature, Hope, and Poesy
When I was young!
                    COLERIDGE.

LORD, thou knowest all things: thou knowest that
I love thee. — JOHN 21 : 17.

The twilight falls, the night is near,
    I fold my work away,
And kneel to One who bends to hear
    The story of the day.

The old, old story; yet I kneel
    To tell it at Thy call;
And cares grow lighter as I feel
    That Jesus knows it all.

Yes, all! The morning and the night,
    The joy, the grief, the loss,
The roughened path, the sunbeam bright,
    The hourly thorn and cross.

Thou knowest all — I lean my head,
    My weary eyelids close;
Content and glad awhile to tread
    This path, since Jesus knows!

And He has loved me! All my heart
    With answering love is stirred,
And every anguished pain and smart
    Finds healing in the Word.

So here I lay me down to rest,
    As nightly shadows fall,
And lean, confiding, on His breast,
    Who knows and pities all!

ANONYMOUS.

AUGUST TENTH.

THAT understanding which we have of our Creator, and of His works, and of ourselves, is the store-house of all wisdom. — A. BZOWSKI.

I know no evil under the sun so great as the abuse of the understanding, and yet there is no vice more common. — STEELE.

The vigorous mind is sympathetic and reflective. It gathers from those around it thoughts similar to its own, and widens and deepens its channels every day.

With curious art the brain, too finely wrought,
Preys on herself, and is destroyed by thought!
Constant attention wears the active mind,
Blots out her pow'rs, and leaves a blank behind.
CHURCHILL.

By earth, and hell, and Heaven,
The shroud of souls is riven,
Mind, mind alone,
Is light, and hope, and life, and power!
EBENEZER ELLIOTT.

The mind within me panted after mind,
The spirit sigh'd to meet a kindred spirit,
And in my human heart there was a void,
Which nothing but humanity could fill.
MONTGOMERY.

Recollect every day the things seen, heard, or read, which make any addition to your understanding. — WATTS.

LET this be the prayer of your heart to-day: Make use of me, dear God, in the way which Thou shalt choose. Thou hast made all things for Thy glory and the good of humanity; Thou hast a mission for me, even me! Give me a heart ready for willing service, O my Father, and then appoint my work.

There is little or nothing in this life worth living for, but we can all of us go forward and do our duty. — WELLINGTON.

Make use of me, my God,
  Let me not be forgot,
Let not Thy child be cast aside,
  One whom Thou needest not.

Thou usest all Thy works,
  The weakest things that be;
Each has a service of its own,
  For all things wait on Thee.

Thou usest the high stars,
  The tiny drops of dew,
The giant peak, the little hill,
  My God, oh, use me too!

Thou usest tree and flow'r,
  The river vast and small;
The eagle great, the little bird,
  That sings upon the wall.

All things do serve Thee here,
  All creatures great and small;
Make use of me, of me, my God,
  The weakest of them all.

                                        H. BONAR.

THERE is not a leaf or a blade of grass, a drop of dew or a ray of light, that hath not God in it. He walks among the hills, and leaves behind the glory of His presence, and the evidence of His power. He beautifies the rivers and seas until they glisten like burnished silver, laughing in His sunlight, and smiling in the soft radiance of His stars. He ushers in the faint, gray dawn, and floods the east with sunrise; He measures the hours of day, and hushes the earth to repose, and guards it while it is wrapped in silence and dreams. Oh, the wonders of God! how divinely and exquisitely are they wrought!

Eternal and Omnipotent unseen!
Who bad'st the world, with all its lives complete,
Start from the void, and thrill Thy feet,
Thee I adore, with reverence serene.
Here, in the fields, Thine own cathedral meet,
Built of thyself, blue-roof'd, and hung with green,
Within all breathing things, in concert sweet,
Organ'd by winds, perpetual hymns repeat.

HORACE SMITH.

O God of Truth,
Make me one with Thee in eternal love. Oft I am
weary,
Reading, listening, but all I wish and long for is in
Thee.
Then silent be all teachers, hushed be all creation at
the sight of Thee:
Speak Thou to me alone.

THOMAS À KEMPIS.

[231]

CHRIST is the Divine Healer; we have not a spiritual disease beyond His reach. Infinitely tender, loving, and sympathetic, He invites us to come to Him and be healed.

In His death, Christ is a sacrifice, satisfying for our sins; in the resurrection, a conqueror; in the ascension, a king; in the intercession, a high priest. — LUTHER.

When across the heart deep waves of sorrow
  Break, as on a dry and barren shore,
When hope glistens with no bright to-morrow,
  And the storms seem sweeping evermore;

When the cup of every earthly gladness
  Bears no taste of the life-giving stream,
And high hopes, as though to mock our sadness,
  Fade and die as in some fitful dream;

Who shall hush the weary spirit's chiding?
  Who the aching void within shall fill?
Who shall whisper of peace abiding,
  And each surging billow calmly still?

Only He whose wounded heart was broken
  With the bitter cross and thorny crown,
Whose dear love glad words of joy had spoken,
  Who His life for us laid meekly down.

Blessed Healer! all our burdens lighten;
  Give us peace, Thine own sweet peace, we pray;
Keep us near Thee till the morn shall brighten,
  And all mists and shadows flee away.

                    CANTERBURY HYMNAL.

GOD pays good wages for good work. The calm consciousness of doing one's best is worth more than dollars and cents, though we may be greatly in need of the latter. Yet whatever price we may receive in exchange for labor is unsatisfactory, if we have with it no inward assurance that we have earned it. God sometimes allows us to have the discipline of waiting, but He knows all of His own by name, and when the place is ready for us, He will call us, and we have only to respond promptly, " Lord, here am I ; send me."

Sum up at night what thou hast done by day,
And in the morning what thou hast to do.
Dress and undress thy soul.

GEORGE HERBERT.

Glory of warrior, glory of orator, glory of song,
Paid with a voice flying by to be lost on an endless sea ;
Glory of virtue, to fight, to struggle, to right the wrong —
Nay, but she aim'd not at glory, no lover of glory she.
Give her the glory of going on and still to be.
The wages of sin is death ; if the wages of virtue be dust,
Would she have heart to endure for the life of the worm and the fly?
She desires no isles of the blest, no quiet seats of the just,
To rest in a golden grove, or bask in a summer sky ;
Give her the wages of going on, and not to die.

ALFRED TENNYSON.

A GOOD listener is a rarity, and as pleasing as rare. I think the reason there are so few good listeners, is because we do not exercise patience enough. It requires considerable patience and self-denial on our part, often, to sit quietly, giving earnest heed to words that do not interest or concern us in the least. But courtesy demands that we should do this even though it may prove a positive infliction on our good nature. Let us be careful not to launch into that dangerous topic which is most interesting to us, but less so to others, — ourselves. To be continually enumerating our ailments, and losses, and crosses, and all the ills we have to bear, — there is no surer way of wearying a listener than this.

It is a secret known to but few, yet of no small use in the conduct of life, that when you fall into a man's conversation, the first thing you should consider is, whether he has a greater inclination to hear you, or that you should hear him. — STEELE.

But 'tis a task indeed to learn — to hear;
In that the skill of conversation lies;
That shows or makes you both polite and wise.
YOUNG.

Nor did we fail to see within ourselves
What need there is to be reserved in speech,
And temper all our thoughts with charity.
WORDSWORTH.

TO what various things has the world been likened!
Hear some of them : —

The true sovereign of the world, who moulds the
world like soft wax, according to his pleasure, is he
who lovingly sees into the world. — CARLYLE.

> Beautiful!
> How beautiful is this visible world,
> How glorious in its action and itself!
>
> BYRON.

> This world is all a fleeting show,
>   For man's illusion given ;
> The smiles of Joy, the tears of Woe,
> Deceitful shine, deceitful flow —
>   There's nothing true but Heaven!
>
> THOMAS MOORE.

> The world is like a bride superbly dressed : —
> Who weds her for dowry must pay for his soul.
>
> HAFIZ.

The world is a comedy to those who think, a tragedy
to those who feel. — WALPOLE.

> The world's a theatre, the earth a stage,
> Which God and Nature do with actors fill.
>
> HEYWOOD.

Such is the world. Understand it, despise it, love
it ; cheerfully hold on thy way through it, with thy eye
on highest loadstars! — CARLYLE.

"GOD is the rock of my heart and my portion for-ever." Can you say this? Can you say that your hope, your faith, your trust is established on the Rock of Ages, and that the Lord is your portion for-ever? If so, you need have no fears for the future. If you have made your peace with Him, He will abide with you, your ever-present, loving Guest, His smile reflect-ing itself in your spirit and filling you with a sweet gra-ciousness that will make you welcome wherever you go. If you trust Him fully and completely, and give your life into His keeping, you can tell others how precious He is. O blessed Rock of Ages, be Thou the strength and the stay of those who trust in Thee!

He taught my heart to trust Him fearlessly
  (Trust oft betrayed, but now misplaced no more);
My Rock! my Rock! my wave-besieged Rock!
  Safe in Thy clefts I rest forevermore.

They that trust in the Lord shall be as Mount Zion, which cannot be removed, but abideth forever. As the mountains are round about Jerusalem, so the Lord is round about his people from henceforth even for-ever. — PSALM 125 : 1, 2.

Rock of Ages, cleft for me,
Let me hide myself in Thee ;
Let the water and the blood
From Thy riven side which flowed
Be of sin the double cure,
Save from wrath, and make me pure.
Rock of Ages, cleft for me,
Let me hide myself in Thee!

TOPLADY.

[236]

AUGUST EIGHTEENTH.

GOD, who is liberal in all His other gifts, shows, by
the wise economy of His providence, how circum-
spect we ought to be in the management of our time,
for He never gives us two moments together. — FÉNE-
LON.

What are all thy boasted treasures?
Tender sorrow, transient pleasures?
Anxious hopes, and jealous fears,
Laughing hours, and mourning years?
Deck'd with brightest tints at morn,
At twilight with'ring on a thorn;
Like the gentle rose of spring,
Chill'd by ev'ry zephyr's wing:
Ah! how soon its colour flies,
Blushes, trembles, falls, and dies.
What is youth?   A smiling sorrow,
Blithe to-day and sad to-morrow;
Never fix'd, forever ranging,
Laughing, weeping, doating, changing;
Wild, capricious, giddy, vain,
Cloy'd with pleasure, nurs'd with pain;
Age steals on with wintry face,
Ev'ry rapt'rous hope to chase,
Like a withered, sapless tree,
Bow'd to chilling fate's decree;
Stripp'd of all its foliage gay,
Drooping at the close of day.

MARY ROBINSON.

Gather the rosebuds while ye may,
Old time is still a-flying;
And that same flower that blooms to-day,
To-morrow shall be dying.

HERRICK.

NATURAL wit is as sparkling as wine; bottled up in the brains of the sage, it is ready to effervesce at the first opportunity. It takes a genius to manage it, for it is a dangerous thing to handle; keen as a lance, it cuts deepest in the hearts that best know how to appreciate it.

> A jest's prosperity lies in the ear
> Of him that hears it, never in the tongue
> Of him that makes it.
>
> SHAKESPEARE.

> True wit is everlasting, like the sun,
> Which though sometimes behind a cloud retir'd,
> Breaks out again, and is by all admir'd:
> A flame that glows amidst conceptions fit,
> E'en something of divine, and more than wit,
> Itself unseen, yet all things by it shown,
> Describing all men, but described by none.
>
> BUCKINGHAM.

> True wit is like the brilliant stone
>   Dug from the Indian mine,
> Which boasts two different powers in one —
>   To cut as well as shine.

> Genius, like that, if polished right,
>   With the same gifts abounds,
> Appears at once both keen and bright,
>   And sparkles while it wounds.
>
> ANONYMOUS.

STRENGTH of character is not mere strength of feeling; it is the resolute restraint of strong feeling. It is unyielding resistance to whatever would disconcert us from without or unsettle us from within. — DICKENS.

A beautiful character makes a beautiful woman. Not long ago I heard a homely woman spoken of as "beautiful"; I looked into her face, and saw plain features, and was disappointed. But a closer acquaintance gave me an insight to her character, whose true key-note was self-forgetfulness. Soul-beauty will not fade, for God has stamped it with eternal youth.

Age cannot wither her, nor custom stale
Her infinite variety: other women cloy
The appetite they feed; but she makes hungry,
Where most she satisfies.
SHAKESPEARE.

Grace was in all her steps, Heav'n in her eye,
In ev'ry gesture dignity and love.
MILTON.

She's a temple
Sacred by birth, and built by hands divine;
Her soul's the deity that lodges there;
Nor is the pile unworthy of the god.
DRYDEN.

The beautiful are never desolate;
But some one always loves them.
BAILEY.

[239]

AUGUST TWENTY-FIRST.

UPWARD, where stars are burning,
　Silent, silent in their turning
　　Round the never-changing pole;
Upward, where the sky is brightest,
Upward, where the blue is lightest,
　　Lift I now my longing soul!

Far above that arch of gladness,
Far beyond those clouds of sadness,
　　Are the many mansions fair!
Far from pain, and sin, and folly,
In that palace of the holy,
　　I would find my mansion there!

Where the glory brightly dwelleth,
Where the new song sweetly swelleth,
　　And the discord never comes;
Where life's stream is ever laving,
And the palm is ever waving—
　　That must be the home of homes!

Where the Lamb on high is seated,
By ten thousand voices greeted,
　　Lord of Lords and King of Kings!
Son of Man, they crown, they crown Him!
Son of God, they own, they own Him!
　　With His name the palace rings!

Blessing, honour, without measure,
Heavenly riches, earthly treasure,
　　Lay we at His blessed feet!
Poor the praise that now we render;
Loud shall be our voices yonder,
　　When before His throne we meet!

H. BONAR.

CARRY the spirit of worship with you; a simple uplifting of the heart to God, sometimes in the busy thoroughfare, and sometimes in the solitude of a walk through the pathless woods, will bring us nearer Heaven than to sit under the preaching of the most learned divine, with our thoughts on things around us.

Sacred Religion! mother of form and fear!
How gorgeously dost thou sit deck'd!
What pompous vestures do we make thee wear!
What stately piles we prodigal erect!
How sweet perfum'd art thou, how shining clear!
How solemnly observed; with what respect!
Another time all plain, all quite threadbare:
Thou must have all within, and nought without;
Sit poorly without light, disrob'd; no care
Of outward grace t' amuse the poor devout.

SAMUEL DANIEL.

Know,
Without a star, or angel, for their guide,
Who worship God shall find Him. Humble love,
And not proud reason, keeps the door of Heaven:
Love finds admission, where proud science fails.

YOUNG.

Love never fails; though knowledge cease,
Though prophecies decay,
Love, Christian love, shall still increase,
Shall still extend her sway.

WILLIAM PETER.

Religious lustre is, by native innocence,
Divinely pure, and simple from all arts.

ROWE.

[241]

A DAY of sweet confidences! Blossom out, O flowers! send upward new shoots, and downward new roots, and whisper to God how thou art growing and thriving for His glory. Dance in the August sunshine, O streams! flow in gladness and brightness, and sing to Jehovah a song of rippling praise! Tell Him thou art watering the dry, parched land, and cooling the woodlands, and how these art His messengers all the day long. And thou, O Heart! what hast thou to say of thy opportunity and thy duty? Pour into His ear the sweet joys of the day, and tell thy dear Lord all thy perplexities. Sit at His feet and rest; confide in Him, for thou hast His messages to bear as well as the flowers and the streams, and if thou hast nothing to tell thy King, thou hast been an unfaithful servant.

If I could trust mine own self with your fate,
   Shall I not rather trust it in God's hand?
   Without Whose Will one lily doth not stand,
Nor sparrow fall at His appointed date;
   Who numbereth the innumerable sand,
Who weighs the wind and water with a weight,
To Whom the world is neither small nor great,
   Whose knowledge foreknew every plan we planned.
Searching my heart for all that touches you,
I find there only love and love's good-will,
Helpless to help and impotent to do,
   Of understanding dull, of sight most dim;
   And therefore I commend you back to Him
Whose love your love's capacity can fill.

CHRISTINA ROSSETTI.

AUGUST TWENTY-FOURTH.

" CAST thy burden on the Lord, and He shall sustain thee."

To every one on earth
God gives a burden to be carried down
The road that lies between the cross and crown.
No lot is wholly free ;
He giveth one to thee.

The burden is God's gift,
And it will make the bearer calm and strong,
Yet, let it press too heavily and long,
He says, Cast it on Me,
And it shall easy be.

And those who heed His voice,
And seek to give it back in trustful prayer,
Have quiet hearts that never can despair ;
And hopes light up the way
Upon the darkest day.

Take thou thy burden thus
Into thy hands, and lay it at His feet,
And whether it be sorrow or defeat,
Or pain or sin or care,
It will grow lighter there.

It is the lonely load
That crushes out the light of Heaven,
But, borne with Him, the soul, restored, forgiven,
Sings out through all the days
Her joy, and God's high praise.

MARIANNE FARNINGHAM.

[243]

I HAVE heard people say they do not like poetry; I always wonder if they understand what it means. Some imagine everything which rhymes to be poetry, while a great deal of it is not poetry at all. On the other hand, some of the finest poems ever produced were wholly without rhyme or measure. It is the delicacy of thought and expression, however clothed, that constitutes real poetry; if you have nothing in you which responds to poetic sentiment, you cannot understand it. Just as well try to explain color to a blind man. It seems to me all true lovers of Nature are fond of poetry, for God has written it on all of His works.

> Poets are all who love, who feel great truths,
> And tell them; and the truth of truths is love.
>
> BAILEY.

Poetry is the breath and finer spirit of all knowledge; it is the impassioned expression which is the countenance of all science. — WORDSWORTH.

That which moveth the heart most is the best poetry; it comes nearer unto God, the source of all power. — W. S. LANDOR.

Poetry is the record of all the best and happiest moments of the happiest and best minds. — SHELLEY.

> A drainless renown
> Of light is Poesy. 'Tis the supreme power:
> The might half slumbering on its own right arm!
>
> KEATS.

REMEMBER us, O Lord, at all times! breathe upon us Thy Spirit, and accompany us through every step of our day's journey. Let us rely upon Thee, knowing that Thou art near; let us not attempt to walk alone, lest we stumble and fall; but let us begin the day aright, asking Thy guidance as soon as our eyes unclose to the light. Let us, in gratitude, make preparation for the new day.

While flowers are wet with dews,
    Dew of our souls, descend;
Ere yet the sun the day renews,
    O Lord, Thy spirit send.

Upon the battle-field,
    Before the fight begins,
We seek, O Lord, Thy sheltering shield,
    To guard us from our sins.

Ere yet our vessel sails
    Upon the stream of day,
We plead, O Lord, for heavenly gales
    To speed us on our way.

On the lone mountain side,
    Before the morning's light,
The Man of Sorrows wept and cried,
    And rose refresh'd with might.

Oh, hear *us*, then, for we
    Are very weak and frail;
We make the Saviour's name our plea,
    And surely must prevail.

C. H. SPURGEON.

[245]

GOD is a tranquil Being, and abides in a tranquil eternity. So must thy spirit become a tranquil and clear little pool, wherein the serene light of God can be mirrored. Therefore shun all that is disquieting and distracting, both within and without. Nothing in the whole world is worth the loss of thy peace; even the faults which thou hast committed should only humble, but not disquiet thee. God is full of joy, peace, and happiness. — G. TERSTEEGEN.

> Well may Thy happy children cease
>   From restless wishes, prone to sin,
> And, in Thy own exceeding peace,
>   Yield to Thy daily discipline.
>
>   A. L. WARING.

We might enjoy much peace, if we would not busy ourselves with the words and deeds of other men, and things which appertain nothing to our charge. How can he abide long in peace, who thrusteth himself into the cares of others, who seeketh occasion abroad, who little or seldom cometh to himself? Blessed are the single-hearted; for they shall enjoy much peace. — THOMAS À KEMPIS.

> Place on the Lord reliance;
>   My soul, with courage wait;
> His truth be thine affiance
>   When faint and desolate;
> His might thy heart shall strengthen,
>   His love thy joy increase;
> Mercy thy days shall lengthen:
>   The Lord will give thee peace.
>
>   MONTGOMERY.

IF you differ with people, don't allow your differences to end in a quarrel. We are here on the earth for such a short time, let us spend it peaceably together. Some men will not brook opposition; they grow irritable and cross if they are contradicted; their example is not a desirable one to follow. You can see how disagreeable they are,—would you wish to imitate them? This quarrelsome sort of individuals are avoided and disliked; but they are really to be pitied, too, for they are greatly afflicted, and yet do not realize that they possess any ailment. A crabbed, self-conceited man, who becomes angry because every one else does not respect his opinions as he does, makes many enemies, and stirs up strife, as he goes through the world. Don't allow yourself to grow like him; live at peace with all men; you have a right to your opinion on all subjects, and there are fitting times when you may express it, but shun quarrelsome debates,—they only end in unkind feelings. Settle differences pleasantly, and part friendly with all men.

Let not opinion make thy judgment err;
The evening conquest crowns the conqueror.

I could never divide myself from any man upon the difference of an opinion, or be angry with his judgment for not agreeing in that from which within a few days I might dissent myself.— SIR THOMAS BROWNE.

Opinion governs all mankind.
SAMUEL BUTLER.

WHAT treasure are you laying up for the future?
While you are gathering in your earthly harvest,
and filling your granaries with all your ripened store,
what are you giving to God? What you give to the
world, in mere shallow pleasures, will only come back
to you as chaff thrown to the winds. May your harvest for Eternity yield a goodly increase, and your
grain ripen for the glory of the Lord of the Harvest!

Ripening harvest rustles in the gale.

.   .   .   .

Here, midst the boldest triumphs of her worth,
Nature herself invites the reapers forth ;
And every cottage from the plenteous store
Receives a burden nightly at its door.
Eternal Power! from whom those blessings flow,
Teach me still more to wonder, more to know :
Seed-time and harvest let me see again ;

.   .   .   .

And let me ever, midst Thy bounties, raise
A humble note of thankfulness and praise!

ROBERT BLOOMFIELD.

These various mercies from above
Matured the swelling grain ;
A yellow harvest crowned thy love,
And plenty fills the plain.

Seed-time and harvest, Lord, alone,
Thou dost on man bestow ;
Let him not, then, forget to own
From whom his blessings flow.

ALICE FLOWERDEW.

[248]

WE must not be too much influenced by what the world says and thinks of us, but, having clear convictions of right and wrong, ever walk in the divine light of God, and as near Heaven as we can.

How happy who is born and taught,
　That serveth not another's will;
Whose armour is his honest thought,
　And simple truth his utmost skill;

Whose passions not his masters are,
　Whose soul is still prepared for death,
Untied unto the worldly care
　Of public fame, or private breath;

Who hath his life from rumours freed,
　Whose conscience is his strong retreat;
Whose state can neither flatterers feed,
　Nor ruin make oppressors great;

Who God doth late and early pray,
　More of His grace and gifts to lend;
And entertains the harmless day
　With a religious book or friend;

This man is freed from servile bands
　Of hope to rise, or fear to fall;
Lord of himself, though not of lands,
　And having nothing, yet hath all.

　　　　　　　　　SIR HENRY WOTTON.

Nothing can work me damage except myself; the harm that I sustain I carry with me, and never am a real sufferer but by my own fault. — ST. BERNARD.

[249]

THE Summer wanes, and, one by one, the long, warm hours melt in the sun. In depths of shade the ivy creeps, its cool green leaves laid lovingly against the oak's great twisted trunk; out-spreading till each friendly bough bears clinging tendrils young and new, and ivy shoots are everywhere.

O Heart, be like the ivy green! send forth thy tender leaves of hope; doubt not, though 'neath the shadows hid, — thou still shalt keep thy gladsome life, and every day be freshly fed by fountains from a Hand divine. The Summer wanes; let it not go, until thou givest to its keep some gift eternal for thy God; some hallowed thought, some treasure rare, some truth, dear Heart, immortal, pure, like Hope, that nevermore shall die. Thus shall thy fadeless ivy twine its beauty round the oak of Time, nor wear a semblance of decay.

Oh, a dainty plant is the ivy green,
  That creepeth o'er ruins old!
Of right choice food are his meals, I ween,
  In his cell so lone and cold.

. . . .

Fast he stealeth on, though he wear no wings,
  And a staunch old heart has he!
How closely he twineth, how tight he clings
  To his friend, the huge oak-tree!

What ages have fled, and their works decayed,
  And nations scattered been;
But the stout old ivy shall never fade
  From its hale and hearty green.
    Creeping where no life is seen,
    A rare old plant is the ivy green.
                    CHARLES DICKENS.

MATTHEW ARNOLD
1822–1888

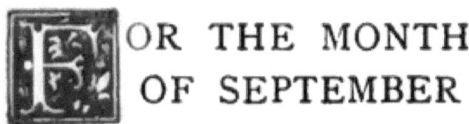# FOR THE MONTH OF SEPTEMBER

SEPTEMBER FIRST.

THE leaves take on their first faint blush, and gold creeps in among the green of waving grass and rustling corn. The skies are tinged with crimson streaks, the fruit hangs glowing from the boughs. The earth is bright and beautiful, as if the Lord had looked from Heaven and bathed it in His smile. I stand with you this wondrous day, and look with you before, behind, and see the glories of the year, outspread in all their bloom and growth; with you I cry, "How marvellous! the selfsame Hand hath made them all!" Behind, the waking, shooting bud, the sprouting oak, the stirring sap; the long, long dreamy Summer days, the tender eves, and starlit nights, and silent growth of grain and fruit. Ah, hush! be still, and hear the song all Nature's tuneful voice repeats:—

Sing hey, sing hey! the Summer days are dying!
Across the hills the first red leaves are flying!
O Heart, dear Heart, in leaf, and fruit, we see
Rich stores of love from God above,
   Dropped down from every tree!
     Sing hey! sing hey! let joyful songs arise!
     Heaven smiles to-day through glad September's
     eyes!

May your soul be like September in its brightness, ripening into fruition for the Eternal Harvest!

SEPTEMBER SECOND.

I SEND thee pansies,
  Yellow as sunshine, purple as the night;
Flowers of remembrance, ever fondly sung
  By all the chiefest of the Sons of Light;
And if in recollection lives regret
  For wasted days and dreams that were not true,
I tell thee that the " Pansy freak'd with jet "
  Is still the hearts'-ease that the poets knew.
Take all the sweetness of a gift unsought,
And for the pansies send me back a thought.
SARAH DOWDNEY.

And there is pansies, that's for thoughts.
SHAKESPEARE.

               Here they grew,
From blue to deeper blue, in midst of each
A golden dazzle like a glimmering star,
Each broader, bigger than a silver crown;
The very sunshine loved them, and would lie
Here happy, coming early, lingering late,
Because they were so fair.
ROBERT BUCHANAN.

And thou so rich in gentle names, appealing
  To hearts that own our nature's common lot;
Thou, styled by sportive fancy's better feeling,
  " A thought," " The Heart's-ease," or " Forget-me-
     not,"
             . . . With humble joy
  Proclaim afresh, by castle and by cot,
Hopes which ought not like things of time to cloy,
And feelings Time itself shall deepen, not destroy!
BERNARD BARTON.

LOVING one another makes better Christians of us; our prayers have more heart in them, and are more acceptable to God, because we love our fellow-men and want them to share God's goodness and mercies. In offering up a petition for others, we receive a double portion ourselves. Our Father has some choice blessing always in store for the unselfish heart. Love makes us forgetful of self, and thoughtful of others; love enables us to bear crosses and to endure losses; love is the loadstar that leads us to the Better Life; love lifts us near and nearer to God.

They sin who tell us love can die;
Its holy flame forever burneth;
From Heaven it came, to Heaven returneth.

SOUTHEY.

He prayeth best who loveth best
  All things, both great and small;
For the dear God who loveth us,
  He made and loveth all.

S. T. COLERIDGE.

Mutual love the token be,
Lord, that we belong to Thee;
Love, Thine image, love impart;
Stamp it on our face and heart;
Only love to us be given;
Lord, we ask no other Heaven.

C. WESLEY.

'Tis Love that makes the heavens shine
With hues more radiant, more divine,
  And turns dull earth to Heaven.

SCHILLER.

THINK not thy time short in this world, since the world itself is not long. The created world is but a small parenthesis in eternity, and a short interposition, for a time, between such a state of duration as was before it and may be after it. — SIR THOMAS BROWNE.

A man's time, when well husbanded, is like a cultivated field, of which a few acres produce more of what is useful to life than extensive provinces, even of the richest soil, when overrun with weeds and brambles. — HUME.

Know the true value of time; snatch, seize, and enjoy every moment of it. No idleness, no laziness, no procrastination; never put off till to-morrow what you can do to-day. — EARL OF CHESTERFIELD.

Time, as he passes us, has a dove's wing,
Unsoil'd, and swift, and of a silken sound.
COWPER.

Even such is Time, that takes on trust
    Our youth, our joys, our all we have,
And pays us, but with age and dust;
    Who in the dark and silent grave,
When we have wandered all our ways,
Shuts up the story of our days.
SIR WALTER RALEIGH.

Years following years, steal something ev'ry day;
At least they steal us from ourselves away.
POPE.

SEPTEMBER FIFTH.

ART thou grieving that the Summer has flown, and its beauty gone forever? Nay, grieve not for that, for other joyous days shall dawn, and other seasons bloom again. Then rather let this thought be thine : Have I improved the passing hours? have I to others been a light to lead them upwards? helped them bear a burden or a heavy cross? have I strown sunshine round my path and given other hearts delight? Has Christ been with me all the way, through changing seasons? Without Him what were earth?

> . . . So shall
> All loved things that vanish or that die
> Return to use in some sweet By-and-By !
>
> ANONYMOUS.

How tedious and tasteless the hours,
   When Jesus no longer I see !
Sweet prospects, sweet birds, and sweet flowers
   Have lost all their sweetness with me ;
The midsummer sun shines but dim,
   The fields strive in vain to look gay,
But when I am happy in Him,
   December's as pleasant as May.

His name yields the richest perfume,
   And sweeter than music His voice ;
His presence disperses my gloom,
   And makes all within me rejoice ;
I would, were He always thus nigh,
   Have nothing to hope or to fear ;
No mortal so happy as I, —
   My Summer would last all the year.

JOHN NEWTON.

BE strong of heart! love on, nor let
  Thy love grow faint, if thou shouldst find
The objects of thy love all changed —
    Unlovely and unkind;
For love, though missing sweet returns,
Makes purer hearts in which it burns.

Be strong of voice! sing on, thy song
Though void of grace, and rough in strain,
May touch some troubled heart, and soothe
    Some portion of its pain;
And all the peace thy songs impart
Shall, sometime, drop into thy heart.

Be strong of arm! support the weak,
From weary shoulders lift the load,
To rest a moment's space; while thou
    Walk'st by them, up life's road,
Be glad, as thus thou toil'st along,
For bearing burdens makes us strong.

Be strong of soul! let every door
Be fast against the foes of right;
And let its walls be strong as truth,
    And proof against unrighteous might,
And let thy Saviour hold the keys;
Then shalt thou surely dwell in peace.

                              ANONYMOUS.

            There is strength
Deep bedded in our hearts, of which we reck
But little till the shafts of Heaven have pierc'd
Its fragile dwelling.
                    FELICIA HEMANS.

A TEMPLE there has been upon earth, a spiritual Temple, made up of living stones; a Temple, as I may say, composed of souls; a Temple with God for its light, and Christ for its high priest; with wings of angels for its arches, with saints and teachers for its pillars, and with worshippers for its pavement. Wherever there is faith and love, this Temple is.—J. H. NEWMAN.

Still may Thy sweet mercy spread
A shady arm above my head,
About my paths; so shall I find
The fair centre of my mind
Thy temple, and those lovely walls
Bright ever with a beam that falls
Fresh from the pure glance of Thine eye,
Lighting to eternity.

R. CRASHAW.

Christ is our Corner-stone,
On Him alone we build;
With His true saints alone
The courts of Heaven are filled.
On His great love
Our hopes we place
Of present grace
And joys above.

JOHN CHANDLER.

Thy spirit should become, while yet on earth, the perfect throne of the Divine Being; think, then, how quiet, how gentle and pure, how reverent thou shouldst be.—GERHARD TERSTEEGEN.

[257]

WE are sowing here what we are to reap hereafter. Through days of darkness, nights of sorrow, it may be, but seed will lie waiting for the touch of the Master-hand to spring into growth. Out of good seed must spring good grain: first the sowing, then the silent waiting, and in His time the golden harvest.

'Tis first the true, and then the beautiful,
   Not first the beautiful, and then the true;
First the wild moor, with rock and reed and pool,
   Then the gay garden, rich in scent and hue.

'Tis first the good, and then the beautiful,
   Not first the beautiful and then the good;
First the rough seed, sown in the rougher soil,
   Then the flower-blossom, or the branching wood.

Not first the glad, and then the sorrowful,
   But first the sorrowful, and then the glad;
Tears for a day — for earth of tears is full,
   Then we forget that we were ever sad.

Not first the bright, and after that the dark,
   But first the dark, and after that the bright;
First the thick cloud, and then the rainbow's arc,
   First the dark grave, then resurrection light.

'Tis first the night — stern night of storm and war;
   Long night of heavy clouds and veiled skies;
Then the fair sparkle of the morning star,
   That bids the saints awake, and dawn arise.

HORATIUS BONAR.

STRENGTH of Will is the quality most needing cultivation in mankind. Will is the central force which gives strength and greatness to character. We overestimate the value of Talent, because it dazzles us; and we are apt to underrate the importance of Will, because its works are less shining. Talent gracefully adorns life; but it is Will which carries us victoriously through the struggle. Intellect is the torch which lights us on our way; Will, the strong arm which rough-hews the path for us. — GEORGE HENRY LEWES.

> Talk not of talents; what hast thou to do?
> Thy duty, be thy portion five or two.
> Talk not of talents; is thy duty done?
> Thou hadst sufficient, were they ten to one.
> MONTGOMERY.

There is always hope in a man that actually and honestly works. In idleness alone is there perpetual despair. — CARLYLE.

Do not fear to take up your work, if God has shown you what it is. Come to a decision regarding it — let it be your determination to make a success of it, using talents and your will-power both. Do not rely on one without the other; each has its place, and each is the gift of God. If you are too self-willed, let it be your aim to conquer and control this fault. Do not abuse your will-power, but use it aright and let it be subject to the divine will of God.

My meat is to do the will of Him that sent me, and to finish His work. — JOHN 4: 34.

[259]

SEPTEMBER TENTH.

TAKE life like a man. Take it just as though it was — as it is — an earnest, vital, essential affair. Take it just as though you personally were born to the task of performing a merry part in it — as though the world had waited for your coming. Take it as though it was a grand opportunity to do and to achieve, to carry forward great and good schemes; to help and cheer a suffering, weary, it may be heart-broken, brother. The fact is, life is undervalued by a great majority of mankind. It is not made half as much of as should be the case. Now and then a man stands aside from the crowd, labours earnestly, steadfastly, confidently, and straightway becomes famous for wisdom, intellect, skill, greatness of some sort. The world wonders, admires, idolizes; and yet it only illustrates what each may do if he takes hold of life with a purpose. — LONDON JOURNAL.

The sweetest lives are those to duty wed,
　　Whose deeds, both great and small,
Are close-knit strands of an unbroken thread
　　Where love ennobles all.
The world may sound no trumpets, ring no bells,
The Book of Life the shining record tells.

It seems so childish to our cultivated intelligences to say, Love God and love one another. The old prophets babbled that, long ago. Yes, and the prophets to come will but repeat the same message in other forms. Truth always comes, as Christ came, in the garb of absolute simplicity . . . Love God and love one another! Is that all? That we have known from our youth up. Yet is there nothing else to say.

RICHARD LE GALLIENNE.

[260]

SEPTEMBER ELEVENTH.

WE all have our faults, and peculiarities; we are all liable to make mistakes, and do things we are sorry for. Then how charitable we should be to others when they do as we have done. When you blame a man for yielding to temptation, do you ever try to bring the question home to yourself: What would *I* have done under the same circumstances? When you hear of some wrong that has been committed, don't judge too harshly the one who is at fault. What would you do if you were in his place? If you had not the sustaining grace of God, you would probably be no better than he is. Therefore be considerate and kindly towards those who err, and be always more ready to pity than to blame.

Then gently scan your brother man,
   Still gentler sister woman;
Though they may gang a kennin' wrang,
   To step aside is human.
One point must still be greatly dark,
   The moving why they do it;
And just as lamely can ye mark
   How far, perhaps, they rue it.

Who made the heart, 'tis He alone
   Decidedly can try us;
He knows each chord — its various tone,
   Each spring — its various bias;
Then at the balance let's be mute,
   We never can adjust it.
What's done we partly may compute,
   But know not what's resisted.

                                        BURNS.

[261]

WHAT have you given to the hours to-day? The busy little hurrying hours that count the pulse-beats of this fleeting September day! What have you entrusted to their keeping that is worth claiming again in the Golden Aftermath? There shall come to you sometime a solemn, immortal Hour, when you shall stand face to face with the Eternal Reaper of earth's ripened harvest; will to-day's record be a source of satisfaction to you then? Has your life given out a glory of gold and scarlet to-day? Has it been drinking in September's dyes to gild other lives, and to make a fabric of beauty and grace for Heaven? Oh, think on the hours! put your best into them; remember they were born for Eternity.

> They all
> Sweep onward.
> These are the immortal Hours
> Of whom thou didst demand. One waits for thee.
>   SHELLEY.

> Hours are golden links, God's token,
>   Reaching Heaven; but one by one
> Take them, lest the chain be broken,
>   Ere thy pilgrimage be done.
>   ADELAIDE PROCTER.

> Happy the man, and happy he alone,
> He who can call to-day his own, —
> He who secure within can say,
> To-morrow do thy worst, for I have lived to-day.
>   DRYDEN.

GUIDE me, O Lord, in all the changes and varieties of the world; that in all things that shall happen I may have an evenness and tranquillity of spirit; that my soul may be wholly resigned to Thy divinest will and pleasure, never murmuring at Thy gentle chastisement and fatherly correction. Amen. — JEREMY TAYLOR.

This is our common lot, — the bitter with the sweet; and if we can drink of this cup unmurmuringly from the Hand of God, He will give us the blessed victory over Self, which is the beginning of the New Life. In this happier and higher state, we shall accept thankfully His wise decree, and with humble submission say, "Thy will be done." We shall then be enabled to comfort other hearts and whisper words of consolation to those who have learned the discipline of sorrow.

Throw thyself on thy God, nor mock Him with feeble
    denial;
Sure of His love, and oh! sure of His mercy at last;
Bitter and deep though the draught, yet shun not the
    cup of thy trial,
But in its healing effect, smile at its bitterness past.

Pray for the holier cup while sweet with bitter lies
    blending,
Tears in the cheerful eye, smiles on the sorrowing
    cheek;
Death expiring in life, when the long-drawn struggle
    is ending;
Triumph and joy to the strong, strength to the weary
    and weak.

              SIR JOHN HERSCHEL.

WE often expect too much of our friends. We sometimes demand more from them than we are willing to give in exchange. We look to them for loyalty at all times; we expect their help in an emergency, and are grieved and disturbed if we cannot depend upon them in time of need. Are we willing to do as much for them? Nothing is more touching than the genuine friendship that some of the poor little newsboys and bootblacks have for each other; they seem to account it a privilege to defend their friends. God bless their little loyal hearts! Many of us, placed in similar circumstances, would not prove so unselfish, I fear, as they, who, though lacking the temporal blessings we enjoy, are staunch and loyal in their friendships.

He ought not to pretend to friendship's name
Who reckons not himself and friend the same.

Such is the use and noble end of friendship,
To bear a part in every storm of fate,
And, by dividing, make the lighter weight.
                                                            BEVIL HIGGONS.

Let falsehood assail not,
    Nor envy disprove;
Let trifles prevail not
    Against those ye love!
Nor change with to-morrow,
    Should fortune take wing,
But the deeper the sorrow,
    The closer still cling!
                                            CHARLES SWAIN.

SEPTEMBER FIFTEENTH.

A GLAD September day! Let us feel the first cool breezes blow inward from the wood; let us ramble through the winding paths, and stoop to gather, here and there, a stray leaf of crimson and amber, that comes fluttering down at our feet. Some uncut fields yet wait the shining sickle, some late roses yet cradle the airy butterflies, and over all the meadow-lark and linnet make music clear and sweet. Rejoice, my heart! this world of September beauty is all for thee!

I take the land to my breast,
  In her coat with daisies fine ;
For me are the hills in their best,
  And all that's made is mine.

JEAN INGELOW.

The world and I are too full of bliss
To think or plan or toil or care ;
  The sun is waxing strong,
  The days are waxing long,
    And all that is,
      Is fair.

Hark to my linnets from the hedges green,
Blackbird and lark, and thrush and dove,
  And every nightingale
  And cuckoo tells its tale,
    And all they mean
      Is love.

CHRISTINA ROSSETTI.

Lo! the hills of harvest whiten,
  All along each distant shore.

CECIL FRANCES ALEXANDER.

PEACE possesses the soul that is strong to do and bear all things for Christ's sake. Be submissive in God's hands; be strong to wait as well as work; with every appointed task, given by the hand of God, comes also the blessing of patience. Peace is one of God's sweetest gifts to His beloved, and is the twin sister of Patience.

The child leans on its parent's breast,
Leaves there its cares and is at rest;
The bird sits singing by his nest,
    And tells aloud
His trust in God, and so is blessed
    'Neath every cloud.

He has no store, he sows no seed,
Yet sings aloud, and doth not heed;
By flowing stream or grassy mead,
    He sings to shame
Men who forget, in fear of need,
    A Father's name.

The heart that trusts forever sings,
And feels as light as it had wings;
A well of peace within it springs;
    Come good or ill,
Whate'er to-day, to-morrow brings,
    It is His will.

ISAAC WILLIAMS.

O my God! I bless
Thy mercy that with Sabbath peace hath filled
My chastened heart, and all its throbbings stilled
To one deep calm of lowliest thankfulness.

FELICIA HEMANS.

[266]

RACE an immortal truth on the hearts of thy
friends while thou livest. Make thy life an ex-
le for others to follow, — a life that is ever point-
Godward. Blend in thy being the loveliness of all
stian graces, — the sweetest of all which are Faith,
e, and Love. Let thy soul outbreathe faith in God
thy fellow-man, hope for the Life Everlasting, and
to all creation. Then shall thy influence be
hless.

There are three lessons I would write, —
  Three words, as with a burning pen,
In tracings of eternal light
  Upon the hearts of men.

Have *Hope*. Though clouds environ now,
  And gladness hides her face in scorn,
Put thou the shadow from thy brow, —
  No night but hath its morn.

Have *Faith*. Where'er thy bark is driven,
  The calm's disport, the tempest's mirth,
Know this, — God rules the host of Heaven,
  The inhabitants of earth.

Have *Love*. Not love alone for one,
  But man, as man, thy brothers call;
And scatter, like the circling sun,
  Thy charities on all.

Thus grave these lessons on thy soul —
  Hope, Faith, and Love — and thou shalt find
Strength when life's surges rudest roll,
  Light when thou else wert blind.

FROM THE GERMAN OF **SCHILLER**.

[267]

SIT not down with idly folded hands; open thy
palms, reach out for thy work, and the Master
Mechanic will give thee a place among His busy work-
men. Then, do thy honest best.

> God did anoint thee with His odorous oil,
> To wrestle, not to reign.
>
> E. B. BROWNING.

To be rich, be diligent; move on
Like Heaven's great movers that enrich the earth,
Whose moment's sloth would show the world undone,
And make the Spring straight bury all her birth.
Rich are the diligent who can command
Time — nature's stock.

DAVENANT.

> 'Tis the bold who win the race,
>   Whether for gold, or love, or name;
> 'Tis the true ones always face
> Dangers and trials, and win a place,
>   A niche in the fane of fame.
>
> ANONYMOUS.

Let me not die before I have done for Thee
Some earthly work, whatever it may be;
Call me not hence with mission unfulfilled,
Let me not leave my space of ground untilled;
Impress this truth upon me, that not one
Can do my portion that I leave undone,
For each one in Thy vineyard hath a spot
To labour in for life, and weary not.
Then give me strength all faithfully to toil,
Converting barren earth to fruitful soil.

ANONYMOUS.

YOUR share and mine! God has divided it out for us and then watches to see how we will accept it, how make use of it. Some bitter with the sweet, some dead leaves with the blooming flowers, some shadows with the glowing sun,— but He hath given it from His Hand Divine. What of the submissive heart that received a bitterer draught than yours? What did it do? Took the cup that God gave, quaffed it to its bitter dregs, and stood calmly beneath His chastening rod, subdued, but not cast down. "Why art thou cast down, O my soul? and why art thou disquieted within me?"

> There are briars besetting my path,
>   That call for patient care;
> There is a cross for every lot,
>   And an earnest need for prayer;
> But the lowly heart that leans on Thee
>   Is happy everywhere.
>
>   ANNA L. WARING.

My God once mixed a harsh cup, for me to drink from it,
And it was full of acrid bitterness intensest;
The black and nauseating draught did make me shrink from it,
And cry, "O Thou who every draught alike dispensest,
This cup of anguish sore, bid me not to quaff of it,
Or pour away the dregs and the deadliest half of it,
But still the cup He held; and seeing He ordained it,
One glance at Him—it turned to sweetness as I drained it.

                          FROM POETRY OF THE ORIENT.

THE particular annoyance which befell you this morning; the vexatious words which met your ear and "grieved" your spirit; the disappointment which was His appointment for to-day; the slight but hindering ailment; the presence of some one who is a "grief of mind" to you, — whatever this day seemeth not joyous, but grievous, is linked in "the good pleasure of His goodness" with a corresponding afterward of "peaceable fruit," the very seed from which, if you only do not choke it, this shall spring and ripen. —
F. R. HAVERGAL.

Sense of wrongs forget to treasure,—
Brethren, live in perfect love!
In the starry realms above,
God will mete as we may measure.
SCHILLER.

Be not you grieved
If that which you mould fair, upright, and smooth,
Be screwed awry, made crooked, lame, and vile,
By racking comments.
So to be bit it rankles not, for Innocence
May with a feather brush off the foul wrong.
THOMAS DEKKER.

Be not o'ermastered with thy pain,
But cling to God, thou shalt not fall;
The floods sweep over thee in vain,
Thou yet shalt rise above them all;
For when thy trial seems too hard to bear,
Lo! God, thy King, hath granted all thy prayer:
Be thou content.
P. GERHARDT.

SEPTEMBER TWENTY-FIRST.

WHO has good deeds brought well to end,
  For him the glowing forests shine;
The whole world is to him a friend,
  And all the earth a diamond mine.

FROM THE POETRY OF THE ORIENT.

Good deeds in this world done
Are paid beyond the sun;
As water on the root
Is seen above in fruit.

WÁSANA'S PROVERB.

Go from the east to the west, as the sun and the stars
    direct thee,
  Go with the girdle of man, go and encompass the
    earth.
Not for the gain of the gold; for the getting, the
    hoarding, the having,
  But for the joy of the deed; but for the Duty to do.
Go with the spiritual life, the higher volition and
    action,
  With the great girdle of God, go and encompass the
    earth.

ARTHUR HUGH CLOUGH.

We live in deeds, not years; in thoughts, not breaths;
In feelings, not in figures on a dial.
We should count time by heart-throbs; he most lives
Who thinks most, feels the noblest, acts the best.

BAILEY.

OUTWARD appearances are often deceitful. Beauties lie hidden underneath rough exteriors, until the touch of a master-hand polishes and chisels and moulds them into loveliness. Who would think the exquisite vase was ever once a mass of sodden clay? Who would believe it possible that the gleaming marble statue was hewn from the dark stone? Ah, who but the great and wise Philosopher could put into the mind of man the ability to reason out these things, to labor, and to achieve? It is the refining process that is needed to bring to light hidden beauties.

> Within this leaf to every eye
> So little worth, doth hidden lie
> Most rare and subtle fragrancy.
> Wouldst thou its secret strength unbind?
> Crush it, and thou shalt perfume find
> Sweet as Arabia's spicy wind.
>
> In this dull stone so poor, and bare
> Of shape or lustre, patient care
> Will find for thee a jewel rare!
> But first must skilful hands essay,
> With file and flint, to clear away
> The film which hides its fire from day.
>
> This leaf! This stone! It is thy heart;
> It must be crushed by pain and smart,
> It must be cleansed by sorrow's art,
> Ere it will yield a fragrance sweet,
> Ere it will shine a jewel meet
> To lay before Thy dear Lord's feet!

ANONYMOUS.

OH, the joy of giving joy to others! Your summer vacation is ended, and how pleasant it has been! You shut your eyes and imagine you are still wandering through the deep green fields and "across the far blue hills." You have brought back some of the fresh country air in your invigorated body, and, besides, have stored up some sweet little lessons from Nature's happy teachings. Your house is full of dust and cobwebs, and there is plenty to be done to get it in habitable order again. There is more yet for you to do; keep on getting ready for winter. Give some of your bottled-up sunshine to others; clear out the store-house of your mind. Every one could not go to the sea-shore, or to the mountains, or even to a quiet country place, as you did. Some stayed in the hot, dry city, walled in by buildings that shut out the blue sky, the sunshine, and the occasional breeze, while you revelled in all three. Now be careful that the dust and cobwebs of selfishness do not accumulate in the corners of your mental house, and keep others from looking in. The poor little sick girl across the way, and the lame bootblack that you pass every day,—how like Heaven it would be to give them some of the brightness you have shut up in your heart, and some of the lessons you have locked away in your mind. Keep brushing down the cobwebs, so the sunlight can have plenty of room to shine in, and so your happiness can have plenty of room to get out. There are a hundred beautiful ways of showing God that you are personally grateful to Him for His goodness to you,—don't fail to take advantage of them.

DO not allow idle curiosity about the affairs of others to rob you of a sense of your obligations to God and man. Many a bright mind has been directed into wrong channels. Endowed with a natural desire to investigate beyond the bounds of sight, it reaches out like a vine for something to cling to, and instead of twining itself around oaks of wisdom and knowledge, finds but brambles of worldly affairs around which to wind its tendrils. Oh, what a pity that a life should be so spoiled by trifles! What difference does it make to you what your neighbor may do, so that you exert the right influence over him, and are never a stumbling-block in his path? Your part is to attend to the duties assigned to *you*, and not, through idle curiosity, to leave your work to see into the affairs of others.

What is it then to me
If others are inquisitive to see?
Why should I quit my place to go and ask
If other men are working at their task?
Leave my own buried roots to go
And see that brother plants shall grow;
And turn away from Thee, O Thou most Holy Light,
To look if other orbs their orbits keep aright,
Around their proper sun,
Deserting Thee, and being undone.

ARTHUR HUGH CLOUGH.

One finger's breadth at hand will mar
A world of light in Heaven afar,
A mote eclipse a glorious star,
    An eyelid hide the sky.

J. KEBLE.

[274]

LORD, who shall abide in thy tabernacle? Who shall dwell in thy holy hill? He that walketh uprightly, and walketh righteously, and speaketh the truth in his heart. — PSALM 15 : 1, 2.

May Truth abide with you through all Eternity!

While the great generation depart,
And full ages and firmaments roll,
Mighty love is the lord of the heart,
And pure truth the bright king of the soul.

ANONYMOUS.

If all circumstances lead me, I will find
Where truth is hid, though it were hid indeed
Within the centre.

SHAKESPEARE.

Rejoice, ye humble, and exult, ye poor; God's kingdom's yours, if ye but walk in truth. — THOMAS À KEMPIS.

It fortifies my soul to know
That, though I perish, Truth is so;
That howsoe'er I stray and range,
Whate'er I do, Thou dost not change.
I steadier step when I recall
That if I slip, Thou dost not fall.

ARTHUR HUGH CLOUGH.

Oh, truth,
Thou art, whilst tenant in a noble breast,
A crown of crystal in an iv'ry chest!

DAVENANT.

[275]

SEPTEMBER TWENTY-SIXTH.

NO one but God understands our hearts: we do not understand them ourselves. They send out words and breathe out thoughts that surprise us, at times. We wonder that we are capable of so much loving or unloving; God looks calmly down and listens to all we say. He knows our hearts from the beginning. The world stamps its image upon us; each heart carries a bit of the world in it, because we are so much with the world, and so much of it. The more our hearts are with God, the more of God we have in us. Let us, then, be less with the world, and more with God.

Each little thronging star that shines
    Below the eternal throne,
Amidst the crowd of burning lines,
    Revolves and burns alone.

Upon its earthly pathway hurled,
    So every human heart,
Even as that lone and burning world,
    Aspires and beats apart.

Mysterious star, and heart as well,
    We little know, alas!
But God can look through both, and tell
    The smallest things that pass.
                        FROM THE FRENCH.

The heart hath its mystery, and who may reveal it,
    Or who ever read in the depth of their own,
How much we never may speak of, yet feel it,
    But even in feeling it, know it unknown.
                        LETITIA E. LANDON.

WHO has not felt the sweet, silent influence of a pure friendship ? It runs through our lives like a thread of gold, and beautifies the fabric of our whole nature.   Happy is he who is such a blessing to others. And when we are called to part from one so dear, his memory never dies ; it is like the perpetual rose of Summer : it keeps on blooming forever, and makes our hearts a never-dying Summer-land.

Friendship's the image of
Eternity, in which there is nothing
Movable — nothing mischievous ; as much
Difference as there is between beauty
And virtue, bodies and shadows, colours
And life, so great odds is there between love
And friendship.

JOHN LILLY.

I count myself in nothing else so happy,
As in a soul rememb'ring my good friends ;
And, as my fortune ripens with my love,
It shall be still thy true love's recompense.

SHAKESPEARE.

Friendship has a power
To soothe affliction in her darkest hour.

HENRY KIRKE WHITE.

The thread of our life would be dark, Heaven knows!
    If it were not with Friendship and Love inter-
        twined ;
And I care not how soon I may sink to repose,
    When those blessings shall cease to be dear to my
        mind.

MOORE.

[277]

SEPTEMBER TWENTY-EIGHTH.

AND you, humble little blades of grass, you are not fair like the flowers, nor have you odors such as they; what have you done to show forth the Father's glory?

> We have fed His humblest creatures,
>   We have served Him truly and long;
> We have no grace to our features,
>   We have neither colour or song.
>
> Yet He who made the flowers
>   Placed us on the self-same sod;
> He knows our reason for being:
>   We are the grass in the garden of God.
>
> FROM THE GULISTAN OF SAADI.

Even the grasses praise God. There is not a blade among them but has a tiny mission to perform, and not one of them but is large enough to hold a drop of dew. What an example for us! When we complain that our strength is too small for the burden laid upon us, why do we not trust our Father to uphold us and give us the power to carry dew-drops of love for our fellow-men? Little smiles, as we pass each other by; a touch of the hand; a word of sympathy, a tear, — ah, what bright drops of heavenly dew they are!

> The merest grass
> Along the roadside where we pass,
> Lichen and moss and sturdy weed,
> Tell of His love who sends the dew,
> The rain and sunshine too,
> To nourish one small seed.
>
> CHRISTINA ROSSETTI.

BEAUTIFUL THINGS TO REMEMBER.

WHO learns and learns, but acts not what he
knows,
  Is one who ploughs and ploughs, but never sows.

Be no imitator; freshly act thy part;
Through this world be thou an independent ranger;
Better is the faith that springeth from the heart,
Than a better faith belonging to a stranger.

  Howe'er the ignorant decry,
  Howe'er oppose the envious crew,
  Since death comes soon, and brief years fly,
  Thy firmly chosen work pursue!

  A friend both wise and true amid all shocks
  Resplendent shines, like fire upon a rock's
  High top, which dissipates the darkness round,
  And fills the travellers by with joy profound.

A wondrous rosary he never needs,
Who tells in love and thought the spirit's beads.
Where'er the face of earnest faith thou bringest, pure,
    and sweet,
Thou then the smiling face of thine approving God
    shall meet.

Name not as friends the men who by you stand
In pleasant times, when peace and welfare please you;
But him indeed call friend who grasps your hand
In that dark day when want and danger seize you.

                    GEMS FROM POETRY OF THE ORIENT.

IT is not until the last golden days of September are slipping away, that we begin to realize that our glad, brief Summer has gone, never to return. True, we have felt the keen little breezes blowing; the nights have grown cooler, and the mornings and evenings take on a mistiness which is as faint and purpling as the bloom on a ripened plum. Oh, let not the season drift by without leaving some tokens of its presence! Give to some heart a harebell of joy, or a torch of love, or a water-lily of purity, to have and to hold during all the winter days to come. Let no season go by without keeping some memento of it; happy is he who can gather blessings in a time of plenty, and scatter them in a time of need.

> But still for Summer dost thou grieve?
> Then read our poets — they shall weave
> A garden of green fancies still,
> Where they who wish may rove at will.
> They have kept for after treats
> The essence of summer sweets,
> And echoes of its songs that wind
> In endless music through the mind :
> They leave stamped in visible traces
> The " thoughts that breathe," in words that shine —
> The flights of soul in sunny places —
> To greet and company with thine.
> These shall wing thee on to flowers —
> The past or future that shall seem
> All the brighter in thy dream,
> For blowing in such desert hours.

THOMAS HOOD.

GEORGE MACDONALD

1824

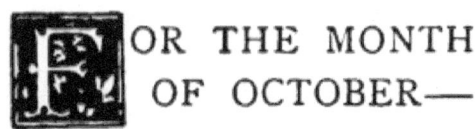

OR THE MONTH OF OCTOBER—

OCTOBER FIRST.

O GRAND October, the whole world has waited thy coming, since first the year began! And now, thou art blushing and glowing and fading and dying all at once. Oh, the splendor of thy forests, the richness and ripeness of thy harvests, how marvellous they are! Earth's best is ready to be garnered; her growing and blooming and perfecting is done, and lo! what an abundance has it yielded! Soul, is thy harvest of good deeds an abundant one? Then for thee will thy Autumn-time be rich in Heaven's glorious colorings, which the frosts of God's wise discipline will bring into ripened fruition.

Inconstant Summer to the tropics flees,
And as her rose-sails catch the amorous breeze,
Lo! bare, brown Autumn trembles to her knees!

The stealthy nights encroach upon the days,
The earth with sudden whiteness is ablaze,
And all her paths are lost in crystal maze!

The ripened nuts drop downward day by day,
Sounding the hollow tocsin of decay,
And bandit squirrels smuggle them away.

Vague sight and scents pervade the atmosphere,
Sounds of invisible stirrings hum the ear,
The morning's lash reveals a frozen tear.

ANONYMOUS.

A BLENDING of rich color lies around us. Here and there a dahlia, crimsoning in the October sunshine, a velvety marigold, yellow as an autumn sunset, and all about the gardens, clustered groups of fringy chrysanthemums, whose spicy breath mingles with the odor of the pines. The orchards hang low their freighted boughs. Truly the year is in its prime.

A second blow of many flowers appear,
Flowers faintly tinged, and breathing no perfume.
But fruits, not blossoms, form the woodland wreath
That circles Autumn's brow.

JAMES GRAHAM.

Life is not quite over,
Even if the year has done with corn and clover,
With flowers and leaves; besides, in fact it's true,
Some leaves remain and some flowers too,
For me and you.
Now see my crops:
I've brought you nuts and hops;
And when the leaf drops, why, the walnut drops.

CHRISTINA ROSSETTI.

What wondrous life is this I lead!
Ripe apples drop about my head.
The luscious clusters of the vine
Upon my mouth do crush their wine.

SAMUEL BUTLER.

God give you many days, and may your whole life be spotless and pure, giving beauty through all the changes, even when the leaf has turned brown and the fruit has ripened. — ANONYMOUS.

[282]

IT is very sweet to us, in our daily life, to catch a little foretaste of Heaven, and feel as if we were a step nearer God. Sometimes there comes to us a far-off vision of the Immortal Land, and we see a dim radiance of its glories. These little glimpses are but a faint revelation of what is to come, when the Heart of Love shall make them all " clear as the noonday."

Yet sometimes glimpses on my sight,
Through present wrong, the eternal right;
And step by step, since time began,
I see the steady gain of man;

That all of good the past hath had
Remains to make our own time glad,
Our common, daily life divine,
And every land a Palestine.

Through the harsh noises of our day
A low, sweet prelude finds its way;
Through clouds of doubt and creeds of fear,
A light is breaking, calm and clear.

That song of love, now low and far,
Ere long shall swell from star to star!
That light, the breaking day, which tips
The golden-spired apocalypse!

.   .   .   .

Henceforth my heart shall sigh no more
For olden time and holier shore;
God's love and blessing, then and there,
Are now and here and everywhere.

GERALD MASSEY.

" GIVE us this day our daily bread." Not this day alone, but all days, doth our Father feed His children. He provides for all our wants; not only those of the body, but of the mind and soul, as well. His goodness is a spacious storehouse, open at all times for our needs. But He desires us to make our wants known: this is why Christ gave us the beautiful prayer which has echoed from lip to lip all over the universe, one of whose sweetest clauses is this: "Give us this day our daily bread." It is an appeal to God to remember us out of His great abundance, and shows our utter dependence on His bounty. Give us, O Lord, mental and spiritual food, as well, that body, mind, and soul may this day be sustained and fed.

The golden harvest field
  Is warmly glowing 'gainst a sapphire sky,
  The orchard trees lift laden boughs on high,
    A fruitage rich to yield.

'Tis thus "Our Father" feeds
  With loving care all creatures He hath made,
  And in His treasure-house hath duly laid
    Sufficient for our needs.

   .   .   .   .

And giveth daily bread
  As He sees well. — With pain, or smiles, or fears,
  Through the brief discipline of early years,
    Are we, His children fed.

HELEN MARION BURNSIDE.

[284]

TRUE courtesy is greatly to be desired; therefore, be courteous.

Seldom yet did living creature see
That courtesies and manhood ever disagree.

SPENSER.

I seldom ride in a car without seeing some evidences of nineteenth century gallantry. While the World's Fair was in progress in Chicago, I was told by a resident of the city that no one had time for civilities, and that I would have no need to make use of those two little gate-openers to desired favors, — "if you please," and "I thank you," — and that it was not expected. I found this a mistaken idea. Sir Walter Raleigh himself could not have been more thoroughly a gentleman in courtesy and deferential politeness than were many of the people who were in attendance at the great exhibition. I cannot now recall a single act of discourtesy at that time. Let us practise true courtesy at all times; it is becoming to everybody.

Serene, accomplish'd, cheerful but not loud;
    Insinuating without insinuation;
Observant of the foibles of the crowd,
    Yet ne'er betraying this in conversation;
Proud with the proud, yet courteously proud,
    So as to make them feel he knew his station
And theirs: — without a struggle to priority
He neither brooked nor claimed superiority.

BYRON.

Civility costs nothing, but buys everything.

LADY MARY WORTLEY MONTAGU.

[285]

L ET the weakest, let the humblest, remember that in his daily course he can, if he will, shed around him almost a heaven. Kindly words, sympathizing attentions, watchfulness against wounding men's sensitiveness, — these cost very little, but they are priceless in their value. Are they not almost the staple of our daily happiness? From hour to hour, from moment to moment, we are supported, blest, by small kindnesses. —F. W. ROBERTSON.

Sympathetic words, looks, and acts are especially dear to us in our home-circle, and are treasured by us as long as we live. Dispense your sympathy as you would your charity. Let it have a bit of Heaven in it; let it be gentle and genuine.

> I lay in sorrow, deep distress:
>   My grief a proud man heard;
> His looks were cold, he gave me gold,
>   But not a kindly word.
> My sorrow passed — I paid him back
>   The gold he gave to me;
> Then stood erect and spoke my thanks,
>   And blessed his charity.
>
> I lay in want, in grief and pain:
>   A poor man passed my way;
> He bound my head, he gave me bread,
>   He watched me night and day.
> How shall I pay him back again
>   For all he did for me?
> Oh, gold is great, but greater far
>   Is heavenly sympathy!
>
> CHARLES MACKAY.

OCTOBER SEVENTH.

THE most necessary talent in a man of conversation, is a good judgment. He that hath this in perfection is a master of his companion, without letting him see it; and has the same advantage over men of any other qualifications whatsoever, as one that can see would have over a blind man of ten times his strength. — STEELE.

'Tis with our judgments as our watches, — none
Go just alike, yet each believes his own.

POPE.

His be the praise, who looking down in scorn
On the false judgment of the partial herd,
Consults his own clear heart, and nobly dares
To *be*, not to be *thought*, an honest man.

CUMBERLAND.

Let none direct thee what to do or say,
Till thee thy judgment of the matter sway;
Let not the pleasing many thee delight,
First judge, if those whom thou dost please judge
    right.

DENHAM.

How much we give to other hearts our tone,
And judge of other's feelings by our own.

LETITIA ELIZABETH LANDON.

Let your judgments be charitable. Look at both sides of the question before deciding which is right. Harsh judgments often occur through ignorance or inattention. Acquaint yourself thoroughly with the facts in the case before you render a decision. In order to be just, you must be accurate.

[287]

ERECT your tabernacles, not out of perishable material, but of substantial stones set up in the name of Christ, and fitted for His habitation.

Methinks it is good to be here,
If thou wilt, let us build — but for whom?
Nor Elias nor Moses appear;
But the shadows of eve that encompass with gloom
The abode of the dead and the place of the tomb.

Shall we build to Ambition? Ah no!
Affrighted, he shrinketh away;
For see, they would pin him below
In a small narrow cave, and, begirt with cold clay,
To the meanest of reptiles a peer and a prey.

Shall we build to Affection and Love?
Ah no! they have withered and died,
Or fled with the spirit above.
Friends, brothers, and sisters are laid side by side,
Yet none have saluted, and none have replied.

Unto Sorrow? — the dead cannot grieve;
Not a sob, not a sigh meets mine ear,
Which Compassion itself could relieve.
Ah, sweetly they slumber, nor love, hope, or fear;
Peace! peace is the watchword, the only one here.

The first tabernacle to Hope we will build,
And look for the sleepers around us to rise!
The second to Faith, which insures it fulfilled,
And the third to the Lamb of the great sacrifice,
Who bequeathed us them both when He rose to the
skies.

HERBERT KNOWLES.

[288]

THE dearest secrets of our heart are known to God. Cover them up, bury them deeply, hide them away from the world as you may, they are always revealed to Him. Do not wish to have anything apart from Him; be glad of His confidence, rejoice in His love, and be comforted through His sympathy. Oh, always remember that God knows, and that *He cares*.

Therefore, our Heavenly Father,
  We will not fear to pray
For the little needs and longings
  That fill our every day;
And when we dare not whisper
  A want that lieth dim
We say, "Our Father knoweth,"
  And leave it all to Him.

For His great love has compassed
  Our nature, and our need,
We know not: but He knoweth,
  And He will bless indeed.
Therefore, O Heavenly Father,
  Give what is best to me;
And take the wants unanswered,
  As offerings made to Thee.

ANONYMOUS

While here, alas! I know but half His love,
  But half discern Him, and but half adore,
But when I meet Him in the realm above,
  I hope to love Him better, praise Him more,
And feel and tell, amid the choir divine,
  How fully I am His, and He is mine.

LYTE.

TO be angry about trifles is mean and childish; to rage and be furious is brutish; . . . but to prevent and suppress rising resentment is wise and glorious, is manly and divine. — WATTS.

When anger rushes, unrestrain'd, to action,
Like a hot steed, it stumbles in its way:
The man of thought strikes deepest, and strikes safest.

RICHARD SAVAGE.

There is not in nature,
A thing that makes a man so deform'd, so beastly,
As doth intemperate anger.

JOHN WEBSTER.

Madness and anger differ but in this,
This is short madness, that long anger is.

CHARLES ALEYN.

If you have inherited a quick temper, learn to control it; wrestle with it, get it under subjection, break it, — master it. There is no grander victory than to conquer a stubborn will, or a hasty temper. It requires patience and perseverance to overcome, every day: keep on trying, you will surely succeed by and by. God will give you the mastery, if you ask Him; He has accomplished greater things than that.

Renew Thine image, Lord, in me,
Lowly and gentle may I be;
    No charms but these to Thee are dear;
No anger mayest Thou ever find,
No pride in my unruffled mind,
    But faith, and heaven-born peace be there.

P. GERHARDT.

OCTOBER ELEVENTH.

IF events change men, much more persons. No man can meet another on the street without making some mark upon him. We say we exchange words when we meet; what we exchange is souls. And when intercourse is very close and frequent, so complete is this exchange that recognizable bits of the one soul begin to show in the other's nature, and the second is conscious of a similar and growing debt to the first. . . . It is the law of influence that we become like those whom we habitually admire. Through all the range of literature, of history, and biography, this law presides. Men are all mosaics of other men. — PROF. HENRY DRUMMOND.

The more we are with Christ, the more we become like Him. The more we study the beauty and loveliness of His character, the more we desire to be like Him. Why should not the flowers be beautiful? They blend in their petals the rose of the dawn, the amber of the noontide, and the flame of the sunset; they drink in the dew and rain, drops that are pure and clear as crystal; why, I repeat, should the flowers not be beautiful with such associations? How could they help it? And you, if your influences are of Christ, will possess a spirit lovelier than the flowers.

Within a caravan of man's trackless spirit
  Is framed an Image so intensely fair,
That the adventurous thoughts that wander near it
  Worship, and as they kneel tremble, and wear
The splendour of its Presence, and the light
  Penetrates their dreamlike frame
Till they become charged with the strength of flame.

PERCY BYSSHE SHELLEY.

MAY God breathe into thy soul the tranquillity of His peace! When Christ stilled the tempest, how must the troubled disciples have been brought near to Him, through this proof of His love and power! How sweet to them must have been those welcome words, how reassuring, how tender — "It is I."

Fierce was the wild billow,
　Dark was the night,
Oars laboured heavily,
　Foam glimmered white;
Mariners trembled,
　Peril was nigh, —
Then said the God of God:
　"Peace! it is I."

Ridge of the mountain-wave,
　Lower thy crest!
Wail of the stormy wind,
　Be thou at rest!
Peril can none be,
　Sorrow must fly,
Where saith the Light of Light:
　"Peace! it is I."

Jesus! Deliverer!
　Come Thou to me!
Soothe Thou my voyaging
　Over life's sea!
Thou, when the storm of death
　Roars, sweeping by,
Whisper, O Truth of Truth!
　"Peace! it is I."

ANATOLIUS OF EPHESUS.

OCTOBER THIRTEENTH.

BY ignorance is pride increas'd;
They most assume who know the least.

JOHN GAY.

Heaven pities ignorance;
She's still the first that has her pardon signed;
All sins else see their faults, she's only blind.

THOMAS MIDDLETON.

Survey our faults, our errors, our vices,— fearful, and fertile field, — trace them to their causes, all those causes resolve themselves into one — *Ignorance!* For as from this source flowed the abuses of religion, so also from this source flow the abuses of all other blessings, of talents, of riches, of power; for we abuse things, either because we know not their real use, or because, with an equal blindness, we imagine the abuse more adapted to our happiness. But as ignorance, then, is the *sole spring of evil*, so, as the antidote of ignorance is knowledge, it necessarily follows that, were we consummate in knowledge, we should be perfect in good. He, therefore, who retards the progress of intellect, countenances *crime* — nay, to a state, is the greatest of criminals; while he who circulates that mental light, more precious than the visual, is the holiest improver, and the surest benefactor of his race! — BULWER.

But 'tis some justice to ascribe to chance
The wrongs you must expect from ignorance;
None can the moulds of their creation choose.
We, therefore, should men's ignorance excuse
When born too low to reach all things sublime;
'Tis rather their misfortune than their crime.

SIR W. DAVENANT.

WHOSOEVER will come after me, let him deny himself, and take up his cross, and follow me. — MARK 8 : 34.

What is your cross? Is it an envious disposition? Is it a hasty temper? Or does it lie in your surroundings? Is it the kind of work you are obliged to do? He has given you this special place, and its special duties, that they may become a *crown* to you. Christ bore His cross with uncomplaining meekness; why should not you?

> I've many a cross to take up now,
>   And many left behind ;
> But present troubles move me not,
>   Nor shake my quiet mind.
> And what may be to-morrow's cross
>   I never seek to find ;
> My Father says, " Leave that to Me,
>   And keep a quiet mind."
>
>   ANONYMOUS.

Take, then, your Cross and follow Jesus,
And your path shall lead to everlasting life.
He went His way before you
Carrying the burden for Himself.
He died for you upon it,
That you might take your own
And die upon it too.
But if you die with Him,
Even so with Him you live ;
And if you are the comrade of His pain,
You shall have His glory too.

                        THOMAS À KEMPIS.

[294]

THERE are times when the Light breaks in upon thy soul, and thou hast a dim idea of what it will be like to be with Christ and His redeemed forever.

Sometimes I catch sweet glimpses of His face
  But that is all.
Sometimes He looks on me and seems to smile,
  But that is all.
Sometimes He speaks a passing word of peace,
  But that is all.
Sometimes I think I hear His loving voice
  Upon me call.

And this is all He meant when thus He spoke,
  " Come unto me "?
Is there no deeper, more enduring rest,
  In Him for thee?
Is there no steadier light for thee in Him?
  Oh, come and see!

Oh, come and see ! oh, look, and look again!
  All shall be right;
Oh, taste His love, and see that it is good,
  Thou child of night.
Oh, trust Him, trust Him in His grace and power,
  Then all is bright!

Then shall thy tossing soul find anchorage
  And steadfast peace ;
Thy love shall rest on His ; thy weary doubts
  Forever cease.
Thy heart shall find in Him, and in His grace,
  Its rest and bliss.

BONAR.

OCTOBER SIXTEENTH.

LET your heart be full of thankfulness and praise to-day ! Walk out into the October sunshine, and breathe in the spicy odors. Go for a drive in the country, if you can; it will do you good. The autumnal breeze is so refreshing, and the woods, kindled with their last dying fires, are a beautiful sight. The orchards are losing their fruited store day by day, and you can hear the song of the harvesters as they gather in their winter hoard. Thank God for the harvest ! Bless Him that the year has been an abundant one, and that He hath given the earth a goodly increase !

> To Thee, Creator of all good,
> Who givest life, and health and food,
>   Sing we Alleluia !

> Praise to God, immortal praise,
> For the love that crowns our days!
> Beauteous source of every joy,
> Let Thy praise our tongues employ.
> For the blessings of the field,
> For the stores the gardens yield ;
> For the fruits in full supply,
> Ripened 'neath the Summer sky ; —
> All that Spring with bounteous hand
> Scatters o'er the smiling land ;
> All that liberal Autumn pours
> From her rich o'erflowing stores ;
> These, to Thee, my Lord, we owe,
> Source whence all our blessings flow ;
> And for these my soul shall raise
> Grateful vows and solemn praise.

ANNA LETITIA BARBAULD.

SUBMIT yourself to the inevitable. How often this is said! Do not allow your temper to become ruffled over trifles; be happy in spite of circumstances; be hopeful in the face of discouragements. Carry a cheerful countenance about with you. The man who is out of work, if he only holds up his head and smiles, and hopes for better things, is much more apt to secure employment than the one who goes around with a mournful, dejected look, seeing nothing but the dark side of everything. Life cannot be all brightness, neither is it all shadow; we have our share of both. You think you have more sorrows than joys, more adversity then prosperity, more bitter than sweet in your life. Do you know why you believe this? Because you forgot to count your blessings. You are only looking out for the trials and ills of life, and when they come you put on a dejected air, and say sadly, "It is no more than I expected." Look out for the bright things,—there are plenty of them in store for you, and when God allows you to walk in the shadow make the best of it, and you will be all the better for it.

A cheerful temper, joined with innocence, will make beauty attractive, knowledge delightful, and wit good-natured. — ADDISON.

What I don't see
  Don't trouble me;
And what I see
  Might trouble me,
Did I not know
  That it must be so.

GOETHE.

[297]

BUILD for Heaven! Keep climbing up by little things; let your commonplace, every-day life be an honor to yourself and your God. Things that seem so insignificant and mean to-day, may grow beautiful by to-morrow. Look at the night-blooming cereus: it is nothing but a reddish-brown folded bud to-day, but in the silence and darkness of the night it bursts into exquisite beauty and fragrance. God sometimes lays His dear Hand on one of His beloved, and says, " Be still, and know that I am God." He whispers tenderly, " Be patient and I will teach thee beautiful lessons, and thou shalt be adorned with grace that thou couldst not otherwise obtain." But the soul-bud, so long folded in the shallow frivolities of earthly happiness, feels for the first time the warm, pure breath of Heaven blowing upon it, and begins to expand, until it becomes a blossom of rare fragrance, fit to be transplanted in the Garden of God.

No cross, no crown — no loss, no gain;
They first must suffer who would reign.

He best can part with life without a sigh
Whose daily living is to daily die.

Youth builds for age; age builds for rest;
Who builds for Heaven will build the best.

SPURGEON.

Out of suffering comes the serious mind; out of salvation, the grateful heart; out of endurance, fortitude; out of deliverance, faith. — RUSKIN.

The truest end of life is to know the life that never ends. — WILLIAM PENN.

[298]

A TIME of ripened fruits and scattered seeds.
Was ever time so beautiful? The year, from its
beginning, has been making preparation for this; you
have been looking forward to it, no matter what your
business is, — everything depends upon the harvest.
A farmer toils all Spring, and waits all Summer for it.
Man revives with the first breath of Autumn, and its
cool breezes are a tonic to body and mind.

Season of mists and mellow fruitfulness!
  Close bosom-friend of the maturing sun;
Conspiring with him how to load and bless
  With fruit the vines that round the thatch-eaves run;
To bend with apples the mossed cottage-trees,
  And fill all fruit with ripeness to the core;
    To swell the gourd and plump the hazel shells
With a sweet kernel; to set budding more,
  And still more, later flowers for the bees,
  Until they think warm days will never cease.
    For Summer has o'erbrimmed their clammy cells.

Where are the songs of spring? Ay, where are they?
  Think not of them, thou hast thy music too,
While barred clouds bloom the soft dying day,
  And touch the stubble-plains with rosy hue;
Then in a wilful choir the small gnats mourn
  Among the river sallows, borne aloft
    Or sinking as the light wind lives or dies;
And full-grown lambs loud bleat from hilly bourn;
  Hedge-crickets sing; and now with treble soft
  The redbreast whistles from a garden croft,
    And gathering swallows twitter from the skies.

                                        KEATS.

WORK while it is called to-day,
   Watch and pray!
With both thine hands right earnestly,
As in the sight of God most high,
   Thy calling ply.

HENRY G. TOMKINS.

Not a prayer, not an act of faithfulness in your calling, not a self-denying or kind word or deed, done out of love for Himself; not a weariness or painfulness endured patiently; not a duty performed; not a temptation resisted; but it enlarges the whole soul for the endless capacity of the love of God. — E. B. PUSEY.

Do nothing without a purpose, and let that purpose be to glorify God. Let every duty be done in His name, and every kindness done for His sake. Let each day's work be rounds upon which you shall climb to Heaven.

Work while life is given;
   Faint not, although 'tis hard;
Work is the will of Heaven,
   And peace is the reward!
   All work is holy.

.   .   .   .

Scorn nought as plain or mean;
   All with thy work impress,
That all where thou hast been
   May day by day confess
   That work is holy.

ANONYMOUS.

[300]

I LOVE and love not: Lord, it breaks my heart
　　To love and not to love.
Thou veiled within Thy glory, gone apart
　　Into Thy shrine, which is above,
Dost Thou not love me, Lord, or care
　　For this mine ill? —
I love thee here or there,
　　I will accept thy broken heart: lie still.

Lord, it was well with me in time gone by
　　That cometh not again,
When I was fresh and cheerful, who but I?
　　I fresh, I cheerful: worn with pain
Now, out of sight and out of heart;
　　O Lord, how long? —
I watch thee as thou art,
　　I will accept thy fainting heart: be strong.

"Lie still," "Be strong," to-day; but Lord, to-morrow,
　　What of to-morrow, Lord?
Shall there be rest from toil, be truce from sorrow,
　　Be living green upon the sward
Now but a barren grave to me,
　　Be joy for sorrow? —
Did I not die for thee?
　　Do not I live for thee? Leave Me to-morrow.
　　　　　　CHRISTINA ROSSETTI.

If we were but contented to leave God all our to-morrows we would not fret and worry so about them. How faithless we are! Oh, let us learn the lesson of submission. Let us give our all into His keeping, — trials, cares, perplexities, heartaches; He wants them all. Shall we not trust Him with everything?

IF you have any special gift, make use of it. That you have *some* gift, cannot be doubted. Perhaps it is music; if so, let your talent be cultivated, that it may brighten other hearts, and sing itself into other souls. The noble band of King's Daughters, who send out messengers into our hospitals and charitable institutions, sometimes select from their number a sweet minstrel, who pours forth a gush of melody to cheer the suffering and afflicted ones; it is like a bit of Heaven to them. Those who possess the gift of song may not recognize it at all; and yet their lives are unwritten music, to which God strikes the key, and sets the chords in harmony. May He give you some pure influence, — some song turned to His love to sing for His glory!

If a pilgrim has been shadowed
  By a tree that I have nursed;
If a cup of cold, clear water
  I have raised to lips athirst;
If I've planted one sweet flower
  By an else too barren way;
If I've whispered in the midnight
  One sweet word of day;
If in one poor bleeding bosom
  I a woe-swept chord have stilled;
If a dark and restless spirit
  I with hope of Heaven have stilled;
If I've made of life's hard battle
  One faint heart grow warm and strong;
Then, my God! I thank Thee — bless Thee
  For the precious gift of song.

ANONYMOUS.

DEAR Heart, keep steadily on thy way, ever trusting, ever singing!

The little birds trust God, for they go singing,
  From northern woods where autumn winds have
    blown,
With joyous faith their trackless pathway winging
  To summer-lands of song, afar, unknown.

. . . .

Let us go singing, then, and not go sighing.
  Since we are sure our times are in His hand,
Why should we weep, and fear, and call it dying?
  'Tis only flitting to a Summer-land.

ANONYMOUS.

Glad is the October sunshine, for it beams so full and free, and the Wind spreads wide and wider, with a wing on earth and sea; and a later crop of apples hangs well-freighted from the tree. Heart, rejoice, the year is ripe! Sing, O Heart, and cease thy grieving! Though thy Summer slips away, though the beauty of the Autumn lose its gold and scarlet dye, there is waiting for thy coming God's blest Summer, by and by!

How calmly may we commit ourselves to the hands of Him who bears up the world — of Him who has created and who provides for the joys, even of insects, as carefully as if He were their father! — RICHTER.

If our love were but more simple,
  We should take Him at His word;
And our lives would be all sunshine
  In the sweetness of our Lord.

FABER.

LEAD us, dear Lord, this day in the green pastures of Thy love, and by the still waters of Thy peace! Feed us, dear Lord, with "food convenient for us," and suffer us not to want for any good thing. Thou art abundantly able to supply all our needs, out of Thy great plenty, therefore we pray Thee that, as "giving doth not impoverish Thee, nor withholding enrich Thee," we, Thy little flock, may be kindly fed and tended, and that when the night cometh, we may be gathered safely into Thy Fold!

When I faint with summer's heat,
Thou shalt guide my weary feet
To the streams, that still and slow,
Through the verdant meadows flow.

MERRICK.

Thy sheep shall hear Thy voice, on plain and hill,
    Through flood or wilderness,
In the green pastures, by the waters still,
    In joy or sharp distress,
Thy call will reach them, sometimes loud and near,
    Then faint and far away;
O thou good Shepherd! grant that heart and ear
    May listen and obey!

SARAH DOUDNEY.

Thou layest Thy hand on the fluttering heart,
    And sayest, "Be still!"
The silence and shadow are only a part
    Of Thy sweet will;
Thy presence is with me, and where Thou art
    I fear no ill.

F. R. HAVERGAL.

ART thou weary? Dear tired heart, be comforted: thou shalt have sweet rest by and by. Beyond earth's cares and sorrows and shadows, there waits for Christ's beloved a never-ending rest.

> Rest remaineth — oh, how sweet,
> Flowery fields for wandering feet,
> Peaceful calm for sleepless eyes,
> Life for death, and songs for sighs.

> Rest remaineth — hush that sigh;
> Mourning pilgrim, rest is nigh;
> Yet a season bright and blest,
> Thou shalt enter on thy rest.

> Rest remaineth — rest from sin —
> Guilt can never enter in;
> Every warring thought shall cease —
> Rest in purity and peace.

> Rest remaineth — rest from tears,
> Rest from parting, rest from fears;
> Every trembling thought shall be
> Lost, my Saviour — lost in Thee.

> Rest remaineth — oh, how blest!
> We believe, and we have rest;
> Faith, reposing faith, hath been
> 'Mongst the things that are not seen.

> Thus, my Saviour, let me be
> Ever here at rest in Thee,
> And at last, by Thee possessed,
> On Thy bosom sink to rest.

FROM "DARK SAYINGS ON A HARP."

THE flood of time is rolling on,
  We stand upon its brink, . . .
To glide in peace down death's mysterious stream.
Have you done well?

SHELLEY.

Look into your heart this autumn day, and ask yourself this question, "Have I done well?" Through
each changing season, while the leaf has unfolded,
taken on its rich green color, and fluttered out into
the air and sunshine; while it grew and waxed strong
and spread itself, with a million other leaves, to make
a restful, cooling shade; while it turned gold, and
crimson, and then russet brown, and lastly ashen gray,
ere it plumed itself for flight, — ah, what have you been
doing? Have you done well? Has your soul been
making preparation for Heaven? As within the grape
the sweet crimson juice is hidden, waiting for the wine-
press to crush it, and for the refiner to clarify it, so the
soul's fruits should reach fruition through passing
seasons; until, crushed and sweetened by the Master
of the Vineyard, it becomes a strengthening draught to
all around it. Learn, then, the lesson of the Grape
and of the Leaf.

The Wine of Life keeps oozing drop by drop,
The Leaves of Life keep falling one by one.

  .   .   .   .

Ah, with the Grape my fading Life provide,
And wash the Body whence the Life has died,
    And lay me, shrouded in the living Leaf,
By some not unfrequented Garden-side.

OMAR KHAYYÁM.

IF thou wouldst be happy, thou must be useful.
Make thyself necessary wherever thy lot is cast;
make thy work acceptable whatever it is; honour thy
calling, no matter how lowly, and then thou shalt be
royal in the sight of God. Mount upward, press forward, and let every day be well and profitably spent,
for the time appointed for thee is short, and life's brief
day soon draweth to a close.

> There will be sorrow
> Beyond to-morrow, if I lose to-day.
> ARTHUR J. MUNBY.

> We have not wings, and we cannot soar;
> But we have feet to scale and climb
> By slow degrees, by more and more,
> The cloudy summits of our time.
> TENNYSON.

All things have something more than barren use;
There is a scent upon the briar,
A tremulous splendour in the Autumn dews;
Cold morns are fringed with fire.

The clodded earth goes up in sweet-breathed flowers;
In music dies poor human speech;
And in beauty blow those hearts of ours
When love is born in each.

Life is transfigured in the soft and tender
Light of love, a volume dun
Of rolling smoke becomes a wreathed splendour
In the declining sun.
ALEXANDER SMITH.

TRUE happiness never flows into a man, but always out of him. Heaven itself is more internal than external. — NEWMAN.

Happiness is a perfume that cannot shed over another, without a few drops falling on one's self. — BYRON.

The happy man is he that hath learned to read himself more than all books; and hath so taken out his lesson that he can never forget it; that knows the world, and cares not for it; that after many traverses of thoughts, is grown to know what he may trust to, and stands now equally armed for all events. — JOSEPH HALL.

The hearts of men are their books; events are their tutors; great actions are their eloquence. — MACAULAY.

If Happiness has not her seat
　And centre in the breast,
We may be wise, or rich, or great,
　But never can be blest.

BURNS.

True happiness is not the growth of earth,
The soil is fruitless if you seek it there;
'Tis an exotic of celestial birth,
And never blooms but in celestial air.
Sweet plant of Paradise! its seeds are sown
In here and there a breast of heavenly mould,
It rises slow, and buds, but ne'er was known
To blossom here — the climate is too cold.

RICHARD BRINSLEY SHERIDAN.

ONLY Heaven is high.
  Only the gods are great.
Above the searchless sky,
In unremoved state,
They from their golden mansions
Look over the lands and the seas;
The ocean's wide expanses,
And the earth's varieties:
Secure of their supremacy,
And sure of affluent ease.
Who shall say, "I stand!" nor fall?
Destiny is over all!
Rust will crumble old renown.
Bust and column tumble down;
Keep and castle; tower and town;
Throne and sceptre; crest and crown.
Destiny is over all!
One by one the pale guests fall
At lighted feasts, in palace hall;
And feast is turned to funeral.
Who shall say, "I stand!" nor fall?
Destiny is over all.

OWEN MEREDITH.

It is a proverbial saying, that every one makes his
own destiny; and this is usually interpreted, that every
one, by his wise or unwise conduct, prepares good or
evil for himself: but we may also understand it, that
whatever it be that he receives from the hand of Providence, he may so accommodate himself to it, that he
will find his lot good for him, however much may seem
to others to be wanting. — WILLIAM VON HUMBOLDT.

DEATH and love are the two wings
Which bear man from earth to Heaven.

MICHAEL ANGELO.

What an empty world this would be without love!
It is the magnetic needle that draws all hearts together
in one common bond of humanity. It is the heart of
Religion, the basis of Benevolence, the twin-sister of
Pity, and the foundation of home.

But Love's a flower that will not die
  For lack of leafy screen,
And Christian Hope can cheer the eye
  That ne'er saw vernal green;
Then be ye sure that Love can bless
E'en in this crowded loneliness.

ANONYMOUS.

Hid in earth's mines of silver,
  Floating in clouds above,
Ringing in Autumn's tempest,
  Murmured by every dove,—
One thought fills God's creation,
  His own great name of Love.

ADELAIDE PROCTER.

I cannot go
Where universal love not smiles around,
Sustains all yon orbs, and all their suns;
From seeming evil still educing good,
And better thence again, and better still,
In infinite progression. But I lose
Myself in Him, in light ineffable!
Come, then, expressive silence, muse His praise.

THOMSON.

LET the golden month go out in prayer. Have thou thine own pure prayer, to suit thy needs, and breathe secretly in the listening ear of Heaven!

O Master and Maker! my hope is in Thee;
My Jesus, dear Saviour! now get my soul free
From this my hard prison, my spirit uprisen
        Soars upward to Thee.
Thus moaning, and groaning, and bending the knee,
I adore and implore that Thou liberate me.

TR. OF PRAYER OF MARY STUART, QUEEN OF SCOTS.
                    (*Written before her execution.*)

Awake in me desires for Heaven!
    Help me to view the world aright;
Far from my heart its wiles be driven
    While endless joys allure my sight:
For Jesus' sake, when flesh shall fail,
With me, O God, may it be well!

AMELIA JULIANA, COUNTESS OF SCHUARZBURG.

Father in Heaven! oh, hear when we call,
Hear for Christ's sake, who is Saviour of all;
Feeble and fainting we trust in Thy might,
In doubting and darkness Thy love be our light:
Let us sleep on Thy breast while the night taper burns,
And wake in Thy arms when the morning returns.
    Father, have mercy; Father, have mercy;
    Father, have mercy thro' Jesus Christ our Lord.

SELINA, COUNTESS OF HUNTINGDON.

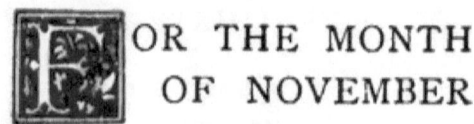

FOR THE MONTH OF NOVEMBER

NOVEMBER FIRST.

IT is November. May you be at peace with all the world, and may you look up into the gray sky and see beyond its shadows the Light of the Eternal, the Sun of Righteousness that declines not with the brooding Autumn days, but steadfast, pure, and clear, shines gloriously forever. Abiding peace is there.

Down below, the wild November whistling,
    Through the beeches' dome of burning red,
And the Autumn sprinkling penitential
    Dust and ashes on the chestnut's head.

Up above, the Tree with leaf unfading
    By the everlasting River's brink:
And the Sea of Glass beyond whose margin
    Never yet the Sun was known to sink.

W. ALEXANDER.

But peace was there: no lightnings blazed;
    No clouds obscured the face of Heaven;
Down each green opening while I gazed,
    My thoughts to Home and you were given.
Oh, tender minds! in life's gay morn,
    Some clouds must dim your coming day;
Yet bootless pride and falsehood scorn,
    And peace like this shall cheer your way.

ROBERT BLOOMFIELD.

CHRISTINA ROSSETTI
1830–1894

NOVEMBER SECOND.

IT does one good to be alone sometimes; to throw care to the winds, and to walk among the rustling leaves, and muse on life,— its changes, its beauties, and its mysteries. Come with me into the dying woods; look, how fast the leaves are falling! how the winds whisper of decay, as they sing their melancholy dirge for the faded flowers. But wait! among the leaves a bit of color peeps, half-sheltered by a friendly bush, a dear memento of the summer days. How loth is Nature yet to lose the flowers she wore upon her breast.

We shall not die nor disappear,
But in these other selves, ourselves succeed,
Even as ripe flowers pass into their seed
Only to be renewed from prime to prime.
                                            THOMAS HOOD.

The constant wheels of nature scorn to tire
        Until her works expire.
                                            FRANCIS QUARLES.

Those few pale Autumn flowers,
        How beautiful they are!
Than all that went before,
Than all the Summer store,
        How lovelier far!

And why? — They are the last!
        The last! the last! the last!
Oh! by that little word
How many thoughts are stirr'd
        That whisper of the past!
                                            CAROLINE SOUTHEY.

[313]

NOW to Thee, gracious Lord of the season, be honour
and glory and praise,
That again in the joy of the harvest our jubilant an-
them we raise.

Though many the fears that beset us, though faith
waxes feeble and cold,
Thy bow, with promise unbroken, glitters still as it glittered of old.

Though weary we grow in our watching the weeks of
the drought as they pass,
When the earth is as iron beneath us, and the heaven
above us as brass.

Yet the showers come back in their season; once more
in the land they are seen,
The brook brimming over with crystals, the grass as
the emerald green.

Though troubled the spirit within us, when the mist
upon valley and plain
Lies thick, and the clouds in their armies return again
after the rain.

Yet the sun cometh forth as a giant, and after the Tempest the morn
Is cloudless and fair, and the colour grows golden and
rich on the corn.

For seedtime and harvest we thank Thee; our fears
as the shadows have fled;
Thou hast given his seed to the sower, Thou hast given
the eater his bread.

ALFRED CHURCH.

[314]

MAY thy soul be as beautiful as the Autumn star-
light, which silvers all the sleeping world. Thou
needst not make any stir or commotion,— only *shine*.
Shine as if God were reflected from thy being.

> There is no end to the Sky,
>   And the stars are everywhere.
>   HENRY BURTON.

It was an eve of Autumn's holiest mood,
                . . . Nature seemed
In silent contemplation to adore
Its Maker.   Now and then the aged leaf
Fell from its fellows, rustling to the ground ;
And, as it fell, bade man think on his end,
On vale and lake, on wood and mountain high,
With pensive wing outspread, sat heavenly Thought,
Conversing with itself. . . .
And up the east, unclouded, rode the moon
With all her stars, gazing on earth intense,
As if she saw some wonder working there.
                        ROBERT POLLOCK.

Ye stars! which are the poetry of Heaven,
If in your bright leaves we would read the fate
Of men and empires, — 'tis to be forgiven
That in our aspirations to be great
Our destinies o'erlap their moral state,
And claim a kindred with you ; for ye are
A beauty and a mystery, and create
In us such love and reverence from afar,
That fortune, fame, power, life, have named themselves
    a star.
                        BYRON.

MAY God preserve and keep thee, "merrie England," noble and illustrious country as thou art! and in every time of danger mayst thou be protected, thy fair name be ever writ in shining letters, and thy rulers be found worthy of thee!

England, with all thy faults, I love thee still,
My Country! and, while yet a nook is left
Where English mind and manners may be found,
Shall be constrain'd to love thee.

                    COWPER.

Happy is England!   I could be content
    To see no other verdure than its own;
    To feel no other breezes than are blown
Through its tall woods with high romances blent.

                    KEATS.

Breathes there a man with soul so dead,
Who never to himself hath said,
This is my own, my native land!
Whose heart hath ne'er within him burn'd,
As home his footsteps he hath turn'd,
From wandering on a foreign strand!

                    SCOTT.

Dear home in England, safe and fast,
If but in thee my lot be cast,
The past shall seem a nothing past
To thee, dear home, if won at last;
Dear home in England, won at last.

              ARTHUR HUGH CLOUGH.

[316]

HOW sweet it is, that no one can ever take the place of those we have loved and lost: they have their own sacred corner in our hearts, their own hallowed shrine in our memory. New friends may endear themselves to us, but they never fill the vacancies made by those who have passed out of our sight into the Better Country.

How much so ever in life's mutations
  We seek our shattered idols to replace,
Not one in all the myriads of the nations
  Can ever fill another's vacant place.

Each has his own, the smallest and most humble,
  As well as he, revered the wide world through;
With every death some love and hope must crumble,
  Which strive to build themselves anew.

If the fair face of violets should perish
  Before another springtime had its birth,
Could all the costly blooms which florists cherish
  Bring back its April beauty to the earth?

Not the most gorgeous flower that uncloses
  Could give the olden grace to vale and plain,
Not even Persia's gardens full of roses,
  Could ever make the world so fair again.

And so with souls we love; they pass and leave us —
  Time teaches patience at a bitter cost;
Yet all the new loves, which the years may give us,
  Fill not the heart-place aching for the lost.

ANONYMOUS.

BE diligent, after thy power, to do deeds of love. Think nothing too little, nothing too low, to do lovingly for the sake of God. Bear with infirmities, ungentle tempers, contradictions; visit the sick, relieve the poor; forego thyself and thine own ways for love; and He whom in them thou lovest, to whom in them thou ministerest, will own thy love, and will pour His own love into thee. — E. B. PUSEY.

The memory of a kindly word
For long gone by,
The fragrance of a fading flower
Sent lovingly;
The gleaming of a sudden smile
Or sudden tear,
The warmer pressure of the hand,
The tone of cheer;
The hush that means I cannot speak,
But I have heard!
The note that only bears a verse
Of God's own word;
Such tiny things we hardly count
As ministry;
The givers deeming they have shone
Scant sympathy;
But when the heart is overwrought,
Oh! who can tell
The power of such tiny things
To make it well!

FRANCES RIDLEY HAVERGAL.

Let this be a day of sweet ministrations.

NOVEMBER EIGHTH.

Some Thoughts about Man.

MARK the perfect man, and behold the upright:
for the end of that man is peace. — PSALM 37 : 37.

In this world there is one godlike thing, the essence
of all that ever was or ever will be of godlike in this
world, — the veneration done to human worth by the
hearts of men. — CARLYLE.

The good great man? three treasures, love and light
And calm thoughts regular as infant's breath,
And three firm friends, more sure than day and night,
Himself, his Maker, and the angel Death.

COLERIDGE.

Men in great place are thrice servants; servants of
the Sovereign or state; servants of fame; and servants
of business. — BURNS.

Man dwells apart, though not alone,
    He walks among his peers unread;
The best of thoughts which he hath known,
    For lack of listeners are not said.

JEAN INGELOW.

Man was mark'd
A friend in his creation to himself,
And may with fit ambition conceive
The greatest blessings, and the brightest honours
Appointed for him, if he can achieve them
The right and noble way.

PHILIP MASSINGER.

THOUGH you may be surrounded by the fog and mist, let your heart keep its sunshine, sending out bright rays to guide and lead through the darkness some one whose love and faith in humanity is shrouded in a mist of doubt.

First, at the dawn of lingering day,
It rises of an ashen gray;
Then deepening with a sordid strain
Of yellow, like a lion's mane.
Scarce an eclipse, with pall so dun,
Blots from the face of Heaven the sun.
But soon a thicker, darker cloak
Wraps all the town, behold in smoke,
Which steam — compelling trade disgorges
From all her furnaces and forges
In pitchy clouds, too dense to rise,
Descends rejected from the skies;
Till struggling day, extinguished quite,
At noon gives place to candle-light.

HENRY LUTTRELL.

No sun — no moon!
No morn — no noon —
No dawn — no dusk — no proper time of day —
No sky — no earthly view —

.   .   .   .

No warmth, no cheerfulness, no healthful ease,
No comfortable feel in any member —
No shade, no sun, no butterflies, no bees,
No fruits, no flowers, no leaves, no birds,
November!

HOOD.

[320]

THESE "gray days" give us plenty of time for thought. Let us enter the "living room" of our brain, and spend a little time with silent Thought. How kind our dear **Heavenly Father** was to give us this means of communing with Him, and of contemplating His goodness!

Our great thoughts, our great affections, the truths of our life never leave us. Surely they cannot separate from our consciousness, shall follow it whithersoever that shall go, and are of their nature divine and immortal. — THACKERAY.

Thoughts, thoughts, thoughts!
Rolling wave-like on the mind's strange shore,
Rustling leaf-like through the evermore.
Oh, that they might follow God's good Hand!
W. ALEXANDER.

Thought can never be compared with action, but when it awakens in us the image of Truth. — MADAME DE STÄEL.

The chariot of Thought
Rolls from the world's ringing walls to its goal,
Urged by Faith, the bright-eyed charioteer of the Soul.
OWEN MEREDITH.

He therefore that would govern his actions by the laws of virtue, must regulate his thoughts by those of reason. — SAMUEL JOHNSON.

Reading seeks, meditation finds;
Prayer asks, contemplation tastes.
ST. AUGUSTINE.

HE who walks with God, who lives in His presence, whose mind is filled with the image of wisdom far above human wisdom, goodness far above human goodness, justice to which a last appeal may be made and with whom justice will ever be found, — he who sees His beauty in this garb of external nature, so exquisite an exposition of the Divine Mind — for shattered and disordered as it is by some evidently external force, enough remains to prove the beauty, grace, and order of the unblemished original; — he who does this lives in a new element; his thoughts, his imagination, his views, are purified and elevated. — ANONYMOUS.

Look in, and see Christ's chosen saint
  In triumph wear his Christ-like chain ;
No fear lest he should swerve or faint ;
  " His life is Christ, his death is gain."
                                        KEBLE.

What shall we be who have in Christ believed —
  What, through His grace, will be our sweet reward?
Eye hath not seen, ear heard, or heart conceived,
  What God for those who love Him hath prepared ;
Let us the steep ascent then boldly climb,
  Our toil and labour will be well repaid ;
Let us haste onward ; till in God's good time
  We reap the fruit — a crown that doth not fade.
                                C. J. P. SPITTA.

Of simple understandings, little inquisitive, and little instructed, are made good Christians, who by reverence and obedience implicitly believe, and are constant in their belief. — MONTAIGNE.

NOVEMBER TWELFTH.

SOME people drift through life without any purpose
or aim. They have nothing in particular to do,
nothing in particular to interest them, and no opinion
worth listening to. What an existence to lead! When
life presents such grand opportunities for doing good to
others, and getting good for ourselves, why should any
one value it so lightly, and make it of so little worth
the living? Choose your work, and try to do it as well
as you can. Make up your mind about things; have
some kind of an opinion, but do not hug it so close
that you would not let it go if you found it to be
wrong. Live for a purpose; work for a purpose; be
decided in what you do; have opinions and ideas of
your own, but do not be either stubborn or conceited
about them. Byron says, "Be something, anything,
but mean." The world always respects a resolute man.

To him, alas! to him, I fear,
The face of death will terrible appear,
Who in his life, flatt'ring his senseless pride,
By being known to all the world beside,
Does not himself, when he is dying, know
Nor what he is, nor whither he's to go.

COWLEY.

Be stirring as the time: be fire with fire;
. . . So shall inferior eyes,
That borrow their behaviour from the great,
Grow great by your example; and put on
The dauntless spirit of resolution.

SHAKESPEARE.

[323]

IN a Devonshire lane as I trotted along
 T'other day, much in want of a subject for song,
Thinks I to myself, I have hit on a strain,
 Sure, Marriage is much like a Devonshire lane.

In the first place, 'tis long, and when once you are in it,
 It holds you as fast as a cage holds a linnet,
For howe'er rough and dirty the road may be found,
 Drive forward you must, since there's no turning
  round.

Then the banks are so high, both to left hand and right,
 That they shut up the beauties around from the
  sight,
And hence you'll allow 'tis an inference plain,
 That Marriage is just like a Devonshire lane.

But thinks I too, these banks within which we are pent,
 With bud, blossom, and berry are richly besprent,
And the conjugal fence which forbids us to roam,
 Looks lovely, when deck'd with the comforts of
  home.

In the rock's gloomy crevice the bright holly grows,
 The ivy waves fresh o'er the withering rose,
And the evergreen love of a virtuous wife
 Smooths the roughness of care, cheers the winter of
  life.

Then long be the journey and narrow the way,
 I'll rejoice that I've seldom a turnpike to pay,
And whate'er others think, be the last to complain,
 Though Marriage is just like a Devonshire lane.

ANONYMOUS.

TEMPTATIONS come to us in so many forms. Not a day passes that we have not need to arm ourselves with fresh courage to meet the battle of life. Overcoming is not easy with any of us: it requires constant vigilance and self-denial, moral courage and strength of will, but each victory over temptation is setting a stone in our spiritual temples which neither time nor decay can destroy. Let us root out the evil habits, overcome the desire to do wrong, and stand up courageously against temptation, not in our own strength, but in the strength of our Lord. He it is that giveth us the victory, in His name.

> Was the trial sore?
> Temptation sharp? Thank God a second time!
> Why comes temptation but for man to meet
> And master, and make crouch beneath his foot
> And so be pedestalled in triumph? Pray
> " Lead us into no such temptations, Lord ! "
> Yea, but, O Thou whose servants are the bold,
> Lead such temptations by the head and hair,
> Reluctant dragons, up to who dares fight,
> That so he may do battle and have praise.
>
> BROWNING.

When life is more terrible than death, it is then the truest valour to dare to live. — SIR THOMAS BROWNE.

> Our business is like men to fight,
> And hero-like to die !
>
> WILLIAM MOTHERWELL.

A man of courage is also full of faith.

> YONGE'S CICERO.

[3•5]

NOVEMBER FIFTEENTH.

MAN carries under his hat a private theatre, wherein a greater drama is acted than is ever performed on the mimic stage, beginning and ending in Eternity. — CARLYLE.

There is a chamber of silence in every human heart. Here our secret thoughts lie hidden away, known only to ourselves and the great Author of our being. Into this chamber we retire when in great joy or sorrow; we seek its seclusion when baffled or defeated, when disappointed, when discouraged, or when successful and happy. What we think while there influences our whole life. We can scarcely understand our own motives often; there is a mysterious something within us which seems to govern our actions, and we obey, as it were, an unseen voice. I think we are in close kinship with the associations of that secret heart-chamber. If our thoughts are pure and ennobling, we carry about with us the reflection of them in good deeds; but if they are not, our influence cannot be wholesome. Oh, this silent, inner life! it only lies revealed to the Eye of God; the world sees but a glimpse of it, but let us keep our hearts so clean and true that we need never fear to have our secret thoughts known.

Thou canst not sufficiently prize Humanity's value;
    Let it be coin'd in deed as it exists in thy breast,
E'en the man whom thou chancest to meet in life's
        narrow pathway,
    If he should ask it of thee, hold forth a succouring
        hand.

SCHILLER.

NOVEMBER SIXTEENTH.

TIME is like a great bird flying ever onward to his nest among the mountains of Eternity. The little minutes make the soft white down on his breast — the countless busy minutes that rest not until they are closely folded under the wings of Time, to be borne away into the trackless past. The days, and weeks, and years gather about him; they form his plumage, and each and every one is eager for flight. What are you giving into Time's keeping to bear away forever? What you give will never return. Let it be something sweet and beautiful that shall be put away for safe keeping, under the wings of the Eternal Years.

The Bird of Time has but a little way
To flutter — and the Bird is on the Wing.

OMAR KHAYYÁM.

How slowly and how silently doth time
Float on his starry journey! Still he goes,
And goes, and goes, and doth not pass away.
He rises with the golden morning, calmly,
And with the moon at night. Methinks I see
Him stretching wide abroad his mighty wings,
Floating forever o'er the crowds of men,
Like a huge vulture with its prey beneath.
Lo! I am here, and time seems passing on:
To-morrow I shall be a breathless thing —
Yet he will still be here; and the blue hours
Will laugh as gaily on the busy world
As though I were alive to welcome them.

BRYAN WALLER PROCTER.

[327]

WHO is the great man? He who has accumulated vast estates, established flourishing institutions, diminished the public debt, won some famous battle, written a popular book, or painted a picture that all London has praised? Ah, perhaps you, in your plain every-day life are greater in the sight of God than the men who have accomplished these things. You think you lead a very humdrum sort of a life; you long to do great and noble things. You have high ambitions, but God had other plans for you. He chose a humble place for you, gave you your work to do, and now is watching the result. He doesn't forget the little wayside blessings you are scattering about you; He notices all the daily kindnesses you are doing for others, and when you whisper to Him that you have lived in vain, do you think your Heavenly Father believes as you do? You have no right to call a life spent for Him, and for the service of others, "useless." They who are greatest in the eyes of the world are often least in the Kingdom of God.

If I am asked, "Who is the *greatest* man?" I answer "The *best*"; and if I am required to say who is the best, I reply, "He that has deserved the most of his fellow-creatures." Whether we deserve better of mankind, by the cultivation of letters, by obscure and inglorious attainments, by intellectual pursuits calculated rather to amuse than inform, than by strenuous exertions in speaking and acting, let those consider who bury themselves in studies unproductive of any benefit to their country, or fellow-citizens. I think not. — SIR WILLIAM JONES.

NO wonder you are troubled and perplexed, and that things go wrong. You are trying to walk alone, and your strength is small. You forget that you are human, and that humanity is solely dependent on God. How would you be clothed and fed and sheltered without Him? Why, you are simply nothing without God; and yet you are trying to rely upon your poor feeble strength. You take your burden to Him, perhaps, and ask Him to carry it for you, but when you finish your prayer to Him, you resume the burden, and go on sighing and wondering why God did not relieve you of it. Learn to rely upon Him; remember He is your Father, and you are His child; trust Him completely, and give into His keeping all that you have.

> With doubts, and cares, and fears opprest,
>   Man's wayward thoughts desponding rove;
> Where shall the troubled soul find rest?
>   Oh! fly to God, for God is love.
>
> Trust, trust in Him — for you He died;
>   By works of love thy faith approve;
> So shall thy soul in peace abide,
>   And know, and feel that God is love.
>   LORD TEIGNMOUTH.

Faith sees the worlds that are not open to any other eye. It has been well said: "The Holy Spirit can put an eye of faith into the soul, and thus make the things of God manifest to it, as He did to the Old Testament saints, who saw things afar off." — ENGLISH CHURCHMAN.

Be not faithless, but believing. — JOHN 20 : 27.

TO be especially loved and cared for, is very sweet to us. To be enshrined in loyal hearts, and set apart as if we were jewels, how precious this is! If we are shining each day for our Master, reflecting His glory, we are truly His jewels.

> Set apart for Jesus !
>   Is not this enough,
> Though this desert prospect
>   Open wild and rough?
> Set apart for His delight,
>   Chosen for His holy pleasure,
>   Sealed to be His special treasure ;
>   Could we choose a nobler joy?
> And would we if we might?
>
> Set apart to love Him,
>   And His love to know ;
> Not to waste affection
>   On a passing show.
> Called to give Him life and heart,
>   Called to pour the hidden treasure,
>   That none other claims to measure
>   Into His beloved hand !
> Thrice blessed " set apart."
>
>   FRANCES RIDLEY HAVERGAL.

Thou art my King—
My King henceforth alone ;
And I, Thy servant, Lord, am all Thine own.
Give me Thy strength ; Oh! let Thy dwelling be
In this poor heart that pants, my Lord, for Thee !

                        G. TERSTEEGEN.

KNOWLEDGE may slumber in the memory, but it never dies. It is like the dormouse in the ivied tower, that sleeps whilst winter lasts, but wakes with the warm breath of spring; it is like the life-germ in the seed; it is like the sweet music of the harp-strings that waits but the master's touch to wake it into utterance. — ANONYMOUS.

> The Almighty wisdom, having given
> Each man within himself an apter light
> To guide his acts, than any light within him,
> Creating nothing, not in all things equal:
> It seems a fault in any that depend
> On other's knowledge, and exile their own.
>
> CHAPMAN AND SHIRLEY.

God intended man to acquire knowledge of his own, this is why He gave him a mind to reason, and to improve his opportunities. Do not depend on the thoughts and opinions of others; lay up a fund of knowledge, and it will be ready to draw from at any time. Add to your store every day; improve the little minutes; make use of everything you can as you pass along. Keep learning; it will help fit you for the life to come.

> Learning is addition beyond
> Nobility or birth: honour of blood,
> Without the ornament of knowledge, is
> A glorious ignorance.
>
> JAMES SHIRLEY.

[331]

WE can't choose happiness either for ourselves or for another; we can't tell where that will lie. We can only choose whether we will indulge ourselves in the present moment, or whether we will renounce that, for the sake of the Divine voice within us —GEORGE ELIOT.

Thou, Lord, my path shalt choose,
    And my Guide be!
What shall I fear to lose
    While I have Thee?
This be my portion blest,
On my Redeemer's breast,
In peaceful trust to rest:
    He cares for me!

Shall I, then, choose my way?
    Never, oh, no!
I, a creature of a day,
    What can I know?
What dread perplexity,
Then would encompass me:
Now I can look to Thee,
    Thou orderest so:

This lightens every cross,
    Cheers every ill:
Suffer I grief or loss,
    It is Thy will!
Who can make no mistake,
Chooseth the way I take;
He who can ne'er forsake,
    Holds my hand still!

FROM THE GERMAN.

WHO has ever been able to mark out a future and have his life exactly as he had planned it? So much depends upon circumstances; for, as we cannot look into the future and see what is before us, what folly it is for us to boast of what we will do in the coming years! Why not leave the future with God? Perhaps these very disappointments are stepping-stones to a better and higher life. We do not consider that God has wisely withheld from us the very thing which might have made us miserable here and hereafter. To be contented with to-day's portion, to be cheerful and bright no matter what comes,—this is the dearest wish I have for you this November day.

Our content
Is our best having.

SHAKESPEARE.

With equal minds what happens let us bear,
Nor joy, nor grieve too much for things beyond our care.

DRYDEN.

Cellars and granaries in vain we fill
With all the bounteous summer's store,
If the mind thirst and hunger still,
The poor rich man's emphatically poor;
Slaves to the things we too much prize,
We masters grow of all that we despise.

COWLEY.

Not he who has little, but he who wishes for more, is poor. — SENECA.

THOUGH we may be always wishing to have what the world calls "a good easy time," we would soon tire of such an existence, could we reach the fulfilment of our desires. A few weeks' vacation at a summer resort refreshes and invigorates us, but as soon as we begin to feel rested we grow impatient to resume our work, and to get back into the daily routine of our former activity. If you have ever been restricted from work by long illness, and your physician tells you that absolute rest is necessary for your restoration to health, then you will fully comprehend the misery of being idle. One has only to have a little experience of this kind to fully appreciate the real luxury of work. Wheels that are allowed to stand still soon rust, and by and by the machinery will not run at all, because the oil and friction are wanting. The machinery of our being needs oiling with cheerfulness; and then if we keep all of the wheels in motion, we shall be happier than if we spent our days in luxurious idleness.

He that embarks on the voyage of life will always wish to advance rather by the simple impulse of the wind than the strokes of the oar; and many founder in their passage while they lie waiting for the gale. — SAMUEL JOHNSON.

Life's cares are comforts; such by Heav'n design'd;
He that has none, must make them, or be wretched.
Cares are employments; and without employ
The soul is on the rack; the rack of rest,
To souls most adverse; action all their joy.
                                        YOUNG.

NOVEMBER TWENTY-FOURTH.

LEARN to be temperate in all things. The man who indulges his appetite too freely starves his mind and neglects his soul. Avoid the use of intoxicating liquors or drugs, — the world has suffered enough through them already; do not run to extremes in anything; let your life be temperate, pure, and blameless, and worthy of imitation. After all, it is not so much what we profess, as how we *live*; this is what the world wants — proofs! If you wish to do anything for the good of humanity, begin with yourself; the truer the pattern, the more it will be copied. If you then would have a temperate world, do your share towards making it so by being temperate yourself.

Temperance is reason's girdle and passion's bridle, the strength of the soul and the foundation of virtue. — JEREMY TAYLOR.

> Philosophy, religious solitude
> And labour wait on temperance; in these
> Desire is bounded: they instruct the mind's
> And body's action.
>
> T. NABB.

There is no difference between knowledge and temperance; for he who knows what is good and embraces it, who knows what is bad and avoids it, is learned and temperate; but they who know very well what ought to be done, and yet do quite otherwise, are ignorant and stupid. — SOCRATES.

> Temperate in every place, — abroad, at home,
> Thence will applause, and hence will profit come.
>
> CRABBE.

BUT we speak the wisdom of God in a mystery, even the hidden wisdom. — I CORINTHIANS 2:7.

We fret ourselves all our life long trying to fathom the mysteries of God, and all to no avail. Why not content ourselves to wait until all the mists that belong to our mortal life shall melt away? Why not be satisfied to worship and adore Him; to read His wisdom written on all His works; and to leave the revelation to Him who orders all things for our good?

God keeps His holy mysteries
    Just on the outside of man's dream!
In diapason slow, we think
To hear their pinions rise and sink,
While they float beneath His eyes,
    Like the swans adown the stream.

Abstractions, are they, from the forms
    Of His great beauty? exaltations
From His great glory? — strong previsions
Of what we shall be? intuitions
Of what we are — in calms and storms,
    Beyond our peace and passions?

Things nameless! which, in passing so,
    Do stroke us with a subtle grace:
We say, " Who passes? " — they are dumb:
We cannot see them go or come:
Their touches fall soft — cold — as snow
    Upon a blind man's face.

ELIZABETH BARRETT BROWNING.

'TIS not a lip, or eye, we beauty call,
But the joint force and full result of all.

ALEXANDER POPE.

The criterion of true beauty is that it increases on examination; if false, that it lessens. There is something, therefore, in true beauty that corresponds with right reason, and is not merely the creation of fancy. — LORD GREVILLE.

Some souls lose all things but the love of beauty;
And by that love they are redeemable:
For in love and beauty they acknowledge good,
And good is God.

BAILEY.

The most natural beauty in the world is honesty and moral truth; for all beauty is truth; true features make the beauty of the face, and true proportions the beauty of architecture, as true measures that of harmony and music. — EARL OF SHAFTESBURY.

Beauty like wit, to judge should be shown;
Both are most valued when they are best known.

LORD LYTTLETON.

Beauty of soul will never fade. Age will not wrinkle it, nor time mar it, nor illness rob it of its attractions. While it is a pleasure to look on a pure sweet face, beautiful and harmonious in tint and feature, yet we cease to care for it, if it is unaccompanied by charm of intellect and depth of soul. Alas, for the beauty that is " only skin deep!"

[337]

LET your heart bring a thank-offering to God
to-day!

Lord of the harvest! Thee we hail!
Thine ancient promise doth not fail;
The varying seasons haste their round,
With goodness all our years are crowned;
    Our thanks we pay,
    This holy day;
Oh, let our hearts in tune be found.

If spring doth wake the song of mirth,
If summer warms the fruitful earth,
When winter sweeps the naked plain,
Or autumn yields its ripened grain,
    We still do sing
    To Thee our King;
Through all their changes Thou dost reign.

But chiefly when Thy liberal hand
Bestows new plenty o'er the land,
When sounds of music fill the air,
As homeward all their treasures bear,
    We too will raise
    Our hymn of praise,
For we Thy common bounties share.

Lord of the harvest! all is Thine,
The rains that fall, the suns that shine,
The seeds once hidden in the ground,
The skill that makes our fruits abound:
    New every year, Thy gifts appear;
New praises from our lips shall sound.

JOHN HAMPDEN GURNEY.

NOTHING can produce so great a serenity of life as a mind free from guilt, and kept untainted, not only from actions, but purposes that are wicked. By this means the soul will be not only unpolluted, but not disturbed; the fountain will run clear and unsullied and the streams that flow from it will be just and honest deeds, ecstasies of satisfaction, a brisk energy of spirit which makes man an enthusiast in his joy, and a tenacious memory, sweeter than hope. — PLU-TARCH.

> Though Wisdom wake, Suspicion sleeps
> At Wisdom's gate, and to Simplicity
> Resigns her charge, while Goodness thinks no ill
> Where no ill seems.
>
> MILTON.

Look for the good in people, then shalt thou grow better thyself. If thou wilt incline thy tastes in a certain direction, thy whole nature will soon tend that way. In continually seeking for beautiful things, thou wilt in time utterly ignore those that are not beautiful. If thou dost pursue goodness, thou wilt become good thyself, and wilt not search for evil in those around thee. Strive to imitate God, who is the sum of true Goodness.

> Goodness is beauty in its best estate.
>
> MARLOWE.

> The soul
> Is strong that trusts in goodness and shows clearly
> It may be trusted.
>
> MASSINGER.

SHALL we allow the camel and the wolf to have more fortitude, more calm endurance, than we? God makes each object, each creature, for some good; we may learn lessons in patience from the slow, plodding ox; lessons in industry from the bee and the ant; lessons in meekness from the lamb; and lessons in perseverance from the tortoise and the snail, as well as lessons in fortitude from the camel and the wolf. Do not scorn to be taught by such as these; they are works of the Divine Hand, thoughts of the Divine Heart. If your burden be, each day, heavy and cumbersome as that which the camel carries, bear it silently and uncomplainingly, until He who loves you shall lift it off. Calm endurance will help to fit you for Heaven.

> Existence may be borne, and the deep root
> Of life and sufferance make its firm abode
> In base and desolate bosoms: mute
> The camel labours with the heaviest load,
> And the wolf dies in silence: not bestow'd
> In vain should such examples be; if they,
> Things of ignoble or of savage mood,
> Endure and shrink not, we of noble clay
> May temper it to bear — it is but for a day.
>
> BYRON.

So, firm in steadfast hope, in thought secure,
  In full accord to all thy world of joy,
May I be nerved to labour high and pure,
  And Thou Thy child to do Thy work employ.

J. STERLING.

May God give thee fortitude and strength for to-day!

FAREWELL, old Autumn, thou wilt not return to
us until another year! May thy sun set in peace:

The mellow year is hastening to its close:
  The little birds have almost sung their last,
Their small notes twitter in the dreary blast —
  That shrill-piped harbinger of early snows;

The dusky waters shudder as they shine,
  The russet leaves obstruct the straggling way
Of oozy brooks, which no deep banks define,
  And the gaunt woods, in ragged, scant array,
Wrap their old limbs with sober ivy twine.

                    HARTLEY COLERIDGE.

Now Autumn's fire burns slowly along the woods,
And day by day the dead leaves fall and melt,
And night by night the monitory blast
Wails in the key-hole, telling how it pass'd
O'er empty fields, or upland solitudes,
Or grim wide wave; and now the power is felt
Of melancholy, tenderer in its moods
Than any joy indulgent Summer dealt.

                    WILLIAM ALLINGHAM.

Dear Heart, thou art not forsaken. Solitude and
Peace are round about thee, and God is over all. Like
a pure white dove with folded wing, His sweet messenger — Peace — is waiting near thee. Thou hearest
a Voice speaking tenderly to thy soul. It is the whisper
of the Eternal, bidding thee cast all thy cares upon
Him. Through the long winter days may His peace
abide with thee and thine!

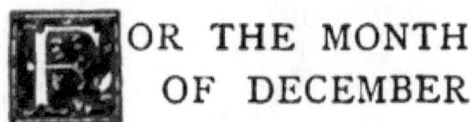

FOR THE MONTH OF DECEMBER

DECEMBER FIRST.

NEXT came the chill December:
  Yet he, through merry feasting which he made
And great bonfires, did not the cold remember;
  His Saviour's birth his mind so much did glad.

EDMUND SPENSER.

Thy heart be like December! Forget the cold, forget the wind. Remember only that the time is now the crown of all the year.

Dimmest and brightest month am I;
My short days end, my lengthening days begin;
What matters more or less sun in the sky,
  When all is sun within?

Ivy and privet dark as night,
I weave with hips and haws a cheerful show,
And holly for a beauty and delight,
  And milky mistletoe.

While high above them all I set
Yew twigs and Christmas roses pure and pale;
Then Spring her snowdrop and her violet
  May keep, so sweet and frail;

May keep each merry singing bird,
Of all her happy birds that singing build:
For I've a carol which some shepherds heard
  Once in a wintry field.

CHRISTINA ROSSETTI.

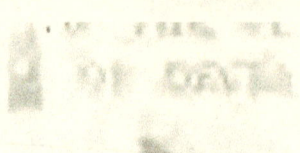

JEAN INGELOW
1830–1897

DECEMBER, — its emblem, the Holly: its motto,
Cheerfulness.

The holly! the holly! oh, twine it with bay —
  Come give the holly a song;
For it helps to drive stern Winter away,
  With his garment so sombre and long;
It peeps through the trees with its berries red,
  And its leaves of burnished green,
When the flowers and fruits have long been dead,
  And not even the daisy is seen.

ELIZA COOK.

Gone are the Summer hours,
  The birds have left their bowers;
While the holly true restrains his hue,
  Nor changes like the flowers.
On his armèd leaf reposes
  The berries tinged like roses;
For he's ever seen in red and green,
  While grim old Winter dozes.

THOMAS MILLER.

And should my youth as youth is apt, I know,
  Some harshness shew,
All vain asperities I day by day
  Would wear away,
Till the smooth temper of my age should be
Like the high leaves upon the holly tree.
   .   .   .   .
So would I seem amid the young and gay
  More grave than they,
That in my age as cheerful I might be
As the green winter of the holly tree.

ROBERT SOUTHEY.

CHERISH a forgiving spirit; do not allow yourself to bear a grudge or harbor an unkind thought against any one. Bury all unpleasant feelings beneath the leaves and snows, deeply let them lie hidden away, no more to wake and haunt you. Christ had more to forgive than you, but He bore no ill-will towards those who persecuted Him. What will it matter in a few brief years if some one injured your pride or hurt your feelings? Better overlook it and forgive it; life is so short. Would you want to stand face to face with your Lord and be obliged to say, " Master, I am unworthy a place in Thy Kingdom, because I could not forgive " ?

Of him that hopes to be forgiven, it is indispensably required that he forgive. It is therefore superfluous to urge any other motive. On this great duty eternity is suspended: and to him that refuses to practise it, the throne of mercy is inaccessible, and the Saviour of the world is born in vain. — SAMUEL JOHNSON.

But O ! *revenge is sweet,*
Thus think the crowd ; who, eager to engage,
Take quickly fire, and kindle into rage.
Not so mild Thales, nor Chrysippus thought,
Nor that good man who drank the poisonous draught
With mind serene, and could not wish to see
His vile accuser drink as deep as he :
Exalted Socrates! divinely brave !
Injured he fell, and dying he forgave ;
Too noble for revenge ; which still we find
The weakest frailty of a feeble mind.

DRYDEN.

[344]

DECEMBER FOURTH.

WE can learn many valuable lessons from children. Their perfect faith and confidence in those they love; their trust in God; their natural simplicity and innocence; their purity and guilelessness of heart; their love for the beautiful, and abhorrence for all that is ugly and unattractive, — these things are the chief charms of childhood. How careful we should be that any influence of ours should mar the loveliness or take from the trustfulness of any child. While we are daily learning sweet lessons of them, let us strive to make ourselves worthy examples for them to follow. Childhood imitates readily; character in the young is easily moulded, and we little think, perhaps, that a careless word or deed of ours will germinate in some tender heart soil, and spring up in a few brief years, — a harvest of wheat or tares.

Every first thing continues forever with the child; the first colour, the first music, the first flower, paint the foreground of his life. The first inner or outer object of love, injustice, or such like, throws a shadow immeasurably far along his after years. — RICHTER.

Happy the child who is suffered to be, and contented to be, what God meant it to be, — a child while childhood lasts. Happy the parent who does not force artificial manners, precocious feelings, premature religion. — F. W. ROBERTSON.

> No sense have they of ills to come,
> No cares beyond to-day.
> Yet see how all around them wait
> The ministers of human fate!

THOMAS GRAY.

[345]

DECEMBER FIFTH.

WHERE are the swallows fled?
     Frozen and dead
Perchance upon some bleak and stormy shore.
     O doubting heart!
Far over purple seas, They wait in sunny ease
    The balmy southern breeze
To bring them to their northern homes once more.

Why must the flowers die?
     Prisoned they lie
In the cold tomb, heedless of tears or rain.
     O doubting heart!
They only sleep below, The soft white ermine snow
    While winter winds shall blow,
To breathe and smile upon you soon again.

The sun has hid its rays
     These many days;
Will dreary hours never leave the earth?
     O doubting heart!
   The stormy clouds on high
   Veil the same sunny sky
   That soon, for spring is nigh,
Shall wake the summer into golden mirth.

Fair hope is dead, and light
     Is quenched in night;
What sound can break the silence of despair?
     O doubting heart!
   The sky is overcast,
   Yet stars shall rise at last,
   Brighter for darkness past,
And angels' silver voices stir the air.

ADELAIDE ANNE PROCTER.

MAY God preserve you from evil-speaking!

But ye, keep ye on earth
  Your lips from over-speech;
Loud words and longing are so little worth,
  And the end is hard to reach;
For silence after grievous things is good,
  And reverence, and the fear that makes men whole,
And shame, and righteous governance of blood,
  And lordship of the soul.

                ALGERNON CHARLES SWINBURNE.

Oh, to be able to keep back the quick words that we so often speak; to suffer reproach and indignity and keep silent! But we only attain to this by constant vigilance, patience, and prayer.

What! never speak one evil word,
  Or rash, or idle, or unkind!
Oh! how shall I, most gracious Lord,
  This mark of true perfection find?

                C. WESLEY.

We say an unkind thing, and another is hindered in learning the holy lesson of charity that thinketh no evil. We say a provoking thing, and our sister or brother is hindered in that day's effort to be meek. How sadly, too, we may hinder without word or act! For wrong feeling is more infectious than wrong-doing; especially the various phases of ill-temper, — gloominess, touchiness, discontent, irritability, — do we not know how catching these are? — FRANCES RIDLEY HAVERGAL.

[347]

THE word of God instructs how we may obtain wisdom, and is continually urging us to increase in knowledge. Solomon says, "Get wisdom, get understanding; forget it not." We are to keep this thought continually before us.

> Would Wisdom for herself be wooed,
>   And wake the foolish from his dream,
> She must be glad as well as good,
>   And must not only be but seem.
>
> .   .   .   .
>
> What's that which Heaven to man endears,
>   And that which eyes no sooner see
> Than the heart says, with floods of tears,
>   "Ah! that's the thing which I would be"?
> Not childhood, full of tears and fret;
>   Not youth, impatient to disown
> Those visions high, which to forget
>   Were worse than never to have known.
> Not these; but souls found here and there,
>   Oases in our waste of sin,
> When everything is well and fair,
>   And God remits His discipline,
> Whose sweet subdual of the world
>   The worldling scarce can recognize;
> And ridicule, against it hurled,
>   Drops with a broken sting and dies.
>   COVENTRY PATMORE.

> Walk
> Boldly and wisely in that light thou hast;
> There is a Hand above will help thee on.
>   BAILEY.

DECEMBER EIGHTH.

I HAVE sought for rest everywhere, but I have found it nowhere, except in a little corner with a little book. — THOMAS À KEMPIS.

Every season has its particular power of striking the mind. . . . To the man of study and imagination the Winter is generally the chief time of labour. Gloom and silence produces composure of mind and consideration of ideas; and the privation of external pleasure naturally causes an effort to find entertainment within. This is the time, in which those whom literature enables to find amusements for themselves, have more than common convictions of their own happiness. When they are condemned by the elements to retirement, and debarred from most of the diversions which are called in to assist the flight of time, they can find new subjects of inquiry, and preserve themselves from the weariness which hangs always flagging upon the vacant mind. — SAMUEL JOHNSON.

A good book is the precious life-blood of a master-spirit, embalmed and treasured up on purpose to a life beyond. — MILTON.

The past lives but in words; a thousand ages were blank if books had not woke their ghosts. — BULWER-LYTTON.

Books are friends, and what friends they are! Their love is deep and unchanging; their patience inexhaustible; their gentleness perennial; their forbearance unbounded; and their sympathy without selfishness. — LANGFORD.

DECEMBER NINTH.

L ET not sleep fall upon thy eyes till thou hast thrice reviewed the transactions of the past day. Where have I turned aside from rectitude? What have I been doing? What have I left undone, which I ought to have done? Begin this from the first act, and proceed; and in conclusion, at the ill which thou hast done be troubled, and rejoice for all the good. — PYTHAGORAS.

Think them all over — the day's events — and sift out the good thou hast done; God grant it may outweigh the evil. What is so helpful to us as to review our past actions, that we may profit by our failures and mistakes, and make a better record in the future?

Moments there are in life — alas, how few! —
When, casting cold, prudential doubts aside
We take a generous impulse for our guide,
And, following promptly what the heart thinks best,
Commit to Providence the rest;
Of shame or sorrow, for the heart is wise,
Sure that no after-reckoning will arise.
And happy they who thus in faith obey
Their better nature; err sometimes they may,
And some sad thoughts lie heavy in the breast,
Such as by hope deceived are left behind;
But like a shadow these will pass away
From the pure sunshine of the peaceful mind.
SOUTHEY.

By all means use sometimes to be alone.
Salute thyself: see what thy soul doth wear,
Dare to look in thy chest; for 'tis thine own:
And tumble up and down what thou find'st there.
GEORGE HERBERT.

DECEMBER TENTH.

SOME persons, I know, estimate happiness by fine
houses, gardens, and parks — others by pictures,
money, and various things wholly remote from their
own species; but when I wish to ascertain the real
felicity of any rational man, I always inquire *whom he
has to love.* If I find he has nobody, or does not love
those he has — even in the midst of all his profusion of
finery and grandeur — I pronounce him a being in adversity. — MRS. INCHBALD.

What wonder man should fail to stay
    A nursling wafted from above,
The growth celestial come astray,
    That tender growth whose name is Love!

It is as if high winds in Heaven
    Had shaken the celestial trees,
And to this earth below had given
    Some feathered seeds from one of these.

O perfect love that 'dureth long!
    Dear growth, that shaded by the palms,
And breathed on by the angel's song,
    Blooms on in Heaven's eternal calms!

How great the task to guard thee here,
    When wind is rough and frost is keen,
And all the ground with doubt and fear
    Is checkered, birth and death between!

Space is against thee — it can part;
    Time is against thee — it can chill;
Words — they but render half the heart;
    Deeds — they are poor to our rich will.

JEAN INGELOW.

THOUGH reason is, as experience assures us, apt to be biassed in such a variety of ways, in its determination of *what is morally right*, yet is it in every man, from his childhood, fitted to apprise him, that it is his duty to act according to *his sense of right*, whatever it may be; and this sense of right is what we call *Conscience.* — ANONYMOUS.

> Knowledge or wealth to few are given,
> But mark how just the ways of Heaven;
> True joy to all is free.
> Nor wealth, nor knowledge grant the boon,
> 'Tis thine, O conscience, thine alone,
> It all belongs to thee.
>
> MICKLE.

> When tyrannizing pain shall stop
> The passage of thy breath,
> And thee compel to swear thyself
> True servant unto death:
> Then shall one virtuous deed impart
> More pleasure to thy mind,
> Than all the treasures that on earth
> Ambitious thoughts can find.
> The well-spent time of one short day,
> One hour, one moment then,
> Shall be more sweet than all the joys
> Amongst us mortal men.
> Then shalt thou find but one refuge
> Which comfort can retain:
> A guiltless conscience pure and clear
> From touch of sinful stain.
>
> SAMUEL BRANDON.

DECEMBER TWELFTH.

DO well the little things now, so shall great things come to thee by and by asking to be done.
— PERSIAN PROVERB.

You are serving God just as much through patience as through active work, if this is what He requires of you. The preparation of a meal, the care of a room, the sewing of a seam, the innumerable little details that must be attended to in the daily routine of life — these require all the patience we can command; the more the better. If you are murmuring and complaining, and doing your duty ungraciously, there is going to be a dark, sorry-looking pattern traced out by your unwilling hands, by and by. But if you are putting in plenty of the golden threads of patience and cheerfulness, your fabric will be like woven sunshine, and an honor to Him who made you.

I love to think that God appoints
    My portion day by day;
Events of life are in His hand;
    And I would only say:
"Appoint them in Thine own good time,
    And in Thine own best way;"
All things shall mingle for my good,
I would not change them if I could,
    Nor alter Thy decree.
Thou art above and I below!
"Thy will be done! and even so,
    For so it pleaseth Thee!"

ANNA L. WARING.

[353]

DECEMBER THIRTEENTH.

IF a man be gracious and courteous to strangers, it shows he is a citizen of the world, and that his heart is no island cut off from other lands, but a continent that joins to them; if he be compassionate towards the afflictions of others, it shows that his heart is like the noble tree that is wounded itself when it gives the balm; if he easily pardons and remits offences, it shows that his mind is planted above injuries, so that he cannot be shot; if he be thankful for small benefits, it shows that he weighs men's minds; . . . but, above all, if he have St. Paul's perfection, that he would wish to be an anathema from Christ for the salvation of his brethren, it shows much of a divine nature, and a kind of conformity with Christ Himself. — FRANCIS BACON.

Then wake into sound divine
The very pavement of Thy shrine,
Till we, like Heaven's star-sprinkled floor,
Faintly give back what we adore;
Childlike though our voices be,
    And untunable the parts,
Thou wilt own the minstrelsy,
    If it flow from childlike hearts.

JOHN KEBLE.

Living monuments do not come of committees — they come from individuals. — JOHN HENRY NEWMAN.

Use the temporal; desire the eternal. — THOMAS À KEMPIS.

[354]

THE happiness of mankind is the *end* of virtue, and truth is the knowledge of the means; which he will never seriously attempt to discover who has not habitually interested himself *in the welfare of others.* The searcher after truth must love and be beloved; for general benevolence is begotten and rendered permanent by social and domestic affections. Let us beware of that proud philosophy which affects to inculcate philanthropy, while it denounces every home-born feeling by which it is produced and matured. The parental and filial duties discipline the heart, and prepare it for the love of all mankind. — S. T. COLERIDGE.

Abou Ben Adhem (may his tribe increase!)
Awoke one night from a deep dream of peace,
And saw, within the moonlight in his room,
Making it rich, and like a lily in bloom,
An angel writing in a book of gold: —
Exceeding peace had made Ben Adhem bold,
And to the presence in the room he said :
"What writest thou?" — The vision rais'd its head,
And with a look made of all sweet accord,
Answer'd : "The name of those who love the Lord."
"And is mine one?" said Abou. "Nay, not so,"
Replied the angel. Abou spoke more low,
But cheerly still; and said: "I pray thee then,
Write me as one that loves his fellow-men."

The angel wrote, and vanish'd. The next night
It came again with a great wakening light,
And show'd the names whom love of God had bless'd,
And lo! Ben Adhem's name led all the rest.

LEIGH HUNT.

MASTER! how shall I bless Thy name
   For Thy tender love to me,
For the sweet enablings of Thy grace,
   So sovereign, yet so free,
That have taught me to obey Thy word
   And cast my care on Thee!

They tell of weary burdens borne
   For discipline of life,
Of long anxieties and doubts,
   Of struggle and of strife,
Of a path of dim perplexities
   With fears and shadows rife.

Oh, I have tried that weary path
   With burdens not a few,
With shadowy faith that Thou would'st lead
   And help me safely through,
Trying to follow and obey,
   And bear my burdens too.

Master! dear Master! Thou didst speak,
   And yet I did not hear,
Or long ago I might have ceased
   From every care and fear,
And gone rejoicing on my way
   From brightening year to year.

And now I find Thy promise true,
   Of perfect peace and rest;
I cannot sigh; I can but sing,
   While leaning on Thy breast,
And leaving everything to Thee,
   Whose ways are always best.

FRANCES RIDLEY HAVERGAL.

HOW rare and beautiful is sincerity! So much is done for self and self-interests, that often what appears to us as a personal favor is nothing more than a means to an end. It is said the Arabs have a prayer like this, "O Lord, I pray that I may never be deceived; but if I am deceived, I pray I may never know it." But most people want to know when they are deceived. To put confidence in a friend, and have him prove unworthy, is always a grief to us. Let us then be sincere ourselves, that no one may be deceived in us.

> First I would have thee cherish truth
>   As leading star in virtue's train;
> Folly may pass, nor vanish youth,
>   But falsehood leaves a poison stain.
>
> ELIZA COOK.

> The man who dares to dress misdeeds,
> And colour them with virtue's name, deserves
> A double punishment from gods and men.
>
> CHARLES JOHNSON.

> What man is wise, what earthly wit so ware,
> As to descry the crafty cunning train,
> By which deceit doth mask in visor fair,
> And cast her colours dyed deep in grain,
> To seem like truth, whose shape she well can feign,
> And fitting gestures to her purpose frame,
> The guiltless man with guile to entertain?
>
> SPENSER.

May you be kept free from deceit!

[357]

MAY this be to you a day of quiet enjoyment! Winter without, Summer within, — this be your portion! Warm the atmosphere of home with your sunny disposition; turn on the electric lights of your good-nature, and illumine every corner of the house; make your place of abode bright with your presence, and keep giving out joy to those around you. Don't sit frowning and brooding over your book or your work, but take time occasionally to give a kind word or a smile to others. Your business will not be any the worse for it; for, although you think it is absolutely necessary to utilize every moment, let me tell you, the world will go on just the same without you, when you have ceased to hurry and worry over things. Take time, then, to be happy and make others so, as you pass along. If you have any joy in you, don't hoard it up; the world needs all it can get; be lavish with it, and you will have plenty left, for it increases with the giving.

> Give me long dreams and visions of content,
> Rather than pleasures in a moment spent:
> And since I know before, the shedding rose
> In that same instant doth her sweetness lose;
> Upon the virgin stock still let her dwell,
> For me to feast my longings with her smell.
> Those are but counterfeits of joy at best,
> Which languish soon as brought into the test,
> Nor can I hold it worth his pains, who tries
> To win that harvest which by reaping dies.
>
> DR. KING, BISHOP OF CHICHESTER.

> It is a joy
> To think the best we can of human kind.
>
> WORDSWORTH.

DECEMBER EIGHTEENTH.

A HEALTHY body is good; but a soul in right health — it is the thing beyond all others to pray for; the blessedest thing this earth receives of Heaven.
— CARLYLE.

> The soul, of origin divine,
> God's glorious image freed from clay,
> In Heaven's eternal sphere shall shine
> A star of day!
> The sun is but a spark of fire,
> A transient meteor in the sky;
> The soul, immortal as its sire,
> Shall never die.
>
> MONTGOMERY.

> The soul on earth is an immortal guest,
> Compell'd to starve at an unreal feast:
> A spark, which upward tends by nature's force:
> A stream diverted from its parent source;
> A drop dissever'd from the boundless sea;
> A moment parted from Eternity;
> A pilgrim panting for the rest to come;
> An exile, anxious for his native home.
>
> HANNAH MORE.

Nature, who has made no two leaves to resemble each other, has endowed our souls with a still greater diversity; and imitation, then, is a kind of death, since it robs each of its individual existence. — MADAME DE STAËL.

May you have "a soul as white as Heaven!"

[359]

THE keener tempests rise:
From all the livid east or piercing north,
Thick clouds descend . . .
Heavy they roll their fleecy world along;
And the sky saddens with the gathered storm.
Through the hushed sky the whitening shower descends
At first thin wavering; till at last the flakes
Fall broad and wide and fast, dimming the day
With a continual flow. The cherished fields
Put on their winter robe of purest white.

JAMES THOMSON.

There is a strange music in the stirring wind!

BOWLES.

Loud wind, strong wind, sweeping o'er the mountains,
Fresh wind, free wind, blowing from the sea,
Pour forth thy vials like streams from airy fountains,
Draughts of life to me.

D. M. MULOCK.

May God keep thee calm of heart and soul, no
matter what may disturb the outer air, or threaten the
outer world. His love protect thee; His care defend
thee; His peace enfold thee, and make thee tranquil
within! Preserve a quiet demeanor; be always hopeful,
bright, and cheerful, but be also gentle of voice and
manner, — not stormy or loud like the Wind. A gusty
nature is never restful; in youth it is bubbling over
with life and merriment, but has no stability; in age it
fumes and frets, and carries a tempest wherever it goes.
Learn how to obtain the inner calm, and thou shalt be
in every season a spirit of rest and peace in the midst
of life's storms.

WHEN your hearth is bright and cheery, and the soft red light flickers on ceiling and wall, when you are surrounded by comforts, and even luxuries, let your heart go out in loving pity to the poor and suffering, the hungry and homeless ones, who are shivering along the cold wintry streets, while you are snugly housed and sheltered from the snowy blasts. Don't stop at mere pity for them ; do something to help them. Pope says,

"In Faith and Hope the world will disagree,
But all mankind's concern is charity."

Oh, poverty is disconsolate! —
 Its pains are many, its foes are strong :
The rich man, in his jovial cheer,
Wishes 'twas winter through the year ;
 The poor man mid his wants profound,
With all his little children round,
 Prays God that winter be not long!

MARY HOWITT.

Winter was at the heart of all things. . . . It was a time when selfishness hugs itself in its own warmth. When the mere wordling rejoices the more in his warm chamber, because it is so bitter cold without. A time when such a man sees in the misery of his fellow-beings nothing save his own victory of fortune....

It was a time, too, when human nature often shows its true divinity, and with misery like a garment clinging to it, forgets its wretchedness in sympathy with suffering. A time when in want, in anguish, in throes of mortal agony, some seed is sown that bears a flower in Heaven. — DOUGLAS JERROLD.

FATHER and King of Powers, both high and low
  Whose sounding Fame all creatures serve to blow;
My Soul shall with the rest strike up thy praise,
And Carol of thy works and wondrous ways.

. . . .

The glorious majesty of God above
Shall ever reign, in Mercy and in Love:

. . . .

As long as life doth last, I Hymns will sing,
With cheerful voice to the eternal King;
As long as I have being, I will praise
The works of God, and all His wondrous ways.

. . . .

Let all His works praise Him with one accord
O praise the Lord, my Soul; praise ye the Lord!

LORD BACON.

Praise Him ever,
Bounteous Giver;
Praise Him, Father, Friend, and Lord!
Each glad soul, its free course winging,
Each glad voice, its free song singing,
Praise the great and mighty Lord!

JOHN STUART BLACKIE.

He is the well of life, for He does give
    To all that live
Both breath and being; He is the Creator
    Both of the water,
Earth, air, and fire. Of all things that subsist
    He has the list;
Of all the heavenly hosts, or what earth claims,
He keeps the scroll, and calls them by their names.

THOMAS HEYWOOD.

LET us keep our faith in God, and in each other. How beautiful is the implicit faith and trust of childhood; and how even more beautiful still is the old person who has preserved a belief in, and love for, all humanity! If we would only see the best in those around us, we should have more faith in them, but we are continually on the lookout for flaws. This is why there are not more Christians in the world: people expect perfection of those who profess to follow Christ, and because they fail to come up to the standard of right, they are often held up as poor examples of Christianity. How wrong this is! We should not expect perfection of any save God, and the man who is trying to imitate Him is to be honored, though he may often make mistakes. He who uses Christianity as a cloak for his sins is not worthy to be called a Christian; therefore *he* certainly is not a fit example to follow. Let us, then, put confidence in God as God, and in man as man, but let us never confuse the two, thinking either that man can be perfect like God, or that God could ever descend to the level of man.

Nought shall prevail against us, or disturb
Our cheerful faith, that all which we behold
Is full of blessings.

WORDSWORTH.

True faith and reason are the soul's two eyes.
Faith evermore looks upward, and descries
Objects remote; — but reason can discover
Things only near, — sees nothing that's above her.

QUARLES.

DECEMBER TWENTY-THIRD.

SEEK not the highest places, but fit yourself for them, so that if they are given to you, you may fill them acceptably and honor them.

Virtue, not rolling suns, the mind matures;
That life is long, which answers life's great end.
The time that bears no fruit, deserves no name.
The man of wisdom is the man of years.

YOUNG.

This is true glory and renown, when God
Looking on earth, with approbation marks
The just man, and divulges him through Heav'n
To all his angels, who with true applause
Recount his praise.

MILTON.

Nobility is not only in dignity and ancient lineage, nor great revenues, lands, or possessions, but in wisdom, knowledge, and virtue, which, in man, is very nobility; and this nobility bringeth man to dignity. Honour ought to be given to virtue, and not to riches. — ANACHARSIS.

Happen what there can, I will be just;
My fortune may forsake me, not my virtue:
That shall go with me and before me still,
And glad me doing well, though I hear ill.

BEN JONSON.

Some there are
By their good deeds exalted, lofty minds
And meditative authors of delight
And happiness, which to the end of time
Will live and spread and flourish.

WORDSWORTH.

WHO art thou that complainest of thy life of toil?
Complain not. Look up, my wearied brother;
see thy fellow-workmen there, in God's Eternity; surviving there, they alone surviving; sacred band of the
Immortals, celestial body-guard of the empire of mankind. To thee, Heaven, though severe, is *not* unkind;
Heaven is kind, — as a noble mother; as that Spartan
mother, saying while she gave her son his shield,
"With it, my son, or upon it." Thou too shalt return
home in honour; to thy far-distant Home, in honour;
doubt it not, — if in the battle thou keep thy shield. —
THOMAS CARLYLE.

Not stirring words, nor gallant deeds alone,
  Plain patient work, fulfilled that length of life;
Duty, not glory — Service, not a throne,
  Inspired his effort, set for him the strife.
                              ARTHUR HUGH CLOUGH.

A trusty workman I would be,
  And well my task pursue;
Work when my Master does not see,
  And work with vigour too.

And whilst I ply the busy foot,
  Or heave the labouring arm,
Do Thou my withering strength recruit,
  And guard me well from harm.
                              JOHN BERRIDGE.

It is just as much to thy credit to do the humble
task well, as to do the great one. It is the *heart* that
God looks at, and not the work itself.

CHRISTMAS-DAY.

A MERRY CHRISTMAS TO YOU!

THIS is the dear Lord's birthday — the time of
rejoicing, the crown of the year !

> Heap on more wood! — the wind is chill;
> But let it whistle as it will,
> We'll keep our Christmas merry still.
>
> SIR WALTER SCOTT.

High cause had they, at Bethlehem, that night
To lift the curtain of Hope's hidden light,
To break decree of silence with Love's cry,
Forseeing how this Babe, born lowlily,

.   .   .   .

Should Mercy to her vacant throne restore,
Teach Right to Kings, and Patience to the poor:
Should by His sweet Name all names overthrow,
And by His lovely words, the quick seeds sow
Of golden equities, and brotherhood,
Of Pity, Peace, and gentle praise of Good;
Of knightly honour, holding life in trust
For God, and Lord, and all things pure and just.

EDWIN ARNOLD.

The shepherds sing; and shall I silent be?
   My God, no hymn for Thee?
My soul's a shepherd too; a flock it feeds
   Of thoughts and words and deeds.
The pasture is Thy word; the streams, Thy grace
   Enriching all the place.
Shepherds and flock shall sing, and all my powers
   Outsing the daylight hours.

GEORGE HERBERT.

[366]

GOD knows what is best for thee; there is not a morning that dawns but He does not think of thee in loving remembrance; He wakes thee again to light and life once more, and yet thou art not half grateful enough to Him; thy every deed is witnessed by Him —fear not to trust Him to guide thee in all thy ways. Be resigned to His will, and know that He loves thee far more than any earthly friend can, and that He holds thy future and all that thou hast in His almighty Hand. He never forgets His beloved, and He will safely keep thee until the years of thy earth-journey have finished their pilgrimage.

> Without an end or bound
> Thy life lies all outspread in light;
> Our lives feel Thy life all around,
> Making our weakness strong, our darkness bright;
> Yet is it neither wilderness nor sea,
> But the calm gladness of a full eternity.
>
> FABER.

And when the tribes of wickedness are strewn
Like forest-leaves in the Autumn of Thine ire:
Faithful and true! Thou still wilt save Thine own!
The saints shall dwell within the unharming fire,
Each white robe spotless, blooming every palm.
Even safe as we, by this still fountain's side,
So shall the church, thy bright and mystic bride,
Sit on the stormy gulf a halcyon bird of calm.
Yes, 'mid yon angry and destroying signs,
O'er us the rainbow of Thy mercy shines;
We hail, we bless the covenant of its beam,
Almighty to avenge, almightiest to redeem!

HENRY HART MILMAN.

AS he that lives longest lives but a little while, every man may be certain that he has no time to waste. The duties of life are commensurate to its duration, and every day brings its task, which if neglected is doubled on the morrow. But he that has already trifled away those months and years, in which he should have laboured, must remember that he has now only a part of that of which the whole is little; and that since the moments remaining are to be considered as the last trust of Heaven, not one is to be lost. — SAMUEL JOHNSON.

An hour once fled, has fled forever.
SCOTT.

To-morrow, and to-morrow, and to-morrow,
Creeps in this petty pace from day to day,
To the last syllable of recorded time.
SHAKESPEARE.

See the minutes how they run,
How many make the hour full, complete,
How many hours bring about the day,
How many days will finish up the year,
How many years a mortal man may live.
SHAKESPEARE.

Our time consumes like smoke and posts away;
Nor can we treasure up a month or day.
The sand within the transitory glass
Doth haste, and so our minutes pass.
WATKYNS.

DECEMBER TWENTY-EIGHTH.

OH, I beseech you, be true! The year is dying fast, how fast! The beautiful Christmas-tide has come and gone; the hearts of the children have been gladdened and all the world is better for its thoughts of Christ, the King. You stand to-day almost at the close of the Old Year; how much you have to think of, as you look backward ! Have you been true to yourself and your convictions? Have you been true to the world, and God? Have you made mistakes? We all do. We all innocently err, but ah! we often do more than this, —we fail to do as well as we might. How about the neglected opportunities? How about the things you might have said and done to help make the world better? Was this being faithful and true to yourself? Were you not deceiving others, when you ignored the chances given you by your Heavenly Father? Perhaps the world has called you good; did you deserve it, when you gave the impression that you were living up to your privileges? "Will a man rob God?" you say, "I would not do *that*," but what else do you call it, when you take His opportunities and throw them away? Have you been true to yourself ? Have you been true to Him?

Where are the great, whom thou wouldst wish to praise thee ?
Where are the pure, whom thou wouldst choose to love thee ?
Where are the brave, to stand supreme above thee,
Whose high commands would cheer, whose chidings raise thee?
  Seek, seeker, in thyself; submit to find
  In the stones, bread, and life in the blank mind.

ARTHUR HUGH CLOUGH.

[369]

WE are led on, like the little children, by a way that we know not. It is a vain thought to flee from the work that God appoints us, for the sake of finding a greater blessing to our souls; as if we could choose for ourselves where we shall find the fulness of the Divine Presence, instead of seeking it where alone it is to be found, in loving obedience. — GEORGE ELIOT.

Calm soul of all things! make it mine
　　To feel amid the city's jar,
That there abides a peace of Thine,
　　Man did not make and cannot mar.

The will to neither strive nor cry,
　　The power to feel with others, give!
Calm, calm me more! nor let me die
　　Before I have begun to live.

　　　　　　　MATTHEW ARNOLD.

Although to-day He prunes my twigs with pain,
　　Yet doth His blood nourish and warm my root;
To-morrow I shall put forth buds again,
　　And clothe myself with fruit.

Although to-day I walk in tedious ways,
　　To-day His staff is turned into a rod,
Yet will I wait for Him the appointed days
　　And stay upon my God.

　　　　　　　CHRISTINA ROSSETTI.

The spirit of obedience and resignation be yours!

DECEMBER THIRTIETH.

WE have had many glances backward, and now let us look forward to futurity, where waits for us the great glad morning of the Better Day. Soon shall dawn the Celestial Spring, when the soul shall leave behind its winter, and mount upward, clad in beauty fresh and fair. All peace, all joy, all happiness be yours; and may you walk with God's redeemed, through the glad Eternal Years!

For what abides that we should look on here?
The heavens are better than this earth below,
They are of more account and far more dear.
We will look up, for all most sweet and fair,
Most pure, most excellent, is garnered there.

JEAN INGELOW.

We are born for a higher destiny than that of earth; there is a realm where the rainbow never fades, where the stars will be spread before us like islands that slumber on the ocean, and where the beings that pass before us like shadows will stay in our presence forever. —
BULWER-LYTTON.

Go wing thy flight from star to star,
From world to luminous world, as far
    As the universe spreads its flaming wall;
Take all the pleasures of all the spheres,
And multiply each through endless years,
    One minute of Heaven is worth them all.

MOORE.

Keep quietly to God, and think
Upon the Eternal Years.

F. W. FABER.

[371]

DECEMBER THIRTY-FIRST.

THE last day of the year; let us give it "God speed!" and as it ends its pilgrimage, may every heart ascend in gratitude to Heaven, for the blessings and mercies so richly showered upon us with all the changing seasons. And it is my sincere wish that from the seed you have sown in the passing year, may spring forth a harvest of good deeds which shall go on ripening through all time, for Eternity. And now we hear the feeble tread of the Old Year, going, going, —and soon he will be sleeping side by side with his departed sires. Oh, may he carry with him many sweet and beautiful things for us to remember in days to come! The Old Year dies; farewell!

And as the moments slip away,
　The midnight bells sweep o'er the sky—
"Good bye, Old Year"—we softly say—
　"Oh dear Old Year—good bye—good bye!"

"Go, long tried friend—we part in peace—
　Thine hour is come, thy tale is told;
Time gives the signal for release—
　And thou art with the days of old!"
　　　　　　　HELEN MARION BURNSIDE.

Oh, New Year, teach us faith!
·　·　·　·　·　·　·　·　·　·

　We'll hold our patient hands, each in his place,
And trust thee to the end;
　Knowing thou leadest onward to those spheres
　Where there are neither days, nor months, nor years.
　　　　　　　DINAH MULOCH CRAIK.